NATION OF THE SWORD
By HR Moore

Titles by HR Moore:

The Relic Trilogy:
Queen of Empire
Temple of Sand
Court of Crystal

In the Gleaming Light

The Ancient Souls Series:
Nation of the Sun
Nation of the Sword
Nation of the Stars (Coming March 2022)

http://www.hrmoore.com

Chapter 1

Raina looked down at her leather cuff. The cuff Jamie—the leader of the Templar nation—was attaching to her wrist. Anger boiled inside her, but she had to play along ... had to be convincing.

He was tagging her, even though she was still a Pagan, according to the magic at least, if not the Registerium's official records.

Jamie stepped back, his eyes boring into her as he delighted in his accomplishment.

'Now you're truly one of us,' he said.

He leaned in, aiming for her lips. Raina turned her head, so he kissed her cheek instead.

'Thank you,' she said with a smile, squeezing his arm to sell the lie.

Aside from his efforts to seduce her, Jamie had been accommodating in the days since she'd signed herself over to the Templar nation. He'd agreed to art classes and playdates in the park for her five-year-old daughter, Callie, so she could hang out with kids her age. He'd arranged trips to the key demon sites Raina wanted Callie to visit. He'd even sent requests to the demon teachers Raina wanted for her daughter ...

Raina *would* give Callie a solid demon education, even if they were Templar hostages.

Most of the teachers on Raina's list had declined Jamie's request. Everyone knew a war was brewing, and no one wanted to be used as leverage ... or become collateral damage.

'I have a surprise for you,' said Jamie, pulling Raina back from her thoughts.

'Oh?' Raina's stomach lurched. Jamie's surprises were usually more of a delight for him than anyone else.

'Alerac,' said Jamie, turning his head towards the door, 'you can come in now.'

Raina's chest constricted. She hadn't seen or spoken with Alerac for hundreds of years. He'd probably heard countless tales about her since then, from any number of enemies. The Pagans—Raina's true nation—and Alerac's Aztec brethren weren't the best of friends.

Alerac entered, his tall frame making short work of the distance to where she and Jamie stood. He wore a bright, elaborately embroidered coat, adorned with a host of magical symbols that Raina hadn't seen in lifetimes. Raina wondered if Jamie even knew what those symbols were ... what they meant.

'I'm happy to see you again,' said Alerac, in his deep, lilting tone. He gave a slight bow as he came to a halt.

'Top of your list, was he not?' said Jamie, looking at Raina expectantly.

'It's a pleasure to see you too, Alerac,' said Raina, mirroring his incline of the head. 'In truth, you're the only teacher on my list who's agreed to come.'

'We Aztecs are friends to the Templar nation,' said Alerac.

'And we're glad ...' Jamie began.

But before he could finish, a wave of power rushed through the room, stealing their breath, crushing their souls. They choked on it, drowned in it, a thick, heavy sensation, like treacle flooding down their throats.

Raina clawed at her chest, her lungs burning, panic stealing all thought. In all of her many lifetimes, she'd never felt anything like this. Callie ... where was Callie?

And then it was gone. They were left winded and unsettled, bent double, heaving in air, unable to speak.

Jamie looked frantically around, as though something in the room could answer his obvious questions. 'What the hell was that?' he said.

'That,' said Alerac, straightening his coat, still breathing hard, 'was a wave of magical power.'

'Where did it come from?' said Jamie, paling. 'Are we under attack?'

'I doubt it,' said Alerac. 'Had that been an attack, we'd all be dead.'

'What?' said Jamie, astonished. Then a flicker of fear crossed his features.

Raina suppressed a smile. Jamie barely believed in magic, and he certainly had no respect for it.

'Can *you* create a wave like that?' asked Jamie.

Raina could practically see the cogs turning in Jamie's mind ... maybe he'd underestimated magic ... should rectify that oversight ...

Alerac fixed Jamie with a disbelieving look. 'No,' said Alerac. 'No power like that has been seen for at least a thousand years.' He turned his eyes to Raina. 'Yes?'

Jamie swiveled his attention to Raina, his features puckered in suspicion.

Oh shit.

'You practiced magic?' said Jamie.

'No,' said Raina, before Alerac could reply for her. 'Not really. I dabbled for a time, very early in my existence. I haven't touched it in many lifetimes.'

Raina concentrated, sending a warning to Alerac. She couldn't send words without preparation—she was rusty—but managed to communicate her discomfort, hoping that would be enough.

Alerac showed no sign of having received her message, but said, 'If you'll excuse me, I'd like to get settled in.'

Alerac left, and Raina fought to hide her relief. He'd kept her history with magic to himself, hadn't sold her out … at least not yet.

Jamie poured himself a drink. He offered one to Raina, but she refused; day drinking had never really been her thing.

He shrugged as he replaced the crystal decanter, then leaned back against the sideboard and took a long sip, letting the silence stretch.

'So,' he said eventually, 'I've fulfilled your every whim and wish …'

That was pushing it. Raina schooled her features into an accommodating smile.

'… now it's your turn to fulfil mine.'

Raina cocked an eyebrow. She was itching to check on Callie after the wave of magic, but she was curious to see which particular wish he'd prioritize.

'We're facing pressure from all sides. We need a plan to fend off our enemies, and the best form of defense is attack.'

Raina looked at him for a long moment, weighing his words. 'You said you didn't want to go to war,' she said calmly, although her pulse picked up.

'I don't. But I can't sit idle while our enemies gain ground. I have no choice but to respond.'

Did he expect her to believe that? 'What are your enemies doing?'

'*Our* enemies are doing many things. Prove your loyalty to me, and I'll tell you more.'

Raina laughed. 'And to prove my loyalty, you want me to formulate a defense? How can I do that without the information I need?'

'You're the great Raina Halabi; I'm sure you have generic strategies you can share. You must understand I can't trust you … and building trust takes time.'

'Trust *me*?' said Raina, scoffing. 'You kidnapped our daughter … and at least twice a week, you slip out and don't tell me where you're going. Did you think I wouldn't notice?' The best form of defense was attack after all …

'You're not ready for that yet.'

She watched as his walls snapped up, shutting her out. She shook her head. 'As you say, trust must be built, Jamie. Let me know when you're ready to do your part.'

Zahora shied back into the shelter of the tunnel that connected the sleeping quarters and the workrooms. She wrung her hands. It did nothing to make her feel better, so she rubbed her face, then re-tied her hair, pulling it almost painfully tight. The pressure only increased her disquiet, so she freed her unruly curls, then dug her fingernails into her palms.

'What are you doing?' asked a male, American voice.

Zahora jumped and spun around, taking in the tall, dark man. Was he here to take her? He didn't look menacing, but if she'd learned anything about demons during her brief time as one, it was they were rarely what they seemed ... his happy-go-lucky look could be a front.

'Sorry, I didn't mean to startle you,' he said, holding up his hands to show he meant no harm.

She appraised him, wondering if she should run, but it was hopeless. She couldn't run from what she'd done. It was bad ... she knew that ... but she didn't know what to do about it.

That was a lie. She knew what she *should* do ... she just didn't want to ... because she was scared witless.

He waited patiently for her to answer, smiling kindly, reassuringly.

Zahora heard voices behind her, and she rushed to the end of the tunnel overlooking the work rooms.

Two demons walked up the path, approaching the hut in the center of the clearing. It belonged to Marla—the Proficient magik who ran this place.

A shiver shot down Zahora's spine. 'Holy crap,' she whispered.

'What?' said the man, now standing beside her.

She pulled him back into the shadows. 'Sussssh. Those are ... well ... never mind who they are, but they're important here.'

'Those two?' he said, his tone disbelieving. 'The old one must be eighty at least. And that one has flowers in her hair!'

'Rose and Talli,' said Zahora. 'You shouldn't judge a book by its cover.'

Talli—the woman with flowers in her hair—who was practically skipping up the path, suddenly turned her eyes to the tunnel.

'Shit,' said Zahora, hastily grabbing the man's sleeve and pulling him back.

'You're not supposed to be here?' he asked with a chuckle.

'I'm supposed to be here. I'm probably supposed to be in that hut ... or maybe they're here to kick me out ... or worse.'

'Am I supposed to understand what you're talking about?'

Zahora took in the man once more. He was lithe, his skin a few shades darker than hers. He had the air of a college athlete. Like he trained all the time, then hung with his bros, full of brash, callous bravado.

No. She was being unfair ... projecting. He did look like a college athlete, but he was kind. She could feel it radiating off him, rippling through the ether, brushing her senses.

'Who are you?' she said. If he was here for her, he was hiding it well.

'I'm Noah. I came looking for a job.'

She gave him an incredulous look. They were on top of a cliff overlooking a lake in the middle of Wales. In other words, they were in the middle of nowhere.

He laughed. 'My dad sent me here on a gap year after college. He won't let me join the family business until I've got *life experience*. He said he'd always wanted to visit Wales, so sent me here first ... he had the grace to let me choose where I go next ...'

'So why not move on? Why get a job?'

'It's nice here ...'

Her features turned stern, calling bullshit.

He chuckled again. 'Dad wouldn't let me bring any money. I have nothing but the clothes on my back, my

9

phone, and a credit card for emergencies—and I only have that because my stepmom insisted. Dad paid for a cottage in the village for a week. After that, I'm homeless too.'

Interesting. Zahora looked at him with fresh eyes, endless questions filling her.

'Zahora,' said a soft voice from the tunnel's entrance.

Oh fuck. This was it …

'Who is this?' said the magik, stepping into the tunnel.

The magik was short and slight. Noah dwarfed him, but somehow it seemed the other way around.

'This is Noah,' said Zahora. 'He needs a job … We can help him, can't we?'

The magik's lips pursed. 'You're needed inside.' When she didn't immediately comply, he scowled, sending her skittering away.

She chastised herself as she went. He was no great and powerful being … why did she let a middling magik affect her that way?

Talli watched as Rose and Marla talked. It was unusual for Talli to be quiet for so long, but despite her hundreds of years, and countless lifetimes, it was still strange to be confronted with a fourteen-year-old who spoke like an adult. More than that, Marla was the Pagans' most senior practicing magik, one of only two

Proficients they had left, and the only one currently incarnated.

Talli had studied under Marla for a few lifetimes. She'd enjoyed learning magic, but only to a point. Talli loved leading the nation's ritual celebrations—and could wield enough magic to do so—but she lacked the interest to devote herself entirely, devoutly. She was social, liked to flit, and those were not qualities that went down well in the Pagans' magical community.

'We have to get Raina back,' said Rose, 'above anything else. And Callie. Until we have them, our hands are tied.'

'We will prepare,' said Marla, resting her hands on the rustic wooden table. 'I will call in all our magiks.'

'We'll try to bolster your numbers through our allies too,' said Rose, 'and a connection with Raina would be an enormous help ...'

Marla nodded. 'We will try. The Templars are sloppy; this will work in our favor.'

'They won't be sloppy for long,' said Talli. 'Not if they realize magic's a true weapon.'

'And by now they may have realized,' said Rose, 'given ...'

A knock sounded from the door.

'Come,' said Marla.

A woman entered, taking tentative steps towards them.

'Zahora,' said Marla, 'meet Rose and Talli.'

Zahora looked to be in her mid-twenties and had a riot of curly black hair. Her tight-fitting shirt and jeans showed off her ample curves, and the way she held her head high, despite what she'd done, made Talli want to respect her. Or maybe she was just young and stupid ... from what Talli had heard, Zahora was only on her second or third incarnation.

'It's a pleasure to meet you,' said Zahora.

Her voice was even, betraying no hint of the discomfort her body put on display. Her fingers twitched, shoulders rigid, lips pursed.

'You too,' said Talli, jumping up and pulling her into a hug. There was no point in torturing the poor thing. What was done was done.

'I ... uh ... I'm really sorry.'

Zahora had never been so nervous, or so excited. Yes, she knew she was in the shit, but at least now she'd get to play in the big leagues. Talli and Rose being here could mean only one thing—they needed her ... finally.

Even though her rational brain knew that, in this moment, she was also terrified. Marla and Rose stared her down. Combined, they'd roamed the earth for thousands of years; gravitas leached from them.

Zahora couldn't stand still ... she kept catching herself fidgeting. She hoped one day she'd be like them ... impervious.

'You should be sorry,' said Marla, 'but you're not.'

Zahora looked at Marla's teenaged form. She was small, with white-blond hair, and skin so white it practically glowed, at least the parts not covered in ink. Swirling patterns and ancient symbols of power, protection, and concealment adorned her. Most senior magiks had similar tattoos to help them navigate the Nexus ... not that Zahora had any idea what that entailed.

'I ...' said Zahora.

'We don't have time to waste on lies, girl,' said Rose. 'We have much to do.'

'I was ... exploring. I just wanted to test my power, to see what I can do. We move so slowly here ... I knew I could do more ...'

'We move slowly for a reason,' said Marla.

'What did I do, exactly?' said Zahora. She was swaying from side to side, her pesky body betraying her again. She rooted her feet to the ground.

'We were hoping you could tell us,' said Talli, kindly.

'Oh.'

'You sent a shock-wave of magic across the world,' said Marla. She always spoke slowly, precisely.

'I did?' said Zahora. That sounded powerful ... she'd always known she was powerful—hell yeah!

'The *entire* world,' said Marla.

'So you can wipe that smirk off your face, because you've just announced your presence to the world,' said Rose.

'I have?' said Zahora.

'Which isn't ideal,' said Talli, 'because we were hoping to utilize the element of surprise. The Templars don't respect magic ...'

'And you've shown to them why they should,' said Rose.

'Oh, shit. Sorry,' said Zahora.

'At least you meant it that time,' said Marla. 'But apologies will not help us now.'

'We need you to work with us,' said Talli. 'We need your help.'

'I'll do whatever I can,' said Zahora, her heart hammering in her chest. This was what she'd been waiting for ... what she'd craved for both of the lifetimes she'd known she was a demon. 'What do you need?'

'We must retrieve Raina and Callie from the Templars,' said Marla. 'To do that, we will gather intelligence from the Nexus.'

'And then transfer Callie to the Pagans,' said Rose.

'We must probe the Registerium's magic, and see if their laws still stand,' said Marla.

'And once we have them back, as Pagans, we'll wipe out the Templar nation,' said Rose.

Silence filled the air as the weight of Rose's words settled. She wanted war, even after Raina and Callie had returned.

'You must help us find a way to do that,' Rose added.

'Wait … you want me to kill them?' said Zahora.

Her head spun as she tried to keep up. Until now, she'd been privy to nothing. She hadn't been given responsibility for a single thing, not even cleaning magical implements. She'd certainly never *killed* anyone …

'No,' said Talli, with a kind smile. 'We want you to disband the nation, magically. It'll strip the Templars of all magical protections, and will change the status of their nation in the eyes of all demons.'

'Oh … is that something that happens a lot?' said Zahora.

'Only once,' said Marla. 'By an Adept.'

'An Adept? Adepts still exist? Wait … you think I'm an *Adept*?' Adepts were rare and powerful magiks. Marla was a Proficient, a step below Adept, and most magiks worshiped the ground she walked on for her power.

A shiver of excitement shot up Zahora's spine. *A freaking Adept?* This was so much better than she'd hoped.

'Don't get ahead of yourself,' said Marla.

The warning in her tone brought Zahora up short. 'So, you don't think I'm an Adept?'

'We have no idea what you are,' said Talli. 'But given the stunt you pulled ... that wave of power ... you're certainly something.'

'What did you do?' asked Rose, the old woman leaning forward in her chair.

'I ... don't exactly know,' said Zahora.

'You connected through the Nexus?' said Talli.

The Nexus—the web of magic crisscrossing the globe, connecting everything. Zahora nodded.

'You felt the Sphere?' Talli prompted.

Had she felt the Sphere—the source of power itself? Zahora wasn't sure, although she thought so. Her teachers had never let her progress past finding the Nexus, and even then, she'd never actually been allowed to engage it, only butt up against it.

Zahora had done more than that today. She'd pushed and shoved against the barrier until she'd slipped right through ...

'I think so,' said Zahora, 'but I've never been allowed that far before.'

'Nor were you allowed that far today,' said Marla, dryly.

'But you got as far as the Sphere,' said Talli, 'and withdrew, without help or protection? That's impressive.'

Zahora smiled at Talli. She was nice—she could see why everyone liked her.

'What happened when you connected?' said Rose, impatiently.

Zahora's eyes flicked back to Rose. 'I saw these ... lines. I wasn't sure what they were, but ... I reached out and touched one.'

The other demons sucked in a collective breath, but they didn't interrupt. Zahora dropped her head ... she'd obviously done something bad.

'It pulled at me, started to suck me away, building in speed. I panicked and dug my heels in, refusing to let it take me.

'I turned and could see the Nexus ... or at least, I think that's what it was ... like a soft shadow. I clawed my way back until I reached it, but the lines wouldn't let me go. I kicked at them, but it didn't help. And then I summoned my magic.'

Zahora looked up at the others. Their faces were uniformly rapt, listening intently. Zahora almost laughed. She—lowly, forgettable Zaha—had these three great demons hanging on her every word. How had this happened?

'What then?' said Rose. 'How did the Sphere react to your magic?'

'I'm not sure,' said Zahora. 'But when I called my magic, there was more than usual. It was easy to repress the pull of the lines. Then the Sphere must have kicked me out, because the next moment, I was on the floor, thrown back from the standing stone.'

'That must be what caused the power surge,' said Talli.

'Maybe,' said Marla, eying Zahora suspiciously. 'Maybe.'

Chapter 2

Caspar and Meredith hurried down the stairs to the nerve center of the Nation of the Holy Star at their headquarters in Israel. Caspar didn't know what Rose did to keep them happy—he didn't want to know—but whatever it was, it was effective … the Holy Star were firm allies of the Pagans, and Caspar couldn't be happier; they possessed modern skills the Pagans did not.

Ira, the Holy Star's most skilled computer engineer, met them at the front desk. He had tanned skin, bouncy black hair, and stubble. He looked about thirty, was lean, and sported a loose-fitting t-shirt and jeans. He had an unassuming, affable air.

'Hello, my friends,' Ira said, with a warm smile and open arms.

He ushered them through the security doors into a circular room that hummed with electricity. Curved monitors encircled them, bigger than usual computer screens, more like enormous televisions, all connected with each other, and currently showing a view of outer space.

The hole where the door had been closed, star-filled blackness now all round them, and claustrophobia took hold of Caspar's insides. He didn't let it show, but he hated everything about the unnatural room … it felt so wrong to him, enclosed by the powerful technology …

In the middle of the room stood a row of strange looking chairs, spaced apart and reclined, almost like beds. And … clothing littered the ground around the chairs, along with the occasional book or magazine.

Ira sat and leaned back in the seat in the very middle. A keyboard, joystick, mouse, and headset suddenly appeared, as if by magic.

'Please, sit,' said Ira, indicating towards the other chairs.

Caspar didn't like it one bit, but he sat, eyeing Meredith to see how she was taking all this. It surprised him to find her entranced, eagerly lowering herself into the chair next to Ira's.

Caspar donned his headset, Ira's voice coming through the earphones loud and clear.

'I'll show you our capabilities,' said Ira. 'Some of them might surprise you … please don't get upset.'

'That good, hey?' said Meredith, raising an eyebrow in Caspar's direction.

'Our business is knowledge,' said Ira, with a wide smile. 'And we're good at it …'

Ira hit a few keys on his keyboard, and the wall of screens jumped to life.

'From what Rose has told us,' said Ira, 'your priority is to retrieve your demons—Raina and Callie—from the Templar nation. We've confirmed they are being held against their will, despite Templar propaganda saying otherwise. We have extensive surveillance in New York, especially around Jamie's apartment.'

Ira tapped his keyboard again, and the screens filled with camera footage.

Caspar frantically scanned the monitors for Raina. 'Do you know where she is?' he asked, his heart thudding loudly in his chest.

Caspar both wanted to see Raina, and didn't. An ache filled him every time he thought of her ... right now, it gripped him so hard, it threatened to choke him. What if Raina and Jamie were together? What if she was looking adoringly into Jamie's eyes? Even if Caspar knew it was fake, it would still hollow him out ... make him sick.

And what if Callie truly believed Jamie was her father? Caspar couldn't bear to see his daughter playing ... bonding with that monster. It should be *him*, not Jamie. But he wanted to see her so desperately. He wanted to see them both.

'Caspar?' said Meredith, looking at him with concern in her eyes. 'Is your headset working?'

'Yes, it's working. I ... just ...'

'Raina's living in Jamie's apartment,' said Ira. 'She comes out most days, either to exercise, or take Callie to classes, or the park. We're trying to identify a pattern to their movements, but the Templars keep changing things up.'

'Jamie's many things, but he's not stupid,' said Meredith.

'Their circle is small,' said Ira, 'although this man— a demon—showed up recently.'

Ira pulled up an image of a man who, judging by his extensive ink, could only be a magik.

'Who is he?' said Caspar. 'And did he arrive before or after the shock-wave?'

'Before,' said Ira, 'but we don't know who exactly he is—he doesn't appear in any of the demon databases we can access. He flew in from South America, so we're assuming he's part of the Aztec nation.'

'Does Jamie have ties to the Aztecs?' asked Meredith.

Caspar shrugged. *Probably.* Once you got old enough, most demons had ties to most nations … unless you'd lived under a rock for hundreds of years.

'The Templars and Aztecs have allied themselves,' said Ira, 'but we don't know of any past connection between the two nation, or any that Jamie has with them specifically. But our access to information from the past is, of course, limited, and we're yet to find a way into the Registerium's databases.'

'Did you hack ours?' said Meredith, with a frown.

'No. Rose gave us access. But we could have …' he said, with a cocky, toothy smile, swinging his head to look directly at Meredith. 'There's always a way in eventually.'

Caspar shuddered. The modern world was … horrifying. He'd lived for hundreds of years, and nothing he'd seen in all his lifetimes made him bat an eye compared to this kind of warfare.

An alert sounded in their headphones, and Ira tapped a key.

'Ah … there,' said Ira, somehow swinging their chairs around, so they faced the other side of the circle of monitors. A box appeared on the screen around the face of a slight, blond-haired woman.

'Jade,' said Caspar.

'Tamsin,' corrected Meredith.

'We think she killed Dean—her human brother,' said Ira. 'He married Raina, right?'

'Yes,' said Meredith.

'Raina annulled the marriage,' snapped Caspar.

'Tamsin's part of Jamie's inner circle,' said Ira. 'I'm surprised to see her actually … she recently travelled to the new West Coast nation … I thought she'd be there longer …'

'Have you got surveillance on the West Coast too?' said Meredith.

'Not as much as we'd like,' said Ira. 'They're clever, whoever they are. But give us time … we love nothing more than a challenge.'

A loud, unfamiliar Irish voice permeated the cocoon of Caspar's headphones, and Ira swung their seats to face the door, which had once again opened.

Caspar ripped off his headset. 'Who are you?' he said, taking in the tall, broad man with ginger hair swept back in a bun. He wore a suit and carried a takeaway coffee cup.

'I'm Torsten,' said the man, 'of the Viking nation. I've come to help … and,' his eyes scanned the room, his features brightening as he found Meredith, 'ah … there you are … and I am here to claim this woman as my wife.'

Meredith rolled her eyes. 'Don't make me kick your arse,' she said. 'No one gets to *claim* me. Your nation may have requested our union, but my nation won't force me to accept.'

'I would be delighted to partake in a pre-coital tussle,' said Torsten. He searched for a place to put his cup, failed to find one, shrugged, and made to place it next to a pile of clothes on the floor.

Ira jumped to his feet. 'No,' he said with surprising force. 'Take your trash, and put it somewhere else.'

'What do you mean, friend?' said Torsten, his features betraying his confusion. 'This place is a shit hole!' He gestured at the stuff all over the floor. 'What difference will it make?'

'Take your cup, and leave this room,' said Ira.

Torsten laughed. 'Okay, okay. But then I'm coming back for my wife.'

'I am not …' Meredith ground out. But another alarm cut her off.

Ira jumped back into his seat and hit a key. 'What the fuck is she doing there?' he said, another box appearing on the screen over a second blond woman. This one was older and curvier than Tamsin.

'Is that … Leila?' said Caspar, studying the woman. 'One of Raina's bridesmaids?'

'Raina's human cousin,' said Ira. 'But I have no idea what she's doing in New York …'

Leila walked across Central Park, heading for her hotel in Chelsea, having just been to Dean's rented apartment on the Upper West Side.

After his breakup with Amari, Dean had disappeared, his body found on a building site a week later. It was a miracle the policeman found it, just as it was about to be covered in concrete … But since they'd found the body, the police had gone quiet.

Someone needed to clean out Dean's apartment and look for clues, but Dean's parents couldn't face coming to New York, and Dean's little sister, Jade, had point blank refused. That, more than anything, had prompted Leila's offer to help.

Leila wasn't even a blood relative … hell, now Amari and Dean's marriage was annulled, she wasn't any kind of relative, but Leila felt … responsible in some way. She'd let that guy—Caspar—into Amari's hotel room the morning after her wedding to Dean …

when Amari had been sick ... vulnerable. That was the only reasonable explanation for Amari's behavior. Well, unless she'd been taken in by a cult ...

Leila had found nothing in Dean's apartment, and when she'd spoken to his former colleagues, they'd been no help either. She'd hoped they would point her to a troubled former client, or a jealous ex-lover with connections to the mafia ... turned out she was wrong ...

Leila walked down Fifth Avenue until she hit Madison Square Park. She grabbed a coffee, then wandered, planning to sit awhile before heading back to her lonely hotel room. She had nowhere to be, no one to call ... she doubted anyone aside from Dean's parents even knew she'd left London ...

She missed her cousin. Leila didn't even know where she was ... maybe she'd never see her again. Last she'd heard was from Dean, when he'd told everyone Amari had broken up with him. Leila had nearly fallen off her chair when she'd heard the news. Sure, Leila had warned Amari a life with Dean would be no picnic—he'd always put his work first—but she'd loved him. Adored him. Had wanted no one but him since they'd met.

And now she was gone. Off to who knew where, doing who knew what, with that strange man ... Caspar.

Leila people watched as she drank her coffee, eventually forcing herself to stand and head back. Maybe she would order room service and watch an old movie. *Dirty Dancing* was made for moments like this ...

'Oh my God.' The words escaped Leila's lips on an exhale as she spotted a familiar face heading out of the park. 'Jade!'

Jade, Dean's little sister, who'd refused to come to New York after the death of her only brother ... this was too much.

'Jade!' she shouted, hurrying after her.

Jade halted, her back ramrod straight. Leila grabbed her arm and spun her around.

'Jade, what the fuck?'

'Hey Leila,' said Jade, blandly.

Something about her was different ... less teenaged angst, and more ... predator.

'What are you doing here?' said Leila. 'You told your parents you couldn't come!'

'That's none of your business,' said Jade. 'Now, if you'll excuse me.'

Leila grabbed her arm again. 'Have you seen Amari? Did she reach out to you ... after Dean's ...' She could only just bring herself to say the word, 'death?'

Jade gave her a long, appraising look, then smiled. It made Leila want to back away.

'Come with me,' said Jade. 'And call me Tamsin.'

'What?'

But Jade—Tamsin—didn't answer. She strode off down the street, leaving Leila with little option but to follow. They walked a few blocks, then entered a small park.

'Ja ... Tamsin, where are we going?'

'You wanted to see Amari?' said Tamsin, her features hard as stone. 'And there she is.'

Tamsin pointed to the middle of the park, to where Amari played with a little girl ... holy shit ... with *Callie*.

Leila's head spun. This was ... weird ... totally fucked up. Amari loathed Dean's spoilt little sister. And now they were hanging out in New York? And with Callie?

Leila came to an abrupt halt, not knowing what to do. Part of her wanted to rush to her cousin, to hug her, make sure she was alright. But her gut screamed at her to run away, that something was wrong … that this was dangerous.

Tamsin was watching her carefully, scrutinizing her every move. She stood rooted to the spot, still not knowing what to do.

'Hey, Raina!' shouted Tamsin.

Raina?

Amari looked up, saw Tamsin, and was about to dismiss her, when Tamsin looked at Leila. Amari's eyes followed, then locked with her cousin's.

Amari held Leila's gaze for a beat, then looked away, barely acknowledging her presence. Hurt cratered Leila's chest … and then she saw red.

She marched towards Amari. 'Where have you been?' she demanded.

'In New York,' said Amari.

'With Jade?'

'Tamsin,' Tamsin corrected, from right behind her. 'Isn't that right, Raina?'

Leila wheeled back to face Amari. 'Why's she calling you Raina?'

'Because that's my name.'

Leila shook her head in disbelief. 'What the fuck is going on here?'

Raina scowled as Callie ran to her side, overhearing the swear word.

'Hey, Callie!' said Leila, leaning down and pulling her in for a hug. 'What are you guys doing here … together?'

'Mari's my Mumma!' said Callie, delightedly.

'You adopted her?' said Leila, looking from Raina to Tamsin and back again.

'In a manner of speaking,' said Raina. 'Callie, why don't you play on the swings; I need to talk to Leila.'

Callie's features turned pleading, urging Raina to let her stay. Raina gave her a stern look.

'Okay,' said Callie, drawing out the word as she turned and reluctantly headed to the swings.

'You can leave too,' Raina said to Tamsin. 'You've done enough damage for one day.'

Tamsin smirked. 'Have fun,' she said, sashaying out of the park.

'Amari ... this is all so weird,' said Leila.

'My name's Raina,' she said, 'and you need to leave. Forget you ever saw me.' Her voice was urgent ... scary.

'Are you in a cult? Did Jade ... Tamsin ... get you involved in something? And Callie too?'

'I'm not in a cult. I don't need your help. You're in danger if you stay here. You need to leave and never come back.'

'That's what you'd say if you were in a cult!' said Leila.

'Why are you here?' said Raina, cold and aloof ... so different to how her cousin usually behaved towards her ...

'Dean's dead,' she said, watching for Raina's reaction.

'I'm sad to hear that,' said Raina, with not even a flicker of emotion.

'I'm looking into what happened for his parents.'

'You should leave that to the police.'

Raina started to turn away, and Leila's frustration boiled over. She grabbed her arm. 'Seriously, Amari, what's got into you? You'd never normally be like this ... at least not with me.'

Raina leaned in close. 'You need to leave,' she said, annunciating each word as her eyes bored into Leila's.

'Tonight. Do not come back here and do not find me again, or you'll put us both in danger ... and Callie too.'

'So you are involved in something shady. Did Dean get you into this? Is that why he's dead?'

Leila examined Raina, looking for a chink in her armor. She found none.

'Callie!' called Raina, pulling away. 'Time to go.'

'Awww,' said Callie, pumping her legs, showing no signs of dismounting the swing.

'Now, Callie,' said Raina.

'Can we just ... talk?' said Leila, catching hold of Raina's arm again, gently this time. 'Even if we don't talk about ... whatever this is. I miss you ... and ... I could use a friend.'

'Leave and never come back,' said Raina, shrugging Leila off. She retrieved Callie and pulled her out of the park, Callie waving frantically at Leila.

Leila plastered a smile on her face and waved back until Callie and Raina disappeared from view. She tried to make sense of it all. Her cousin had turned into a cold, heartless bitch. She'd never been the warm, cuddly type, but this was a different level ...

Leila wasn't going anywhere ... it wasn't like she had anywhere to go. She would get her cousin back, and Callie too.

Tamsin took a deep breath, steeling herself, then pushed open the door to Jamie's bedroom.

'Tamsin?' said Jamie, whirling around. He wore nothing but a towel.

'Good workout?' said Tamsin, letting her eyes glide across the contours of his chest.

'What are you doing here?' said Jamie, scanning the doorway behind her. 'What happened?'

'The demons of the West Coast wouldn't see me, and I couldn't find their headquarters.'

Jamie's features blackened. 'So you gave up?'

'San Francisco's teaming with demons from other nations. If I hang around there, it'll make us look desperate. I left two of our lesser-known demons … they'll report back if they find anything.'

Tamsin kept her head up, her voice even. She was his equal … even if he didn't realize it yet. She looked directly into his eyes, then raised an inviting eyebrow.

Jamie's gaze dipped to her lips, then lower.

Her insides contracted with triumphant glee. He still wanted her, even if Raina had put a wrench in the works …

Tamsin moved towards the window, walking slowly, swinging her hips. She cast around for signs of Raina, but there were none … not a single indication she'd been here.

Tamsin paused by an upholstered chair and placed a hand on the soft velvet. She smirked, turning it into a seductive pout as she looked back over her shoulder at Jamie.

He came up behind her, standing close.

'You're a lesser-known demon too,' he said, his breath caressing her neck. 'No one knows who you are.'

'Hmm,' she said, in a noncommittal fashion.

His fingers skirted the outside of her thigh, playing with the fabric of her dress, gathering it up in his fist, while his other hand went to her waist. She took hold of it, guiding it to her braless breast. He squeezed and kneaded, then pinched. She gasped and pressed back into his arousal.

His hand slipped under her rucked-up dress, his fingers—no underwear to contend with—pushing inside her.

'Fuck, Tamsin,' he growled into her neck. 'Fuck … we …' His tone changed, and he hesitated.

I don't think so. Tamsin reached back and pulled his towel free, dropping it to the floor. She grasped him, pumping only twice before his hesitance disappeared, chased away by her hand.

He bent her over the chair, hiked up her dress, and entered without preamble. They both gasped.

'Jesus,' he said, pounding into her. 'Fuck … I … needed this.'

'Me too,' said Tamsin, hiding her triumph, 'but guess who I bumped into in the park …'

Jamie stilled.

'Don't stop.'

'Who?' he said, moving again, slowly.

'Raina's cousin, Leila.'

Jamie's fingers skated to her core, caressing her as he slid in and out. Tamsin moaned.

'And? What did you do?'

'I … uh … Jamie …'

'Seeing as Tamsin's a little distracted, I'll tell you,' said Raina, from the open door.

They both froze, but Jamie didn't pull away, Tamsin trapped beneath him.

'Why don't you join us?' said Jamie. 'It would be so much better …' He thrust into Tamsin again, as though demonstrating. 'When's the last time you …'

Tamsin saw red. *Fucking Raina.* She'd had Jamie exactly where she wanted him … and she was nobody's plaything. She pushed Jamie backwards, freeing herself from his grasp, and headed for the exit.

'Stop,' said Jamie, his voice cold like steel.

Tamsin stopped, but didn't turn.

'I didn't dismiss you,' he said. 'And I wasn't finished.'

'You're going to force her to have sex with you?' said Raina, her tone mocking.

Tamsin could fight her own battles … she certainly didn't need *Raina* to defend her.

'Go,' said Jamie, with a wave of his hand.

Tamsin screamed, and swore, and thrashed, and threw things … but only in her mind.

'Couldn't keep it in your pants any longer?' said Raina, running scathing eyes over his naked body.

'She offered it on a plate,' said Jamie. 'What was I supposed to do?'

He sauntered to his walk-in closet and disappeared into the cavernous space, returning moments later wearing a robe.

'You did exactly what I expected,' said Raina, dropping into an armchair, lounging back.

'Oh, don't be like that … How was your cousin?'

'How can this work if I can't trust you? You told me it was over between you and Tamsin … and she's been back … what? Two minutes?'

'Baby …'

Raina shuddered at the brash endearment. Caspar would never call her that. Loyal, clever Caspar who she missed with all her heart. He'd never needed women the way Jamie did ... he only needed her.

'Raina, come on. You're *still* shutting me out ... You expect me to be celibate?'

'I need to be able to trust you. You say you want us to be together, but everything you do tells me that's a lie. You want me to help you, but you're withholding information, and disappearing to secret meetings ... are you meeting allies? Or prostitutes? Or ...'

'I don't pay for sex,' said Jamie, stepping towards her. 'And ... what?' He waved his arm in frustration. 'You want full disclosure? You know if I give you that, and you ever leave me, I'll have to kill you.'

Raina took a breath. She wanted nothing less than to know Jamie's secrets. 'I don't need full disclosure— I'd never ask that from any demon—but at the very least, I need to know your goals. How can I create a strategy if I don't know what it's for?'

'It's better we start small ...'

'No.'

'Raina ...'

It was all so easy with Caspar, so natural. From when they'd first met, they'd clicked into an uncomplicated rhythm. They challenged each other ... disagreed ... but the trust, respect, alignment, had just ... existed, almost from the first moment, when they'd stood assessing one another from opposite sides of a room. With Jamie, it had always been a dance ... exciting to start, but now just ... urgh, she couldn't think like this ... she was here for Callie ... to protect her daughter.

'Raina,' Jamie said again.

'You might surround yourself with kid demons, but I'm not one,' she said, standing. 'When you're ready for the big leagues, come find me.'

Chapter 3

Zahora sat and tried to listen as Marla—the Pagans' only incarnated Proficient—drew a symbol on the back of her hand. The sound of trickling water filled the air from the spring feeding a circle around the standing stone. A channel connected the standing stone to the circle, amplifying its power.

The stone stood in a cave, enclosed on all sides, but open to the elements above, trees partially obscuring the bright blue sky. Zahora tried to concentrate on Marla's words, but her head was fuzzy ... that often happened here.

She looked down as Marla finished drawing a Shield Knot on her hand—a circle with four looping points intersecting it. It was a symbol of protection to help ward off evil. Many magiks used it, hoping it would afford some measure of safety when using the Nexus ... hoping it would mean they didn't lose themselves there.

To Zahora, it felt wrong. She fought the urge to shake her hand, to rid herself of the symbol.

'Zahora,' said Marla, her quiet annoyance permeating Zahora's thoughts. 'You're not listening ...

again. You wonder why your progress has been so slow? This is why ... but you have a duty to your nation now ... you must concentrate.'

'It's just ...' She tried to collect her thoughts, but it was difficult, like swimming against the tide. 'I ... don't ... this symbol ... doesn't feel right.'

Marla scrutinized her. 'As I have explained, we will try multiple symbols. It may not feel right, but that doesn't mean it won't work.' Her tone contained unmistakable anger.

Marla exhaled loudly, as though centering herself, letting her annoyance wash away.

Zahora wanted to tell her exactly what she thought of this approach ... wanted to refuse to do things this way, but she didn't have a way of her own ... was too inexperienced for that.

Frustration bubbled inside, and Zahora tried to imagine what Rose or Talli would do in this situation ... It was a vain thought; they would never be in this situation. They were too powerful, too knowledgeable, too old ...

'We will try many symbols,' Marla repeated more calmly, as she followed the channel of water to the stone. 'Now, come here ...'

Zahora sat with her back against the stone. The Nexus immediately brushed her senses, calling to her, but then it shut her out.

'It's not working,' said Zahora.

'We are yet to *do* anything,' said Marla, snappily. 'You can't know if it's working.'

'It just shut me out. I ...'

'Zahora, please concentrate. Focus. Find the Nexus ... reach for it ... but do not touch it.'

'It's not there,' she said.

'*Try*,' Marla insisted, uncharacteristically ruffled.

'But ...'

33

'Zahora, how can I teach if you won't listen? You must work at it. Not everything is as simple as a click of the fingers. I will leave you to practice. Search for the Nexus. You may need to push through the symbol. It may be hard ... and time-consuming. I have other pupils to attend. I will return later to check on your progress. *Do not* cross the Nexus.'

Rage filled Zahora as Marla walked away. Why did no one ever listen to her? Marla was too careful, lacking in vision ... no sense of adventure. She knew how to drag the life out of any situation.

The other Neos—trainee magiks, or magiks with little power—sucked up to Marla, hanging off her every word. She was so used to adoration, she didn't know what genuine feedback looked like. Zahora was only trying to tell her how it felt ...

She prepared to try again, attempting to clear her head, to focus. At least the fuzziness had gone, along with her sense of the magic ... She sought the Nexus, reached for it, called to it, but nothing happened. Again and again, nothing happened.

Oh, screw it. She'd never feel the Nexus with that symbol on her hand, no matter how hard she tried ... she knew it in her soul.

She plunged her hand into the frigid water, scrubbing at her skin until the symbol washed away. The water was calming despite the cold, and rightness settled over her when the last traces of ink disappeared.

The magic returned, and she smiled, luxuriating in the sensation, breathing it in. *Now ... let's try some that feel right ...*

She ran through the symbols in her mind, letting them tick past her eyes, one by one.

Three symbols called to her: The Triskelion, for motion. The Dara Knot, for endurance, strength, and power. And the Serch Bythol, which was probably best left alone for now, seeing as that symbol was for eternal love ...

Zahora picked up the brush Marla had left behind and dipped it in the ink. She drew the three spirals of the Triskelion on the back of one hand, and a twisting, looping Dara Knot on the other. It wasn't perfect—she wasn't used to using her left hand—but as soon as she'd finished, she felt ... different. Powerful. Restless.

Zahora discarded the brush and sat with her back to the stone. She'd only just skimmed the rough, cold surface when the Nexus reached out to her, sucked at her. That had never happened before ...

A bolt of unease filled her ... of uncertainty. Was this usual? Was it safe? The senior magiks had never allowed her to practice magic ... not properly, so all of this was new.

She tentatively reached out, brushing against the Nexus. It seemed ... happy. *At least the Nexus appreciates me ...* The thought had barely formed when something yanked at her soul, throwing her off balance. It took hold and pulled her in, although, unlike last time, it didn't urge her through to the other side, into the Sphere. She was thankful for that, at least.

But it moved her across the Nexus, faster and faster, the motion unstoppable. *Oh shit.* She had to stop ... she was going too fast. Could she get back to the stone? Panic coursed through her. Maybe the Triskelion had been the wrong choice ... she was out of control. But she also had the Dara Knot. She should use that ... but ... how? What should she do? What would Rose do? Or Raina? Raina ... the legend of legends ... a Pagan she'd never met, but who was feared and revered in equal measure ... who needed Zahora's help ...

Raina needed *her*. That was ... elating, liberating, made her feel commanding. The Dara Knot burned.

She *was* commanding, even more so with the knot. But …

Zahora careered to a halt, the jolt in her chest so hard it winded her, or at least that's how it felt. *Could one wind one's soul?* She could do nothing for several long moments, struggling to catch her breath. And then she heard voices.

Oh Gods. Where was she? Where had the Nexus taken her? She still didn't know how to get back, but she forced that thought aside, concentrating on the voices, following them until she was looking into a room outside the Nexus, in the physical world.

'Despite Jamie's disdain for magic, this building's on a ley line,' said a male voice.

'Well, it's not like Jamie started the Templar nation,' said a female voice. 'Those who did probably respected magic.'

Zahora's heart lurched. This was a Templar building? Had the Nexus brought her to Raina?

'Quiet,' said the man.

'What? Why?' said Raina, her voice low.

'Take my hand,' said the man.

A force clamped around Zahora's chest, squashing her, choking her.

'Stop!' Zahora hissed. 'I'm a friend … a Pagan.'

The force lessened, although it didn't leave entirely.

'The Pagans are no friends of ours,' said the man, squeezing again.

'I'm … lost,' said Zahora, straining for breath. 'I didn't mean to come. The Nexus … it brought me.'

The man's grip loosened again. 'What?' he said. 'How?'

'I don't know. I thought about Raina, and it brought me to her.'

'What are you?' the man said.

'What do you mean?'

'What level of magik?'

'I'm a Neo.'

'And I'm Marilyn Monroe.'

'Are you?'

'No, girl. I'm not.'

Embarrassment flooded her, despite her predicament. You never knew who demons had once been ...

'I'm ... young.' Despite how much Zahora hated the fact, maybe it would save her. 'Can you help me get back?'

The man was quiet for a long time.

'Let her go,' said Raina, her voice strained.

'I could finish her right here and now. I have her soul in my hand ...'

'Alerac ...' said Raina. 'She's a baby.'

'Who will grow up,' said Alerac.

Rushing filled Zahora's ears, her heart racing wildly as she awaited her fate. And then something called to her ... a melodic ringing ... a sound she could almost take hold of, that spoke to her soul. And her soul answered.

She shook off the shackle of Alerac's grasp and galloped towards the music, a second tone joining the first in perfect, ringing harmony, then a third. The sound filled her up, made her hair stand on end, made her unequivocally happy.

And then she was back, leaning against the stone, Noah's face hovering over her.

'Thank God,' he said, silencing two of the sound bowls.

'Don't,' she said, grabbing his hand before he could silence the third. 'I ... the bowls ... you ... I think you just saved my life.'

Noah paled. 'Are you okay?' he said, looking into her eyes.

He held up a finger from his free hand and waved it back and forth in front of her eyes. She followed it, then looked at him … really looked at him … into him. Her magic reached for him, and she lifted her free hand to his face.

'You have fire in your eyes,' she said. 'Hidden depths, and … guilt, fear, longing. But your soul is good. Did you know that?'

She felt drunk, her magic running away with her. It was never usually like this … the magic fuzz didn't normally jumble her brain.

Then she remembered the symbols. 'Oh, shit. Help me wash these off?' she said, pushing their joined hands into the water. He pulled his fingers from her grasp and gently rubbed her skin.

Zahora tipped her head back against the stone, suddenly exhausted. 'Why were you here?' she said sleepily, enjoying his caress, the cold bite of the water keeping her present.

'They gave me a job. Thank you, by the way. They said they were expecting more people to arrive, so they could use an extra pair of hands. They told me to bring the sound bowls in here and set them around the edge of the cave.

'When I got here, it looked like you were unconscious, then you started to shake, and your lips moved, and your fingers twitched. I tried to wake you. I shook you and called your name, but it didn't work.'

'So you used the bowls?'

'I'm a musician,' he said shyly, looking down at her hand, avoiding her eyes. 'Or at least, I want to be.'

'I knew I liked you,' she said, fighting her drooping eyelids.

Noah dried their hands on his t-shirt, giving her a view of his washboard abs. It was a good thing she was so tired, or she might have reached out and stroked them … that would definitely be against the rules.

'What happened?' he said, releasing her hand. 'What were you doing?'

'Special kind of meditation.'

'You said I saved your life? What did you mean?'

'It saps your energy … I'm sleepy.'

'Come on,' he said, pulling Zahora to her feet, wrapping an arm around her to keep her upright. 'Do I need to take you to the nurse's office?'

'The nurse's office?'

'It was a joke.'

'Oh. No,' she said, resting her head against him, breathing him in. 'I just need to sleep.'

Raina and Alerac looked at each other for a long time, neither speaking. They were on the precipice, and once they went over, there was no coming back.

Raina had known Alerac once, had respected him. He'd taught her magic—was one of the best—but he was an Aztec first and foremost. And the Aztecs were allied with the Templars. If she revealed her loyalty was still with the Pagans, would he rat her out to Jamie? If Jamie had proof she was lying to him, her escape would become exponentially harder.

But … if she could enlist his help … well, then her chances of success would skyrocket. What she'd just seen him do … that was rare. Powers like those were mostly lost.

Raina racked her brain, trying to remember Alerac's history. Her memory had never been good, and their paths hadn't crossed in a long time. Did he once have a lover who'd been killed by the Templars? Or was that another magik she'd known? Damn it, she couldn't remember. And to make matters worse, Alerac had all but drained her power, had used her life force to amplify his abilities. She could barely think straight.

'Your magic is impressive,' said Raina, hedging.

'Thank you,' said Alerac. 'I thought the Pagans had no one more skilled than a Proficient ...'

'She was more?'

'She was something I've never seen,' said Alerac.

A bubble of excitement rose inside Raina. 'How so?' she said.

'You don't travel around the Nexus like she did,' he said. 'You use the Nexus to access the power of the Sphere, then use that connection to amplify sendings, or to speed recovery, or to spy ... listening across the ley lines. But whatever she did ... her very soul was in the Nexus, here, when it should have been thousands of miles away.'

'How did you keep her here?'

'I grabbed her soul,' he said with a smile. 'She had no defenses ... I could have crushed her ... should have crushed her ...'

'Then she can't be more than a Proficient, if it would have been so easy for you to end her.'

'She said she was young,' said Alerac. 'She lacks training. But she's extremely powerful ... more powerful than anyone I've seen in many lifetimes ...'

'Gods ...' Raina's blood heated with a mix of wonder and terror. The Pagans had a weapon, a force that could make a difference in this war ...

'We should tell Jamie, presumably ...' said Alerac, raising an eyebrow.

'Hmmm,' said Raina, 'but we don't understand what she is, not really. We don't want to worry Jamie with something that could turn out to be nothing …'

Alerac fixed Raina with a penetrating stare, the air weighed down with unsaid words.

Raina's legs gave way and she slumped to the floor.

'Gods, woman, when did you last use your magic? You're shot.'

'Hundreds of years ago,' Raina said weakly.

'Up onto the table,' he said, helping Raina onto the massage table in the center of his small workroom. She lay face down, her eyes trying to close. 'You need to use the Sphere.'

'I don't like using magic …'

'You don't have a choice. I took a lot … you used to be so strong …'

Raina tried not to let his words sting. He hadn't meant them as an insult, but they hurt like one.

'You remember how to use the Nexus at least? To access the Sphere?'

'I'm assuming this room doesn't have a hidden stone?'

'No. You'll have to feel the magic for yourself. I'll help,' he said, lifting her top, exposing the skin of her back. 'Go now.'

Alerac splayed his hands across her back, pressing into her flesh, and Raina loosed a long breath. She inhaled and searched for the Nexus, surprised when she found it with ease. On the exhale, she connected with it, pushing through to brush against the Sphere.

'Don't go too far,' said Alerac. 'Stay there, and let the energy diffuse towards you. It'll take longer this way, but you can't risk getting sucked in … no one survives that.'

Raina sat on a cliff above the raging power of the Sphere. From this distance, she benefited only from the smell of hot metal, the sight of the lines, and the odd bit of spray, but it soothed her nonetheless.

It had been a long time since she'd been here, so close to the raw magic. It called to her. It had always called to her. And it had cost her dearly.

Raina heard the door open, heard male voices, felt Alerac's tension through his hands, and pulled her unwilling soul back from the Nexus.

'What are you doing?' said Jamie, striding to Raina's side.

'Massage,' said Alerac, his hands kneading her knots.

Raina winced as he dug into a tender spot. 'He's got some of the best hands I've ever known,' she said.

Jamie's hand brushed her foot, and she tried not to tense.

'Is that so?' he said, tugging on a toe.

Raina hated herself, but it felt good.

'You can leave,' Jamie said to Alerac.

'We only just started,' said Raina. 'I'll find you when we're done.'

'You're done,' said Jamie, his tone predatory.

Raina inhaled in an irritated fashion, but said nothing. Alerac left without a word. Raina made to get up, but Jamie stopped her with a hand on her shoulder.

'My hands are excellent too ... this you know ...'

It was true; if he'd retained any of the skill from his previous lives, Jamie knew how to deliver a massage.

He stood by her head and pulled up her top.

'Off,' he said, urging her up so he could pull it over her head.

Raina let him. She couldn't care less about nakedness, and it would make the massage better.

He unclipped her bra, then ran his hands down her back. Raina suppressed a hum of pleasure. She'd been training hard, forcing her body into shape, not to mention the toll Alerac's use of her magic had taken. She was tired and bruised and ached all over.

Jamie stopped, walked to the shelves housing Alerac's lotions and potions, and selected an oil. He dropped a liberal quantity on her back, her body contracting against the shocking cold. She relaxed when the smell of lavender filled her lungs, bringing back memories of the south of France, of Caspar.

She imagined it was Caspar's hands caressing her back, her shoulders, her backside, kneading the knots, finding her pressure points.

She wondered what Caspar was doing ... where he was. She could try to find him using magic, but that was dangerous—Alerac would sense it—and her magic wasn't strong these days.

'I like this body,' said Jamie, his voice a purr.

Raina fought her body's attempt to tense at his words.

'I'd like to explore it properly,' he said, running a single finger up the back of her leg.

'You don't seem picky,' said Raina, images of him and Tamsin flashing before her eyes.

He kissed her lower back.

She exhaled, fisting her hands into balls. The carnal part of her wanted him to do it again.

'It's different with you,' said Jamie. 'I want you as an equal, not a plaything. But you can't expect me to be celibate ... I'm not a Buddhist.'

'It's different with me?' She laughed. 'I bet you say that to all the women. You don't even trust me …'

'Do you blame me?'

He ran his hands over her backside, then down her legs to her toes. He pulled each one gently, then worked his way up her leg, slowing as he reached her thigh.

'What do you want, Jamie?' she said, trying to ignore his fingers, circling ever closer.

'I told you; I want us to be a family.'

'Then you need to let me in. You treat me like a captive … you keep secrets, you screwed Tamsin two minutes after she returned … You want to have your cake and eat it, and that's not how family works.'

His fingers skirted her core, and she pulled away, pushing herself up to sit on the table. Her breasts were bare, and Jamie's eyes flicked down to them.

She shook her head. 'You would have thought, with all the breasts you've seen, over so many lifetimes, you'd be able to ignore them for thirty seconds.'

'That's not how it works,' he said, echoing her words as he stepped into her space.

Raina placed a hand on his chest, halting his approach. 'Sex won't make us what you say you want … we're not sleeping together until we have … something meaningful.'

'Is this because of Caspar?'

Raina's heart lurched. She slid off the table into his space, pushing him back out of her way as she reached for her top. 'I have no need for an insecure, jealous little man.'

He grabbed her hand, spinning her back to face him. 'I am no such thing.'

Her eyes locked with his. 'Is that so?' she said. 'Go screw Tamsin; you won't get what you want from me.'
And you'll never compare to Caspar.

Chapter 4

Jon stared at the face on his computer screen in disbelief. 'You've got to be kidding, right?'

'No,' said Caspar, losing his patience. 'Go to New York and retrieve Leila; she's a liability.'

'How's she a liability?'

'Seriously?' said Caspar. 'She's looking for Dean's killer. The Templars murdered Dean, they already know Leila's there, and she's Raina's cousin. They could use her as leverage.'

'Raina would never choose Leila over saving Callie, or helping our nation,' said Jon. 'And so what if they kill her?'

'For fuck's sake, Jon,' said Caspar, grabbing handfuls of his hair.

'Why me? I've got responsibilities at work ... I can't just up and take off to New York ... I might lose my bonus ...'

Caspar growled. 'There's no one else, and it's not like we need the money you earn.'

'It's the principle,' said Jon. 'What about Elliot? He doesn't have a job any longer ... or Gemma?'

'Rose sent them to the West Coast, to sound out the new nation.'

'Talli or Christa?'

'They need to plan for the equinox, and they're looking for an Adept.'

'Urgh,' said Jon. 'Meredith?'

'She's needed here with me.'

'Why?'

'Jesus Christ,' said Caspar. 'Do I need to call Rose? You're young. Hardly anyone knows who you are. You've kept your head down, so you're likely off the Templars' radar, and not in their database.'

'Unless they have access to the Registerium's database ...'

'If they have that, we're all screwed,' said Caspar.

'How am I supposed to convince her?'

'And here was me thinking you had *some* ability to think for yourself ... Just get on the next plane to New York, find Leila, and get her out the way.'

'Oh, fine,' said Jon, jabbing his finger at the red button. He missed. *Really?* 'But I'm flying first class.'

'What's up?' said Meredith, as she joined Caspar in the orange grove at the heart of the Holy Star's headquarters.

'Your boyfriend,' said Caspar.

Meredith scowled.

'Boyfriend?' said Torsten. Meredith's newly acquired Viking-shaped shadow appeared behind her. He sat next to Meredith on a bench in the shade.

'He's the love of my life,' said Meredith, giving Torsten a look so fierce he got to his feet. 'So you might as well give up already.'

Torsten looked uncertainly at Caspar.

'It's a running joke,' said Caspar. 'Jon's a baby demon ... nothing to worry about.'

Torsten nodded, then ran a hand across his perfectly slicked ginger coiffure, making sure not a hair had been shaken out of place.

Meredith rolled her eyes. 'Jon's not such a baby any longer,' she said. 'You should remember that.'

'He's going to New York to retrieve Leila,' said Caspar.

'Good,' said Meredith. 'Was that all you wanted?'

Caspar looked from Meredith to Torsten, planning his next words carefully. 'I've spoken to Sofie and Henrik,' he said, watching them with interest.

'My king and queen are not happy about my lack of engagement,' said Torsten.

Meredith growled.

Caspar nodded. 'In a nutshell,' he said. 'However, we've settled on a new arrangement to secure our alliance.'

'If I have to marry a different Viking, ask them to send someone less ... prissy,' said Meredith.

'Prissy?' said Torsten, rounding on her. 'I'll have you know, I'm the most feared warrior in my nation.'

'Could have fooled me ...' said Meredith.

'Guys,' said Caspar, 'quit bickering. If aggressive flirting's your thing, that's fine, but save it for when I'm not around.'

Meredith scowled again.

'Does that mean she's into me?' said Torsten.

Caspar shook his head in exasperation. 'Sofie and Henrik have one condition to seal our alliance ... they want information on the West Coast nation.

'Between the work Ira's doing, and Gemma and Elliot's trip to the West Coast, we should have it covered, but you two need to stick around here, help Ira however you can, and relay information to both our nations.'

'Where are *you* going?' said Meredith, her tone objectionable.

'On a roadshow,' he said. 'You're welcome to schmooze the leaders of the other nations if you'd prefer that job ...?'

His words were harsher than he'd intended, and Meredith looked away.

A tiny part of Caspar felt sorry for Meredith. He'd secretly hoped Torsten would turn out to be her soulmate. But then, there was still time ...

Zahora had been avoiding Noah for three days. She couldn't recall exactly what had happened when he'd put her to bed after her near disaster at the stone, and that was probably for the best.

In the days since, she'd reined herself in, told herself she had to suck it up, to follow Marla's slow method. She'd done it too, studiously testing one symbol at a time. None of them had given her the same feeling as the symbols she'd chosen herself, but she couldn't tell Marla that ... it would mean revealing what she'd done; how she'd nearly ruined everything … maybe she had ruined everything. Maybe that man with Raina, whoever he'd been, had run straight to the Templars' leader. But also, maybe he knew more about magic than anyone here …

She looked down at the Dara Knot she'd painted on her arm; it was like part of her went missing when she washed it off … it made her feel … prepared somehow. *Urgh*, she was supposed to be meditating, restoring her inner balance … or … something. She shouldn't allow her mind to wander.

She lay on a large flat stone in the middle of a circle of smaller flat stones that protruded from a waist-deep pool of water. The pool was further into the same cave complex as the standing stone, the water flowing to this pool after it passed there.

Candles and sound bowls sat on the smaller stones around her. She reached for a bowl, turning it over in her hands. They'd never helped focus her before … only that one time with …

'Zahora?' said Noah's smooth, soothing voice.

She jumped, dropping the bowl onto the stone. 'Oh damn it, that's one of Marla's favorites,' she said, reaching to pick up the dented metal.

'It's a piece of shit,' said Noah. 'It's so full of flaws, she won't notice a new scratch or two.'

'I wouldn't be so sure,' said Zahora. She was certain it was exactly the kind of thing Marla would notice.

'What are you doing here?' they both said together, then smiled.

'I'm exploring,' said Noah. 'I don't think I'm supposed to be in here, but curiosity got the better of me.'

Zahora laughed. 'Marla would probably fire you if she knew.'

'Then for God's sake, don't tell her!'

'Do you believe in God?' said Zahora. She wasn't sure what made her ask … 'Sorry. You don't have to …'

Noah gave an easy laugh. 'It's fine, and I do believe in God. My parents are religious, so I guess it rubbed off on me. Although, I'm not as strict as they are … I guess I'm more … spiritual. How about you?'

Zahora wasn't sure how to answer, so instead said, 'I'm supposed to be meditating—Marla's orders—but I can't seem to concentrate.'

'I'm guessing that happens a lot to you?' said Noah, sitting on the edge of the pool and removing his flip-flops.

'You really shouldn't …' said Zahora, as he lowered his feet into the water.

'Too late …' said Noah, mischievously.

'Seriously, if Marla finds you, I had nothing to do with …' she waved her hand in his general direction, '… this.'

'It was all me,' Noah confirmed. 'But I can't help you relax from over here.'

Help me relax? A zing of awareness travelled through her. 'Woah there tiger. What do you mean?'

'You can't concentrate, and I can help,' he said with a shrug.

'I'll be … fine.'

'You're the most restless person I've ever met; there's no way you can do this by yourself.'

Zahora furrowed her brow. 'What do you mean, restless?'

'I can practically feel it radiating off you. You're impatient … itching for momentum; it's got to be exhausting.'

Zahora thought his words over. Was it exhausting? She wasn't so sure. It was … something. Frustrating?

Irritating? Like the whole world wanted to hold her back ... but ... exhausting?

'You're wrong,' she said. 'I'm not exhausted. I'm just getting started.'

Noah said nothing. He looked at her, really looked, then pushed himself over the edge, into the water.

It was freezing, Zahora knew, but he didn't seem to notice. He gave not a wince, nor sign of tension about the shoulders.

'It's deeper than I thought,' he said, pulling off his t-shirt, revealing the full splendor of his ridged torso.

Zahora stared. She knew she shouldn't, but she couldn't help it ... it wasn't like fine male specimens littered the place. Her pulse rocketed ... how was this supposed to help her meditate?

'What are you doing?' she said, tracking his progress, the gap narrowing.

'Lie down,' he said.

Zahora laughed. She wasn't sure why exactly ... was he making her nervous? People weren't usually so self-assured ...

'There's no way I'm lying down. I don't know you ... and you're half naked!'

Noah stopped, processing her words. 'Then let's get to know each other.'

'Aren't you supposed to be working?'

'Day off.'

'There's such a thing?'

'Where shall we start?' he said, moving towards the biggest of the small stones. 'Will this fall over if I sit on it?'

'I don't know,' she said. 'I doubt it, although if it does, they might literally hang, draw, and quarter you.'

'Good to know,' he said, gingerly resting his weight on the stone. It held.

'So, where are you from?' he asked.

'You first.'

He gave her an indulgent look. 'I'm from America.'

'Where?'

'I've lived all over, but I went to school on the West Coast, much to Dad's despair. He wanted me to stay on the East Coast ... Ivy League.'

'Do you get on with your parents?' asked Zahora, lapping up each piece of information as though it were sustenance.

'I don't think so ... your turn. Are you from around here?'

'Yes and no,' said Zahora. She couldn't tell him the truth—that she'd been born in Cornwall over a hundred years ago, this her third life ... that she had an estranged human family not ten miles from where they sat. They'd been devastated when she'd left them five years ago, still a teenager. She settled on, 'I am now.'

'Do your parents live nearby?'

'They died,' she said, which wasn't wholly untrue. Her parents from her first two lives were dead.

'I'm sorry.'

'Do you get on with your parents?' she asked.

'Yes and no,' he said with a smile.

'Don't be evasive.'

He raised an eyebrow.

She splashed him.

'Hey!' he said. 'Do that again and I'll dunk you.'

It took all Zahora's self-control to resist, but going there, to all that physical contact, seemed like crossing a line.

'Tell me,' she said, her voice soft.

He looked at her for a beat, their gazes locked. 'I get on okay with Dad. I guess we have a typical father-son relationship. He wants me to be like him, and I want to do my own thing ... live my own life.'

'What about your mum?'

52

He went still, then looked away. 'Mum was from Africa. I can't remember her ... she's dead.'

Oh. 'I'm sorry,' she said, feeling like an arsehole.

He still refused to look at her.

'Hey,' she said, 'don't make me splash you ...'

'It wouldn't be the worst thing ...' he said, flicking his eyes to hers.

Her stomach lurched. 'I thought you were going to help me relax.'

He jumped off his stone. 'Lie down,' he said. 'On your front.'

Zahora reluctantly did as he said, using her arms as a pillow.

'Close your eyes.'

She gave him a look, but did it, feeling vulnerable, acutely aware of every sound and movement he made.

A metallic rubbing filled the air and a sound bowl sprang to life, a soft ring rolling out across the cave. Zahora's hair stood on end. After a few gentle splashes, another bowl sounded, then two more, bathing the cave in music.

The sounds both relaxed and invigorated, waking her on the inside. The Dara Knot on her arm heated, pulling at her, but not as strongly as before. She hadn't used the Triskelion ... in her case, extra motion wasn't needed.

She tried to meditate, but the magic called to her, the Nexus only a breath away. She wasn't touching the standing stone, but she was still on a ley line, and the water connected her to it. She hesitated. Last time she'd touched the magic, she'd come close to destruction, saved only by Noah. The time before had been no different, and she'd announced herself to the world. She should be cautious ... listen to Marla. She should use this time to relax, recuperate, learn ...

But when would she next be able to access the Nexus with Noah by her side? He knew how to call her back … She'd gone three days with no progress at all, and time wasn't on their side …

She didn't make the decision, not consciously at least. Her soul longed for the Nexus. More than that, it longed to touch the Sphere—the raw power of the lines. Going that far was a bad idea, so she brushed against the Nexus instead, let it feel her power.

It liked her power, sucked at her, trying to draw her to the other side. She fought back, calling on the strength of the Dara Knot to resist, to help keep her safe. She thought of Raina, willing the Nexus to find her, to transport her there.

It did her bidding with surprising speed, and when she jolted to a halt, Zahora had to breathe deeply, to listen to the music grounding her in the outside world, to center herself.

Raina's voice pierced her nausea, every ounce of focus snapping to attention, following the words.

'You have to go,' said Raina, her tone coaxing.

'I don't want to,' said a second voice, that of a young girl.

'Callie,' said Raina, 'we've been through this. It's important for you to learn magic.'

'The Templars say magic's stupid,' said Callie.

'Alerac is very old. He can teach you many things … not only about magic. And I have to go out … so your other option is to sit here by yourself.'

'Urgh, fine. I'll go. But I'm not going to listen to him …'

The door opened and Callie stormed through.

'Have fun!' said Raina.

Callie slammed the door. Raina ran an exasperated hand through her hair, then slipped her shoes on.

Zahora knew she had to do something; there was no telling how often Raina was alone …

'Raina,' said Zahora, but Raina headed for the door, as though she hadn't heard.

'RAINA!' shouted Zahora.

Again, nothing. *Shit. Shit. Shit.*

Just as Raina's hand landed on the door handle, Zahora reached for Raina's soul and tugged. Raina fell backwards onto the floor, clutching her chest. A force batted Zahora away so hard she cried out, startled.

Raina jumped to her feet, looking wildly around.

'I'm a friend,' said Zahora, again and again, willing the words towards Raina. She'd heard the other magiks talk of sendings—magical messages sent around the Nexus. Zahora had never done one, had never been taught … it was a skill the Pagans reserved for Proficients. But she willed her words towards Raina, hoping against hope her message would get through.

'I'm a friend. I'm Pagan. I'm a friend. I'm Pagan.'

Raina relaxed a little, her movements less frantic. 'Hang on,' she said, casting her eyes around the room.

Raina took a candle from a low table, then rummaged under her bed, pulling out a piece of stone. She threw aside the rug and placed the stone on the floor. She lit the candle and held it aloft, turning in a circle, muttering words Zahora couldn't make out.

Raina blew out the candle, but continued turning, so the smoke wafted around, then sat next to the stone, touching it with both hands. 'Can you hear me?' Raina said.

'Yes,' said Zahora, 'but I've been able to hear you all along … Can you hear me?'

'I can, but I haven't much time,' said Raina. 'Who are you?'

'I'm from the Pagan nation. I'm training with the magiks.'

'You're the one who came the other day?'

'Yes,' said Zahora.

'Why are you here?'

'I ...' Why was she here? Because Raina was a living legend? Because she was supposed to be helping her escape ...? 'I'm here because I want to help ... but I need you to help me first.'

Raina tipped her head to the side, but stayed silent.

'I've got power ... a lot of it ... but I don't know how to use it. Marla wants me to slow down, to do everything methodically, but I don't work that way. I thought ... I thought you might understand ... might be able to help me ... with a different method or something ...'

Raina swung her head to the door. 'I've got to go. I can't help you ... not directly at least. I don't have the training for what you need, but Alerac does.'

'The man from the other day?'

'Yes.'

'Is he on our side?'

Raina shook her head. 'That's the problem ... I don't know. I'll be in touch when I do.' Raina replaced the carpet, then left the room. Zahora followed.

'I was coming to get you. Are you ready to go?' said a man.

'Yes,' said Raina, completely composed.

Zahora trailed them, curiosity getting the better of her, but it was harder and harder the further they went, exhaustion pulling at her soul. Still, she followed them down the clear acrylic stairs, where a raft of long swords adorned the wall, then out a huge front door that slid side to side on rollers.

Raina and the man left the building, and Zahora tried to keep up, but everything became confused, blurry, more difficult to focus. Zahora picked up sounds and snippets of vision, but nothing concrete.

56

Her connection to the Nexus waned, and Zahora panicked. What would happen if she lost the Nexus entirely?

And then she felt something hot and ... sensual run down her back. A deep, decadent ringing filled her head and she felt the Nexus more keenly ... knew how to get back to its safety. She could feel the lines of the Sphere running under the building, and allowed them to tug at her soul, to pull her back to her body.

Zahora came back to herself, the cold of the stone the first thing that registered in her conscious mind. Thank the Gods: She'd made it back unharmed, or at least, she thought she had ...

She opened her eyes, about to roll over, but the sensation on her back came again, low on her spine, against her bare skin. It was hot ... too hot? No, it was cooling ... then another patch of heat, lower. Candle wax, she realized. Noah.

It continued, travelling lower still, then stopped. A metallic scraping filled the air, this one higher pitched than the last. It sent a buzz of euphoria through her, and she basked in the rich, beautiful, flawless note resonating around her.

'Mmmm,' she said, 'that is the most perfect sound I've ever heard.'

Noah breathed an audible sigh of relief. 'Thank God you're back,' he said. 'I was about to get Marla.'

Or maybe his voice was the most perfect sound ... 'Gods, never do that!' she said, unable to lift her head. 'She'd kill me.'

'I wouldn't let her,' said Noah, placing a reassuring hand on her shoulder.

Heat radiated out from his touch, and a shiver zinged down her spine. She hummed again, realizing too late she probably should have stopped the sound ...

Noah chuckled, then put his other hand on her back.

'Your hands are so hot,' she said, 'but that water must be freezing ...'

'I'm a furnace,' he said. 'Always have been.'

'It's nice. No one's touched me in ... well ... a long time.'

He slid his hands down her back, to where the wax stuck to her skin.

Zahora breathed out and closed her eyes, trying to ignore the growing heat in her blood. She didn't want him to stop ... she wanted to lie here forever with his hot, healing hands.

'I'll take the wax off,' he said. 'It was the only thing I could think of ... aside from rolling you into the water ... the sound bowls didn't work like last time, and I splashed you a bit, and shook you ...'

'It was a great idea,' she said.

Noah pushed up her top as he peeled off the wax. She wanted him to slide his hands up further, under her clothes ... she tried to banish the unhelpful thought, but then he pulled at the wax on her spine, and it was ... it was erotic. She had to bite her lip to keep from moaning. *Oh for goodness' sake* ...what was she doing? She couldn't get involved with a human ...

But he was such a good-looking human, and his hands were so ... hot.

He traced his fingers across her skin, picking off the last bits of wax. She hummed again; she didn't want the contact to end.

He pulled down her top, and the air went taut in the growing silence. Was it just her, or could he feel that too?

'Done,' he said, with a gentle pat.

'Shame,' she said, the word out before she could stop herself.

Noah chuckled again. 'You know, I give a mean head massage,' he said, leaning so his lips were close to her ear. 'Next time, I'll try that.'

She lifted her head. 'Next time?'

He gave her an incredulous look. 'Oh, come on. You don't expect me to believe there won't be a next time? How are you planning on getting back from ... wherever it is you go? Going to ask Marla to help you?'

Damn it; he had a point. 'How do you know when to help? And ... why were you even in here?'

'They told me to set out sound bowls again, and you twitch and shake and make little yelping noises like an injured puppy.'

That's embarrassing ... 'I do not.'

'I can film it next time if you'd like?'

She sat up, dangled her legs in the freezing water, and looked him squarely in the eyes. 'No one can know about this ... Marla would ...'

'She'd kill you; I know.'

'Seriously ...'

'I can keep a secret.'

She paused, searching his eyes. She didn't even know him ...

'I just want to help,' he said, 'to be useful, and ... I don't want you to hurt yourself.'

He shouldn't be privy to any of this ...

'What are you doing anyway?' he asked. 'Some kind of deep meditation?'

She took a breath. Was his curiosity a good sign or a bad one?

'Kind of,' she said, fighting her closing eyelids. She eyed the water, not relishing the idea of wading through it ... maybe she could just sleep here on the cold, hard stone. 'Why do you want to help me?'

'Because I'm a great guy!' he said, nudging her.

She shook her head.

'And I like you,' he said quietly.

He likes me! She should put an end to this right now … demon-human relationships never worked out.

She gave him an encouraging smile. 'I like you too,' she whispered. It was getting hard to talk. 'But I don't know you.'

'What else do you want to know?'

Lots of things, probably, not that she could think of a single question right now. All she could think about was sleep. Her eyes fluttered closed for a second, then another. It was so hard to force them open. They should be open. She would open them …

Strong hands grasped her shoulders. 'Hey,' said Noah. 'I'll help you back to your room.'

Zahora nodded, or at least tried to … she wasn't sure if her body was still doing her bidding … but then warmth and strength and Noah's musky male scent were all around her, and she sighed. She burrowed into him, wishing she could crawl inside and pull him closed around her, like a mouse nesting for the winter. She'd happily spend a whole season here.

'I've got you,' said Noah's deep voice, vibrations rumbling through his chest and into her. His lips brushed her hair, and, unable to fight it any longer, she tumbled into the dark, deep clutches of sleep.

Chapter 5

Jamie stood back and waved Raina ahead, up a shiny flight of stairs. They'd walked to the financial district, their conversation stunted, Raina intrigued to see where he was taking her.

They entered a modern skyscraper with a large entrance hall, a man behind a reception desk looking up as the door swung shut behind them.

'Good afternoon, Mr. Vanderveld,' said the receptionist. 'The Grand Master will be with you shortly.'

Grand Master? Of what? Jamie was the only Grand Master of the Templar nation …

'He's in the shooting range,' said the receptionist. 'Please select robes.'

Jamie nodded, motioning for Raina to follow him towards a room off to the side of the reception area. She took in every detail of her surroundings—the Christian insignia, shooting certificates, Latin mottos—and dread crept up her spine. She spun to face Jamie, her eyes wide.

'That was quicker than I expected,' he said with a smug smile.

Raina took steps back towards the exit, but Jamie stopped her with a hand on her arm.

'You're not in any danger,' he said. 'You wanted to know where I've been, and this is it. We've got a ... strategic partnership with the Slayers.'

'The most righteous Order of Knights of the Hospi,' corrected the receptionist, his hawk-like eyes trained on them.

Jamie inclined his head.

'This way,' said Jamie, his voice low.

Raina hesitated. It felt wrong to be in the lion's den, but she needed to find out more about this *strategic partnership* ... it would be invaluable information, if she could get a message to the Pagans.

She followed Jamie into a room full of red robes, accepting the robe he threw round her shoulders without protest. Jamie raised his hood, and Raina did the same. She followed him back to the reception area, her mind racing. This was not at all where she'd thought Jamie had been spending his time ... the most dangerous place for a demon to be ...

A short Black man, clad as though headed to the Hamptons for the weekend, waited for them, a red robe slung over his arm.

'Grand Master,' said Jamie, shaking the man's hand.

'Jamie,' said the Grand Master.

'This is Raina Halabi,' said Jamie.

Raina shook his hand, fighting the urge to use it to throw him to the floor.

'The famed Raina,' said the Grand Master. 'What an *honor*.'

'I'm sure the *honor* is all mine,' said Raina, matching his sarcastic tone. 'Is someone going to tell me why I'm here now?'

The Grand Master cocked an eyebrow, then swung a questioning look at Jamie.

'Our nation has a partnership with the Slayers,' said Jamie. 'We both know our chances of success are higher if we work together. The Slayers have freedoms that the Templars—as a demon nation—do not. I've brought you here as I thought it pertinent to acquaint our key strategist with our most valuable ally.'

Chances of success? With what? What was Jamie's grand plan? If it involved the Slayers, that could only mean death and destruction ... assuming they weren't walking into a trap right here and now.

'Come,' said the Grand Master, 'or we'll be late.'

They followed the Grand Master along a gleaming, ultra-modern corridor, then through a set of ancient looking wooden doors. The juxtaposition was stark, and unease trickled down Raina's spine; everything about this place felt wrong.

They entered a hexagonal stone chamber—a church, but with no pews, and symbols adorning the six paths to the central altar. Six columns circled the altar, which was flooded with light from above. They must have built the skyscraper around an old church ...

People stood in the areas between the paths, dressed in red robes, their hoods up so Raina couldn't see their faces.

A chant began as they entered, and Raina shuddered at the sound. The Grand Master processed to the center, past the candles that lined the path, the only source of light aside from the skylight above the altar.

Jamie peeled off after only a few steps, pulling Raina to stand with him at the back by the wall, close enough to the path to have a good view of the altar.

'This place has been here since the Dutch first came to New York,' said Jamie. 'Cleverly concealed, don't you think?'

Raina raised her eyebrows in agreement. From the outside, the building was identical to all the other corporate monstrosities. No one would guess an old church lay inside.

'They own the whole building,' Jamie murmured.

'This entire building's full of Slayers?' hissed Raina, horrified.

The chanting ceased, and Jamie threw her a conspiratorial look, like there was more he would tell her later. She had questions, that was for damn sure.

The Grand Master reached the altar. He knelt before another robed Slayer—a priest—who held two weapons in the shape of a cross above the Grand Master's head.

Raina froze. Those weapons had been crafted to kill her people. And not just temporarily—so they could reincarnate—but permanently. They were scoops to remove a demon's eyes ...

At her great age, there were few things that truly scared her, but the Furor was one of them. Demons spent their lives avoiding the terrifying instruments. To get this close—on purpose—was insanity.

Raina could feel Jamie's gaze, but she couldn't tear her eyes from the threat. If she had to fight her way out, she probably could. She'd have to sacrifice Jamie, of course, but she'd make it. She'd be out before they could raise the alarm ... assuming they hadn't locked the doors already ... deep breaths ... it would be okay ... Jamie wouldn't put himself in danger ... not on purpose anyway ...

The priest finished his incantation and lowered the Furors. A set of doors on the far side of the chamber swung open, and two robed Slayers entered, dragging the limp figure of a woman between them.

More Slayers stepped forward, unhooking chains from the pillars by the altar. They attached the chains to the unconscious woman's wrists and ankles, laying her flat on the floor. The light from the ceiling illuminated her slack features.

The Grand Master now held the Furors, the priest fixing the woman's head in a brace. The woman woke, took a second to realize what was happening, then screamed. Raina closed her eyes. She couldn't watch, not when she had met the woman, had so recently seen her living life to the full. Had danced with her in the hall of the Vikings'.

Jamie would be watching for any sign of weakness, but he couldn't see her face hidden inside the hood of her robe. Raina was no stranger to death, had killed many times ... but she'd never caused the final death of a demon, at least not on purpose.

She tried to block out the sounds of screaming, scraping, sucking, the Grand Master's instructions, the smell of burning flesh as they destroyed the Viking's eyes as she lay whimpering on the floor. But it was futile. She heard it and smelt it and tasted it on the air. She focused on settling her roiling stomach, using a small magic to help. The magic came more easily now, thanks to Alerac's relentless instruction.

She thought of Caspar, of his deep brown eyes and soothing voice, transported to a previous life, to the aftermath of a death such as this. They'd been too late to save a friend, and had clung together in their grief, covered in the blood of the Slayers responsible. She could almost imagine the chapel's incense smelled like her soulmate ... But the sound of a knife impaling flesh interrupted the memory ... and then, silence.

Raina opened her eyes and took in the pool of blood seeping out across the flagstones.

'The Lord be with you,' said the priest.

'And also with you,' the Slayers chanted back.

'What the fuck, Jamie?' said Raina, as soon as they'd escaped the Slayers' building, and she was sure they weren't being followed. Raina hadn't felt like this in lifetimes—out of control ... blindsided.

'We need them,' said Jamie, with a dismissive hand wave.

'For what?'

'To rid the world of the unworthy.'

'Jamie ... what had that Viking woman done?'

Jamie stopped walking and spun to face her. 'Only the strong should be allowed to survive. We demons live constrained lives ... it's unnatural ... not the way it's supposed to be, and that woman was nothing ... no one. Demons like us are superior, and it's time we started acting like it.'

'By killing each other?' said Raina. It wasn't the first time demons had spouted such nonsense, not by a long shot ... And it wasn't like the humans were any better ...

'If that's what it takes to bring our race to heal.'

'Why?' said Raina.

'Because I deserve to rule ... you and I ... we were born to do it. And once we have our own race in hand, we can turn this world around. Sort out the mess the humans have made. Create our own utopia ... for our daughter. We can make the world a better place.'

Inside the safety of her own mind, Raina smirked, then laughed, then cringed, then raged. Outside, her face was blank. Had Jamie learned nothing from his hundreds of years? Didn't he know that killing only led to more killing? That dictatorships led only to suffering? That large tech companies, spouting the same rubbish, were literally killing the world at this very moment, for the *good of humanity*?

'Okay, Jamie. Tell me more.'

Leila watched as her cousin—along with a handsome companion who was not Caspar—stopped on the other side of the street. They were obviously discussing something contentious, and Leila longed to know what it was. Who was this strange man, and what was her cousin doing with him?

Leila had been scouring the area around the park where she'd seen Amari and Callie for days, but to no avail. And then here Amari was, right in front of Leila's favorite brunch spot, only a couple of blocks from the park.

Amari and the man moved on. Leila hastily threw money on the table and jumped up to follow them, but she'd made it only a handful of steps when someone grabbed her arm and dragged her into an alley.

'It's okay, I'm not trying to hurt you,' said a brash male voice. He relinquished his hold, and Leila whirled to face her accoster.

'Who the hell are you?' said Leila, eyeing the tall, blonde, self-assured man in an expensive suit before her ... not your average mugger ...

'I'm Jon—your knight in shining armor.'

His accent was British. Was this to do with Dean? Or … 'Are you one of those weirdos with a superhero complex? Because, in case you hadn't noticed, I don't need saving.'

'The fact you think that tells me I was right to come.'

'I'm going now,' said Leila, turning away, a spike of fear hitting her as she exposed her back to him.

'I know you're following Raina,' said Jon. 'And it's a bad idea.'

'What did you say?' said Leila, spinning back to face him.

'You heard me. And if you keep doing what you're doing, you're going to get yourself killed.'

Leila's usually fast mouth went dry. She didn't know what to say, possibly for the first time in her life. So she just stared at the beautiful, arrogant man before her.

'I'll tell you everything, but we should get off the streets,' said Jon. 'We're in the Templars' heartland, right under their noses, and if we're caught, they'll kill me too.'

The way he talked about their possible demise was so casual. Wasn't that strange?

'Where do you suggest we go?' said Leila.

'I have an apartment not too far away,' said Jon. 'Or we can go to your place.'

'Or we can do neither of those things,' said Leila. 'I've literally just met you. You could be a serial rapist, or a murder, or a rapist and a murderer.'

Jon rolled his eyes and took an audible breath. 'You should trust me.'

Leila gave him a look that said, *seriously?*

'This is why I hate jobs like this,' said Jon. 'People like you are always so unreasonable. You know I'm supposed to be eating a seven-course tasting menu right now? At one of the world's top restaurants? Celebrating my money-making genius? And instead, I'm standing in a filthy alleyway, with a stroppy woman.'

'Excuse me, Mr. Fancy-Pants,' said Leila. 'I never asked you to accost me in the street, and I couldn't give a rat's arse about your seven-course dinner. I probably know ten restaurants right here in Manhattan that would knock the socks right off your fancy-pants dinner.'

'I doubt it,' said Jon. 'I'm something of an expert ... and you said fancy-pants twice.'

'I bet it's got a celebrity chef and everything,' said Leila.

'I don't see what that has to do with anything ...'

'And my cousin is probably the most sought-after food critic this side of Istanbul. I know a thing or two myself.'

'What ... Raina?' said Jon, his features scrunching in disbelief.

'Amari,' said Leila.

'She's called Raina.'

'Her name is Amari, Jackass.' Leila made for the street. 'Are you coming or not?'

Chapter 6

Caspar made his way down the dazzling corridor of a Shindu temple in northern India. He hated the bling, the incense, the landscape, the heat, the sweet freaking tea. He couldn't wait to leave ... and he'd only just arrived.

'Caspar,' said a woman at the end of the corridor. She was short, round, and insufferably self-important.

'Eka,' said Caspar, 'it's a pleasure to see you again so soon.' Caspar gave her a respectful half bow.

'Indeed, it is,' said Eka, inclining her head. 'I must say I was surprised, given our conversation at the Buddhist caves. You assured me you hadn't kidnapped Raina, and yet she's currently with the Templars, is she not?'

Talk about diving straight in ... 'Raina registered as a Pagan as soon as she awoke,' said Caspar. 'That should tell you all you need to know.'

'Then why is she currently with the Templars? Why has the Registerium confirmed her transfer to the Templar nation?'

'A good question,' said Caspar. 'And if you're interested in justice, in finding the truth, then you should work with the Pagan nation. The Registerium did not follow protocol during Raina's nation transfer: We were not informed, and the transfer was not completed through the standing stone ...'

Eka raised her eyebrows. 'If that's true, I will concede my interest is piqued.'

'And you must have heard about Raina's reunion with Jamie? She told him, in front of a room full of demons—including an envoy from the Buddhist nation—that we did not kidnap her. I'm sure you'll be able to confirm that if you try.'

Eka nodded her head once. 'That we will,' she said. 'And in the meantime, we will discuss the potential terms of an alliance.'

Eka stood back, and the colossal ornate doors behind her cracked open, revealing a lavish hall full of gold leaf and plush cushions.

Caspar nodded and smiled, but inside he raged. This bullshit would take hours. Hours that would do little to help Raina or Callie. Caspar had no cards to play, and the Shindus knew it ... they would make ridiculous demands. It had been a long time since Caspar had been so powerless in a negotiation. He and Raina had been the ones everyone else had to please. And they would be again ... that he vowed.

'Yes?' said Meredith, answering Caspar's call. She'd been trying—and failing—to avoid Torsten for days on end. Everywhere she went, there he was. Every time she trained, or ate, or tried to have a conversation with Ira—the tech wizz who could teach her things of genuine interest, like how to strengthen her nation's defenses—but every time, there he was, making inane comments about her prowess.

It was infuriating … and worst of all, he could not take a hint. Her rebukes barely even landed glancing blows. He would simply smile and take her venomous words as invitations to try harder. At least Ira seemed to feel the same way about the irritating Viking, not that he'd offered much help …

'You're not going to like this,' said Caspar, his voice pulling her back to the phone call.

'What now?' said Meredith.

'The Shindus have a request to secure our alliance …'

Meredith didn't fill the silence.

'As you know, they never much liked Raina … after the incident in the fifteen hundreds …'

'Oh, for Gods' sake, Caspar, just spit it out,' said Meredith. It felt good to snap.

'They want you to dig up treasure they buried in the Dead Sea.'

'Why can't they do it themselves?'

'They don't have the best relationship with the Holy Star,' said Caspar, 'and they're not sure where it is, exactly.'

'Are you freaking kidding me? You're sending me on a treasure hunt?'

'You're the closest,' said Caspar. 'And Torsten can help.'

'No,' said Meredith, warming to the task. 'Torsten can stay in Tel Aviv and help Ira. I'll go by myself.'

'I'm afraid that won't be possible,' said Caspar. 'The Vikings want to see the treasure before we hand it over …'

'In case they decide it's really theirs?' said Meredith. 'What is it with Vikings and other people's stuff?'

'Well, in any case, Torsten needs to come with you.'

'Torsten can go by himself, and I'll stay here. Ira's a genius ... the things he's teaching me will be invaluable to our nation.'

'You know as well as I do, if the Vikings get their hands on the treasure unsupervised, it'll disappear before you can say the word *alliance*.'

'Urgh,' said Meredith, resisting the urge to hurl her phone at the head of the man who had just appeared around the nearest corner. 'I'm assuming you've already cleared this with the Holy Star? They're happy for us to go treasure hunting in their territory?'

'Yes,' said Caspar. 'They said to watch out for raiders ... I think the Persian Zoros got wind of the treasure too and have been skirmishing to try and find it.'

'Oh for ... fine,' said Meredith. 'Nothing I can't handle.'

Meredith hung up the phone.

'You heard the good news?' said Torsten.

It was such a shame he was so irritating ... his accent was a delight. She rolled her eyes.

'The Dead Sea's so romantic,' said Torsten, 'and, Gods willing, the Zorros will give us the chance to fight back to back. Nothing like a tussle to get the blood pumping ...'

'Jesus Christ,' said Meredith. 'When will you take the hint?'

'When you open your eyes and see what's right in front of you? Maybe then.'

His words were stern—unusual for him—and they landed like a knockout punch.

Zahora lay back in the freezing water. It sucked the heat from her skin, sapping her, and then she felt it … the sustaining magic of the Sphere, buoying her, filling her. She closed her eyes and let it in, greedily sucking up as much as she could get.

This pool was even further into the cave complex than the others. Only a handful of senior magiks were allowed so far into the caves, which made them blessedly quiet. Marla had given Zahora special dispensation to be here, seeing as she was integral to the effort to rescue Raina and Callie … not that she'd made any headway on that either. Raina still hadn't been in contact, and Zahora needed to reach out to her again, but she couldn't. It was too dangerous while she was preoccupied with thoughts of … other things.

The magic made her tingle, every nerve coming alive, and then it made her restless … even more restless than the magik demons that kept arriving, causing disturbance in the ether, and taking Noah from her. She hadn't seen him in days … he'd been helping cook and clean, preparing beds and meditation spaces.

All she could think about was him. Even now, while the magic of the ley lines was pulsing in her veins, she couldn't concentrate, except for on him.

It was holding her back, and she had to do something … but there was only one solution she could come up with, and that involved pouncing on him.

There was nothing for it … and it *was* for the good of their nation, after all. She stood, making for the pool's edge, then grabbed her towel and wrapped it around her naked body. She slipped on her flip-flops and stalked off in the direction of the cookhouse.

It was just after lunch, in the lull before prep for the evening meal got underway, and Zahora didn't know where Noah was. She hadn't seen him today, and his schedule varied wildly. She looked around, staying hidden—given that she was wearing a towel—but couldn't find him anywhere.

She looked in the communal hall, the teaching chambers, and in the stores. Still no sign. She looked in the library, then endless meditation rooms—nothing. Her irritable state worsened. How could it be so hard to find someone in a compound as small as this?

She walked back towards her hut via the impressive vegetable garden, and finally struck gold, catching a glimpse of his back disappearing into an old potting shed. Zahora marched forward with renewed vigor. She followed him into the shed, which was filled with old pots, soil, tools, and had windows down the side overlooking the garden.

Noah turned when he heard her enter, his face betraying first his shock, then his delight at seeing her. His eyes traveled down the length of her, taking in her towel and flip-flops, then flicked up to her face.

They stared at each other for a beat, forbidden fruit hanging in the air between them, and then, in unison, they moved. They crashed together, mouths meeting in a frantic press, then opening, each inviting the other to explore.

Noah picked her up and put her on the potting bench, their hands roaming until they found skin. His long, lean stomach muscles rippled under Zahora's icy fingers, and she felt him everywhere, enhanced by the magic from the pool.

Noah's fingers dipped between her legs, and she moaned, pressing into his touch. It was so, so good, but she was impatient for more, so her hands went to his trousers, making quick work of the button and zip.

'Zahora, we can't ...' he ground out, sending a guilty look through the windows.

'Why not?' she said, pumping her hand up and down his length.

'We don't have protection ... oh God,' he gasped, moving his hips in time with her fist. 'Don't stop.'

'I can't have kids,' she said, shunting herself to the edge of the bench, his erection brushing her core. She shivered as she moved him against her.

He grabbed her hair and tugged, forcing her eyes up to meet his. 'Not ever?'

The last thing she needed was for him to have an emotional breakdown about her demon lack of fertility ... 'It's extremely unlikely I'll ever conceive a baby,' she said, 'like ninety-nine-point-nine percent certain. I've made peace with it.'

'Fuck,' he said, 'this is ... when did you last get tested? I'm clean. I was tested before I left the States.'

'Me too,' she said, 'I'm clean.' She wasn't about to tell him she'd never had sex in this body ... that would ruin everything, and lead to endless questions. Now she thought about it, that probably explained a lot of this lifetime's angst ...

'Are you sure you want to do this? Here? Like this?' he said, his cock nudging against her.

'Yes,' she said. 'Right now. Do you?'

He gave her an incredulous look, then pushed into her, lifting her off the bench as he pumped his hips. She tipped her head back and her towel fell open, her breasts bouncing with every thrust. 'Oh my God,' he said, burying his face in her cleavage, slowing his pace.

She linked her hands behind his head and writhed, seeking more friction. He sucked a nipple into his mouth, and she gasped, bucking against him.

He lowered her back onto the bench, pushing tools out of the way, neither caring when they clattered to the ground.

She moaned as his fingers explored, and he moved faster, more frantic with every thrust. They tipped over the edge together, and she convulsed around him, rolling her hips, riding the aftershocks, eking out every last ounce of pleasure.

Noah lifted her against him, then sank to the floor, leaning back against the wall, still inside her. She rested her head in the crook of his neck, nuzzling at his pulse point as his hands caressed her.

She pulled back and looked him in the eye, then held his face in both hands and kissed him, the kiss deep and languid and luxurious. He hummed, and she rocked her hips.

He smiled into her mouth, and she rocked again, then again, feeling him stiffen. He palmed her breast, then pinched her nipple, rolling it between his fingers. She arched her back, moving along his length.

'How is this so good?' he murmured, then took her ass in his hands, moving her faster.

'Yes,' she moaned, dropping her hand between them.

'Fuck ... that's so hot.'

She rode him harder, pulsing her hips, so close to oblivion.

'Zahora ... baby.'

And then it hit. Great pulsing shock-waves racking through her, intensifying as he too found release.

Zahora and Noah snuck back to Zahora's hut, taking pains to avoid being seen, and trying to make it look like they weren't together. As soon as they reached the small stone shack Zahora called home, they collapsed onto the low double bed and cuddled up together under the covers.

Zahora curled herself into Noah's side, having to stop herself from purring as he stroked her back. It felt so good to be touched ... no one had ever touched her like this. And she needed it ... it made her feel whole. No matter how much she took from the Sphere, nothing else could replenish her this way ... intimacy had such power.

Noah's hand went to her hair, gently scratching her scalp, and a purr broke free. She couldn't help it ... she must have died and gone to heaven.

'Never stop,' she said, nuzzling him.

'I won't.'

'Do you want to work for your dad?' she asked, stroking the ridges of his stomach.

He dropped a kiss on her forehead and left his lips there. 'I don't know,' he said. 'I want to make him proud, but I really want to be a musician. I know I won't make as much money, or at least, it's unlikely, but it's what I want ... what I'm passionate about.'

'Like a pop star?' she asked.

'I'm more into country.'

'Will you show me?'

'Of course. I was thinking I might try it, to bring you back from your meditation next time.'

'I like that idea,' she said, kissing his neck.

'What about you? Was your calling always to this place ... whatever it is?'

'You know what it is,' she said.

'A bunch of back-to-nature hippie weirdos who meditate all the time?'

She swatted him. 'I guess you're not too far off,' she said with a smile. 'Although I'm not sure the others would appreciate that description ... especially not Marla.'

'What would they prefer?'

'I don't know ...' She knew perfectly well, but wasn't about to tell him they went by the title *magik* ... 'I guess they'd call themselves ... spectral, or ... extrasensory.'

'Did that sound better to you?' he joked, giving her a playful squeeze.

She squirmed. 'I guess not ... but you live with us ... so that makes you a hippie weirdo too.'

Rose and Marla watched as Zahora and Noah crept out of the potting shed. They knew exactly what they were up to ... had known it would happen for some time.

'Is he a distraction?' said Rose, still watching their retreating backs.

'Everything that isn't training or recovery is a distraction,' said Marla.

'Is he helping her get what we want?'

'She's connected with the Nexus several times without permission. I am yet to speak with her about it, but I believe, without him, she would have been lost.'

Rose started, then rounded on Marla. 'And you let her do it more than once? Without knowing if she could return?'

'I sent him to her, just in case. She's young and headstrong ... needs to make her own way. She wants to rail against me.'

'Then he's helping her ... he stays ... but, who is he?'

'An American on a gap year.'

'Is he a spy?'

'I don't think so ... We think he's a baby demon, but haven't been able to check for sure, and I don't have a trusted hunter on hand ...'

Rose's gut sent her a deep sense of foreboding. 'And he just showed up one day?'

'He was sent by his father, apparently ... a successful businessman. None of the checks showed anything strange, and he hasn't been snooping around.'

'Just shagging our most valuable magik ...' said Rose, her voice dripping with sarcasm. 'Let them keep going, but watch him. It's odd, his showing up here at this moment in time. And if we have to remove him, make sure you're there to pull her back yourself.'

Rose turned as if to leave, then looked back. 'And find out what she's been doing in the Nexus. In case you've forgotten, the longer Raina and Callie remain with the Templars, the higher the chance we lose them forever ... them and the coming war.'

Zahora hid at the back of a cave that was full of newly arrived magiks. Rose moved to stand at the front, stepping up onto a large rock so she could more easily address the crowd. Talli and Christa were there too, and a buzz of anticipation filled the air at the presence of such celebrity. A hush fell over them as Rose prepared to speak.

'I'm sure you're all eager to know why we've called you here,' said Rose. 'Some of you will have heard that Raina has left the Pagan nation to join the Templars. This is a lie. The Templars forced Raina to transfer to their nation, because her demon child is in their possession.'

A collective gasp went up.

'The Registerium, in an unprecedented move, approved Raina's nation transfer without notifying the Pagan nation, which, I need not remind you, is against protocol. They also transferred her remotely, meaning a magical transfer has not taken place.'

'Then she's still a Pagan!' called a woman near the front.

'Exactly,' said Rose, turning to face the woman. 'We believe the Templars will try to complete the transfer through the Registerium's stone, but it is unclear when. This gives us a window of opportunity—potentially a brief window—in which to rescue Raina before they complete the magical transfer.

'However, Raina's daughter, Callie, is a full Templar, and the Templars do not allow their members to transfer without permission. So we must find a way around this convention … find a way to transfer Callie to the Pagans without Templar permission.'

A rustle of disquiet went through the group as their mission finally became clear … a mission that could put them in a sticky situation with the Registerium if their work was ever discovered. Zahora felt nothing but scorn for their reaction, because she relished the challenge.

'The Registerium has aided the Templars, and has broken many rules in the process. We hope this means the Registerium's magic is weak … weak enough for us to gain access and discover a way to transfer Callie … which is where you come in.'

'You're hoping because the Templars have broken the rules, we can too?' said the man next to Zahora.

'Exactly,' said Rose. Her eyes found the man, and then Zahora. Rose smiled, and Zahora returned the gesture, having to pinch herself that their leader had picked her out of a crowd. 'Magic—like everything—degrades over time. Maybe the rules are null and void. Maybe the Registerium's stone is no longer needed for transfers. Maybe the Templar stipulation that demons may not leave without permission is no longer enforceable … these are the questions we need you to help us answer.

'We *must* transfer Callie. If we can access other Registerium records, so much the better. If we can determine how much of the original agreement is still in force, that will be helpful too. But the primary objective, the one thing we *must* achieve, is to transfer Callie to our nation without the Templars' help.'

Zahora tried to slip out of the cave before anyone saw her, but the call of her name halted her retreat. 'A word please,' said Rose.

Dread slithered down Zahora's spine. Did she know about Noah?

'I know you've been accessing the Nexus,' said Rose.

Shit.

'Don't worry, I'm not here to reprimand you. I want a debrief.'

Zahora's heart leapt. Rose—freaking Rose—wanted a debrief from her! 'Sure,' she said. 'You want to know everything?'

'Yes, please.'

Zahora told Rose about the two times she'd visited Raina, about the Aztec magik, and how she hoped the Aztec would teach her.

'I'm waiting for Raina to contact me. Other than that, I don't know what to do. The Aztec grabbed hold of me ... I think he could have killed me through the Nexus ... I don't want to risk getting caught again.'

'Then you'll join the team testing the Registerium,' said Rose, 'at least until you hear anything from Raina. We can't have you sitting idle ... who knows what you might do ...'

Jon had to admit Leila's crab shack had been good ... better than good ... not that he would tell her that. But Jon could do better. Everyone knew New York was about bagels, and he knew where to find the best Manhattan had to offer.

They met on the Upper West Side, at a shop you'd only find if you knew where to look. The Holy Star had been giving Jon constant updates on Leila's whereabouts, and he'd trailed her since she left her hotel that morning, just in case.

'You think this place is going to beat last night?' said Leila, eying the unassuming frontage.

'Would we be here if I didn't?' said Jon, sweeping his arm back in a grand gesture, ushering Leila inside. 'Prepare to have your mind blown.'

They sat, and Jon ordered on behalf of them both; to start, a toasted onion bagel with cream cheese.

'Now,' said Jon, as they waited for their food, 'I have a private plane waiting to take us to London. We can finish our bagels, declare me the winner, take a few to go, and be back on the right side of the pond in time for dinner. I'll even let you pick the location ... yes?'

Leila gave him a long, hard look. 'First, if you think I'm getting on a private plane with you—a stranger— you have another thing coming. Second, I'm not finished in New York. And third, there's absolutely no way a *bagel* is going to beat last night.'

'The only thing you're going to find in New York is your demise,' said Jon, leaning back in his seat and crossing a leg over his knee.

'What is it you think I'm doing here?' said Leila.

They hadn't talked about Raina last night; they'd been too caught up in the delectable crab. Jon cast his eyes about the place ... it had too high a turnover for anyone to linger without it being obvious, and he found no one suspicious.

'You're trying to find out what happened to Dean,' said Jon, with his trademark smile.

'How do you know that?' said Leila, shifting uncomfortably.

'You haven't been discrete.'

'Do you know what happened to Dean?'

'Yes. The people holding Raina hostage killed him.'

'What?' said Leila, with an expression of shocked disbelief. 'How ...' She fell silent.

Maybe Jon had been a little too blunt ...

'Look,' he said, trying to be reassuring, 'I know this probably sounds crazy, but Dean's sister, Tamsin, is mixed up in ... in a kind of cult.'

'And you think they're holding Amari hostage?'

'Raina, and yes.'

'She didn't look like a hostage ...'

'Well, she is, and if you keep snooping around, they'll kill you.'

'People don't go around killing because someone asks a couple of questions ...'

Jon gave her an incredulous look. 'Don't they?'

Leila visibly shuddered. 'I don't even know who you are. You say you're a friend of Amari's ... Raina ... whatever, but I'm not going anywhere with you without proof. What if you're the one who killed Dean?'

'You can't prove a negative,' said Jon, flippantly, as their bagels arrived.

Leila balled her hands into fists, then picked up her food. 'Do not follow me, and don't contact me again.'

Jon took a bite of his bagel as he watched her leave, which was even more delicious than he remembered ... definitely had the edge on last night's crab ...

He could have handled the conversation better ... he was man enough to admit that to himself ... which was annoying, because now he'd have to put his back into it. He ordered two more bagels ... sustenance was needed before writing up this morning's progress report, and then he had to come up with a plan that might actually work on this stubborn, irrational woman.

Raina knocked once on Jamie's bedroom door, then entered without waiting for an answer. What she saw made her start, but neither of the men looked in her direction. Alerac was magic-massaging Jamie.

Thoughts raced through Raina's mind. Was Alerac passing information to Jamie? Was he playing her? Or was he just keeping Jamie sweet? Maybe Alerac was trying to extract information from Jamie to funnel back to the Aztecs ... fucking politics.

'Jamie, I need to speak with you,' said Raina.

'Hello, darling,' said Jamie. 'You seem tense ... maybe you need a massage.'

'We're done,' said Alerac. 'I'll leave you.'

Jamie raised his head from the table and nodded. 'What can I do for you, darling?' he said, securing a towel around his waist and sitting on the table.

'Don't call me darling.'

'Would you prefer sweetie?'

'I'd prefer Raina.'

'You are tense.'

'Can't imagine why ...'

'Darling, working with the Slayers is a necessary evil. I assure you, I wouldn't be doing it if I had another way ...'

'I'm not here about that specifically,' she said. 'I need more information about your plans. Otherwise, I can't help.'

Jamie's features twisted. 'How's Caspar?'

Raina threw her hands up. 'I have no idea! I haven't communicated with him since I got here. How's Tamsin?'

'Fine, I should think,' said Jamie, with an infuriating half-smile.

'What's the point in me being here if you won't tell me anything substantial? And even if you won't trust me for my own sake, you have a trump card ... I can't go anywhere.'

'I need your loyalty,' said Jamie. 'Not because our daughter is under Templar protection, but because you are truly loyal to our nation.'

'I've declared my loyalty,' said Raina, thinking of Callie ... how she made all this worthwhile. 'What more can I do?'

'I can think of a couple of things ...' said Jamie, his tone full of suggestion.

'Can you focus for one second?'

'You steal my focus ... I can't help it.'

Raina paused ... she'd have to try a different tack. 'The Slayer building ... is that full of Slayers trained to kill us?'

'No.'

Silence settled over them.

'Care to elaborate?'

'Their Order is split into three parts: military, religious, and charitable. The building houses a hospital of sorts, as well as their most sacred church. We assume their military headquarters is there too, although from what we can tell, they have outposts all over the world.'

Raina fought the urge to shudder. 'What's your agreement with them?'

'We share intelligence on enemy nations. In return, they leave the Templars alone.'

'What happens when they decide to take out the Templars?'

'They can't. We own controlling interests in their largest companies; we've boxed them into a financial corner. If they move against us, we'll destroy their finances, and humans really don't like it when their money disappears. What would they do without their private jets and five star retreats?'

'And you get to blame any hostile activity on the Slayers,' said Raina.

'You say it like it's a lie,' said Jamie. 'All hostile activity *is* down to the Slayers. We point them in the right direction, that's all.'

'But they want to annihilate our entire race ... your allies ... what will you do when the Slayers attack them?'

'*Our* allies,' said Jamie, letting silence settle to hammer home his point.

'You won't tell me who they are,' said Raina, 'so I don't know if they are mine ... and you didn't answer the question.'

'They won't go after our allies. If they do, there'll be financial consequences. Although, if they kill the odd demon here or there, that can't be helped.'

'Like the Slayers you sent after me in London?'

'They were there to rescue you.'

'That's why they threw knives?'

'I can't say I'm impressed with their training,' said Jamie. 'But there's only so much I'm willing to teach them.'

'How long have you been working with them?' she asked. She tried to put from her mind the images of her last two deaths. They'd been gruesome—she'd had to kill herself both times because she'd been cornered by Slayers ... or maybe Jamie had been the true cause.

'Not long,' said Jamie, his tone telling her not to push.

Not long could mean anything from five minutes to a hundred years for a demon. If he'd had nothing to do with her deaths, surely he would just say so ...

'Do you know how I died in my last life?' said Raina. She didn't care if he didn't want to talk about it, because she did.

'Of course ... it was in my territory, after you turned down my proposal of marriage.' Jamie's face turned to stone.

Rose had sent Raina on a diplomatic mission to seduce him—taking advantage of her time away from Caspar—but Jamie's proposal had made her feel sick. She loved Caspar ... only Caspar ... even when she hated him. Jamie wasn't even a worthy second best.

'Muuuuuum!' said Callie, rushing into the room. 'Alerac won't let me play! He says I have to practice stupid magic.'

Callie attached herself to Raina's leg.

'Callie, we've been over this,' said Raina, thinking for the hundredth time that day that parenting was the hardest thing she'd done in all her lifetimes—kids were not rational beings. 'You have to learn magic, and Alerac is the best there is … you're lucky to have him.'

'But I don't want to … it hurts my head, and,' she paused to think, 'I'm tired.' Another pause. 'I want to play … and … I'm hungry … will you play with me?'

'If you do your lessons, I'll throw you a party,' said Jamie, crouching in front of Callie.

She glanced at him suspiciously. 'What kind of party?'

'A Halloween party,' said Jamie. 'And we'll all dress up.'

Raina inwardly groaned.

'With balloons?' said Callie.

'Yep.'

'And cake?'

'Absolutely.'

'And … what else?'

'Games, and candy, and music.'

'We can invite my friends from the park!' said Callie.

'No,' said Jamie. 'Only family.'

Confusion hijacked Callie's features. 'Only you and me and Mummy?'

'And all the people who live here,' said Jamie.

'Alerac?' said Callie, sulkily.

'Yes,' said Raina. Callie stormed off. 'You're going to ruin her …'

'What's the point of having an heir if I don't spoil her?' he said.

Raina's stomach clenched. Callie was an heir alright, but not to Jamie's poisoned chalice. She was heir to Raina and Caspar's dynasty.

Raina imagined how Caspar would have dealt with their sulky, entitled child. He'd probably have her eating from the palm of his hand by now …

How she missed him. His brilliance, the unassuming air that hid his ruthlessness, the cradle of his arms. The world thought it was Raina who was cold and cutthroat, never ceasing in pursuit of a challenge. And she was, but he was too. He was just better with people, so they assumed he was softer. But he was single-minded, devoted, unwavering. That's why they were soulmates ... his soul matched hers. They would stop at nothing to get what they wanted. And right now, they wanted their family safe and together, and back on Pagan soil.

Chapter 7

'We have three tasks,' said Christa, standing in front of the assembled magiks. Christa was Talli's partner and a total enigma. Zahora had only met her once before today, and her shell had been impermeable, which made Zahora nervous.

Zahora's mind wandered to Noah. She hadn't seen him in days ... not since Rose, Talli, and Christa had turned up and banished him from all meetings. Rose had even lectured Zahora about not sharing information with him, because they didn't know who he was ... not really.

Zahora knew Rose was right, but that didn't stop her from missing him. And instead of lying wrapped in Noah's muscular arms, here she was, in another pointless meeting. When would it end?

'Zahora?' said Christa, her features stern.

Zahora had always wondered what exactly Christa added to the leadership, other than following Talli around. Over the last few days, it had become clear. Christa was the management mastermind behind Talli's creative flair. Talli brought bold ideas, dramaticism, and charisma, but Christa brought ruthless practicality and focus on delivering. She was scary, and everyone fell over themselves to do her bidding.

'Ah ... yes? Sorry,' said Zahora, feeling her cheeks redden.

'We have three tasks,' said Christa, addressing everyone again. 'And we will split into three task-forces to achieve them. The first group will probe the Registerium's magic. The second will focus on hacking the Registerium's archives, which these days are electronic. The third will concentrate on finding those who instated the Registerium's magic in the first place, so we can glean information from them.

'The third task will be managed by myself, Talli, and Caspar, who is currently meeting with other nations. The second task—the electronic records—will be headed up by our ally nation, the Holy Star. The first task will be led by Marla, and is where everyone in this room comes in. Any finding, regardless of how insignificant, must be shared with the other two groups.

'Should you need to access our ambassador at the Registerium—Malcolm—please go through your group leader. Questions?'

The room went silent. Zahora pondered how she would organize the magical probing of the Registerium if she were in charge ...

'Great!' said Talli, stepping forward with a clap of her hands. 'You should also know we're holding Mabon celebrations here this year. The planning will be a little rushed, given we have other things on our plates, but we can't let a successful harvest go uncelebrated! More details soon.'

Christa gave Talli a long-suffering look, then headed for the exit, saying, 'Marla, over to you.'

'You're sure this is the only way?' said Caspar, moving his head slowly from one angle to another, trying to dislodge the hammer that kept coming down on his brain. Too much travel, too much drinking—it would be rude to refuse his hosts' hospitality—and not enough sleep.

Ira, from the Holy Star, shrugged on the other end of the video call. 'The Templars might not respect magic, but turns out they respect hackers. I mean, there's always a way in eventually, but nothing we've tried so far has got close.'

'You've already sent the device to Jon?'

'Yep,' said Ira. 'Should get there today. And we'll keep hunting for another way in, but they've trained their people well. Not a single one of them opened our emails. I'm wondering if they have a central team monitoring everything as it comes in … that's what we do.'

'Maybe we should too,' said Caspar, wondering how big brother email monitoring would go down with the leadership …

'Sorry I don't have better news,' said Ira.

'Don't be. You guys are the best in the world,' said Caspar. 'We're glad you're on our side.'

Ira hung up and Caspar took a moment, waiting for another hammer blow to pass before calling Jon.

'Alright grandad?' said Jon's cocky voice down the line.

'I have bad news,' said Caspar.

'Makes a change,' said Jon sarcastically. 'What now? I need to fly to Beijing and take apart the Great Wall to uncover some long-lost treasure?'

'You've been reading Meredith's reports then,' said Caspar.

'She called me; she's pretty pissed.'

'Well, it's not like there's a *war* on or anything … I'm so sorry to get in the way of everyone's plans … Do you know where I am, Jon?'

'No.'

'Neither do I, because the Egyptians blindfolded me, threw me in the bed of a truck, then drove the rough route to god-knows-where. At one stage, I was knocked unconscious. So please, do tell me how terrible it is eating bagels in New York, and how your five-star hotel suite is a hardship.

'And the worst thing that's happened to Meredith is a man declaring his undying love for her … so maybe she should take a hard look at herself as well.'

'Alright, keep your knickers on … I'm just saying …'

'Well next time, keep your trap shut, or I'll have Rose kick you off the leadership. You're supposed to bring something to the table, not drain the life out of everyone with your incessant *whining*.'

'Okay, okay,' said Jon, having the good sense to sound abashed.

'Now listen up; change of plans. You need to convince Leila to stay in New York long enough for her to give Raina a USB stick. Ira already sent it. It should arrive with you today. It's the only way for us to get into the Templars' network.'

'Okay,' said Jon.

Caspar was relieved Jon didn't complain, but his lack of backchat was a little off-putting. No doubt he'd bitch to Meredith as soon as they hung up …

Caspar was about to end the call when his phone buzzed. 'Hang on Jon, it's Ira.'

Caspar put them on a three-way call, and Ira got straight to the point. 'Leila's booked a flight back to London and a car to the airport,' he said. 'She's leaving in twenty minutes.'

'Shit,' said Jon. 'I'm on it.'

Jon flung open his hotel room door and raced outside. He sprinted the two blocks to Leila's hotel, then stopped, realizing he didn't know what to say. Caspar's outburst was unusual, and had preoccupied his thoughts as he'd run … he was usually so calm under pressure, but something had riled him up … just Raina? Or something else? Jon had to concentrate … right now he had bigger fish to fry.

Leila had said she never wanted to see Jon again, and this was borderline stalker behavior. Oh, Gods, it was worse than that. He was about to convince her to put herself at risk, for the sake of an organization who'd brought her nothing but heartache.

The door to Leila's building opened, and she appeared with only a wheeled carry-on and a sports bag slung over her shoulder. Jon hadn't pegged her as a "travel light" kinda woman.

She stopped short when she saw him, dumping her sports bag on the sidewalk. 'I told you I never wanted to see you again,' she said, and then burst into tears.

Jon froze for a split second, then some subconscious part of him propelled him forward. He embraced her, and she clung to him, sobbing into his shirt. Jon had no idea what to do next. He was wholly unequipped for this situation. Sure, everyone cried, but all the women he knew were likely to punch you if you tried to hug them when they were.

He stroked her back ... that seemed like the kind of thing one should do. 'It's going to be okay,' he found himself saying. That sounded right ... although, it was most probably a lie ... did that matter?

She pushed away and wiped her eyes. 'This is so embarrassing,' she said.

'For you or me?'

She swiped him and choked out a laugh.

'Want to talk about it?' said Jon. He was on fire! That was definitely an appropriate response.

'Not really.'

'Come on, it'll help ... and I'm probably the only person this side of the Atlantic you can talk to ... certainly if you don't want to land yourself in a psychiatric ward.'

She tried to fight it, but another sob escaped her.

'And I happen to know a steak restaurant that'll blow your socks off,' he said.

'I'm getting on a flight,' she said. 'I have to go.'

'They have Wagyu ...'

She looked at him with sadness in her eyes. 'I've paid for the flight.'

'I'll buy you a new one.'

Her eyebrows knitted with suspicion.

Damn damn damn. 'I'm not a stalker, I promise.'

She frowned.

'I know that's what I'd say if I were a stalker, but I swear I'm not.'

'Then who are you? How do you know about Dean? Why did you care about me leaving so much, but are now bribing me to stay? What's going on with Amari? None of this makes any sense!'

'I'll explain everything … over Wagyu …'

'Every anti-stalker advice unit would tell me to say *no*.'

'We've already established I'm not a stalker,' he said, flashing his most charming smile, 'and steak's got to beat a flight back to London by yourself, with bad food and no leg room … I'm assuming you didn't book a first-class ticket …?'

'Economy.'

'No rational person would turn down this dinner for an economy flight,' he said. He was about to add that he'd buy her a replacement first-class ticket, but thought better of it.

'Fine,' she huffed, as more tears trickled down her cheeks, 'but you're giving me answers.'

He fished a handkerchief out of his pocket and offered it to her.

She looked dubious as she took it. 'Who has these any longer?'

Jon smiled, marveling as … something unfurled in his chest. 'I'm a traditionalist.'

They dumped Leila's bags with her building's concierge, then walked to midtown. Jon could feel Leila's mood brightening with each passing step, and it buoyed him.

They reached a small steak joint nestled between two large buildings. The host's face split into a beaming smile when Jon mentioned Elliot, and he ushered them inside the dimly lit interior.

'Full disclosure,' said Jon, in a low, conspiratorial tone, 'I've never actually been here, but my friend

Elliot—who's the most food-obsessed person I've ever met—swears it's the best steak outside of Japan.'

'You lured me here under false pretenses,' whispered Leila, in a matching tone.

'I apologize profusely,' said Jon.

'Don't lie,' said Leila. 'It doesn't suit you.'

Jon raised an eyebrow. Was she flirting with him?

The host settled them at a secluded table in the back. There were only ten or twelve tables in the whole place, and beautifully intricate Japanese-inspired screens had been strategically placed to give all the tables a sense of privacy. Everything else was ultra-modern, including forks with only two prongs that looked like weapons from a bad sci-fi movie.

Their host told them their food would be out shortly, not giving them the opportunity to order, then brought cocktails, which they gratefully accepted. Leila downed half of hers then leaned across the table.

'Why were you crying?' said Jon, not wanting her to launch her interrogation … not yet.

Leila dropped her eyes to her hands. She twiddled her thumbs. 'I don't want to go into it,' she said eventually. 'And you promised me answers if I came with you … so spill.'

Jon sighed and took a sip of his cocktail. 'What do you want to know?'

'Everything. What's happened to my cousin? Why did they kill Dean? Why's Callie here? Who are you? How do you fit into all of this? Why did you want me to leave, and now you're frustrating my effort to?'

'Is that all?' said Jon, with a sardonic smile.

'That's just for starters,' she said sternly. 'Quit stalling and get on with it.'

Jon took a deep breath, then leaned forward into her space, their faces close. 'Okay,' he said, 'but promise to hear me out, keep an open mind, and try not to think I'm crazy.'

'Oh … that bad?'

'Worse,' said Jon. 'It's going to sound ludicrous … so don't say I didn't warn you.'

Leila visibly steeled herself. 'Okay, fine … now spill.'

Jon looked her in the eye for a beat … two. This wasn't allowed … could get him thrown out of his nation … but it was the only way … *Here goes nothing.*

'There are groups of people around the world who reincarnate,' said Jon, taking in every twitch she made.

She raised an eyebrow, but stayed silent. What could she say to that?

'Most of us …'

'You're one of these … people?' she said, rearing back. *Great.*

'Yes, and most of us belong to a nation. Nations are spread across the world and have varying beliefs … not unlike human countries.'

'You don't count yourself as human?' said Leila, her body going still … worried her heart had actually stopped.

'We're human enough,' said Jon. 'I belong to a nation called the Pagans, and so does Raina. Our territory is in Europe. A different nation—the Templars—own New York and most of North America.'

Leila listened as Jon told her about Raina's past with Jamie, about Caspar, Dean, how Callie fit in, and about the Templars' hostile intentions.

He finished just as their steak arrived, but neither of them even looked at it.

'If what you say is true,' said Leila, although, how could it be? 'then we both need to get the hell out of here. Now.'

'That is what I've been telling you,' said Jon.

She shot him a warning look.

'So why the change of heart?' she said.

'We, and our allies have been trying to hack into the Templars' computer network. We can't find a way in, and are hoping you'll help us.'

Leila did nothing for a beat. 'Are you serious?'

Jon ate a slice of steak. 'Wow. You need to try this.'

'Don't deflect,' she said, but when would she get the chance to eat Wagyu again? Some of the best Wagyu in the world, if Jon could be believed. She took a mouthful. 'Oh my god.'

She savored the succulent buttery sweetness in silence, transported to a near spiritual plane.

'Seriously,' said Leila, her mind blown. 'That is …'

'Elliot strikes again,' said Jon.

'What exactly is it you think I can do?' said Leila, picking up her red wine and swirling her glass. She had to resist the temptation to scoff down every last morsel on her plate in two seconds' flat. 'I can only just use my own laptop.'

'We need you to get a USB stick to Raina. One meeting, and then we'll get you out … we'll protect you.'

'Oh, is that all?' said Leila. 'You want me to risk my life for you people, after all the shit you've put me through? You've taken the only true friend I had … the only person who gave a shit about me. And now …

now I have no one, you want me to help *you*?' Tears filled her eyes again, and that made her even more angry.

Jon reached across the table and took her hand. She snatched it back, although, he'd said he could protect her ... it was scary how good that sounded, even if the offer had come from someone who genuinely seemed to believe he could reincarnate ...

She closed her eyes and breathed in and out. Meditation was all the rage these days ... maybe some deep breathing could help her.

'I know this is a lot to take in.'

'No shit. How do I know you're not getting me to smuggle something illegal? Or ... something ... I don't know ... whatever weird stuff you people are into? And do you really expect me to believe you actually reincarnate?'

'Well, it was a longshot, but I had hoped ...'

'You're obviously in a cult. A particularly bizarre one, where you all fight each other, and ... steal people.'

'I know it sounds ludicrous ... I told you it would, but think about Raina ... she must have felt *different* somehow, after her demon self awoke?'

'Her *what*?'

'Sorry ... I didn't mean to bring up the d-word ... it's a ridiculous name and I don't know why we still use it ...'

'A satanic cult ...'

Leila was on the verge of flight. She shoveled another mouthful.

'Actually, the original word *daimōn* means deity, or genius.'

'It gets worse ...'

'Did Raina feel different?' Jon pressed.

'Yes ... but she's joined a cult! Of course she feels different.'

'People don't just change overnight. She feels different because she *is* different ... fundamentally. Before, she only had her memories from this life. Now, she has memories going back millennia. And she's old. Imagine what she knows ... what she's seen ...'

'I ... don't know what to say ... I ...' She paused, looking everywhere but at him. This was insane. She'd thought her life couldn't get any worse, but the universe once again proved it could screw you over in special ways ... especially when you were down.

Jon's hand moved as though it was going to take hers again and her eyes flicked to his face. His hand stilled.

'I know this is a lot,' he said. 'By all means, take time to process ... but we need to get out of here as soon as we can. The longer you're here, the more danger you're in. Tamsin—Dean's sister—doesn't like Raina. She's looking for ways to hurt her, and hurting you would do it.'

'I doubt that,' said Leila, realizing the tears had started again. 'Raina told me to leave ... to never contact her again.'

'She's trying to protect you.'

Leila turned away as the server refilled her glass, trying to hide her distress.

'It's going to be okay,' said Jon, putting a hand on her arm.

She didn't pull away and the gesture made her sob harder. 'It's not that,' she said, 'it's ... without Raina, I'm alone.' He squeezed, and she took a shuddering breath. 'If what you say is true ... she's lost to me forever.'

Meredith trudged in front of Torsten, a spade slung over her shoulder. They'd finally found the treasure, and had only been attacked by four raiding parties while retrieving it. Not too bad, considering … and at least Torsten could fight, even if he was ceaselessly annoying.

'So, my love,' said Torsten, who had the treasure chest balanced on his shoulder, 'how shall we celebrate our victory?'

'By taking a hot shower and sleeping in a warm, comfortable bed,' said Meredith. 'Separately,' she added, as a hopeful look crossed Torsten's face.

Their days and nights had been long and arduous, and Meredith was glad it was done. Her phone buzzed, and she answered. 'I told you, we found it. We're on our way back now.'

'Great,' said Caspar's voice down the line. 'I've got another mission for you when you've delivered the chest.'

'Only me?' she said hopefully.

'Torsten will be tagging along too. The Egyptians want a necklace hidden in a cave near Cinque Terre in Italy.'

Meredith rolled her eyes; there was no use arguing. 'Send me the details,' she said, and then hung up.

'Good news?' said Torsten brightly.

'Hardly,' said Meredith. 'We're going to Cinque Terre.'

'Wonderful!'

'To find a necklace.'

'Sad there won't be anyone there to attack us,' said Torsten, hefting the treasure onto his other shoulder.

'I can attack you if you'd like.'

Torsten smiled broadly. 'As a matter of fact, I would like ...'

Meredith said nothing, traipsing in silence through the twilight gloom to their truck. Torsten put the treasure in the back, and she chucked in her spade. She was preoccupied, which was why she didn't see the two men.

But Torsten—facing the attackers—sensed movement and launched himself at Meredith, throwing her to the ground, as two knives sailed through the air where she'd been. Torsten and Meredith rolled to a crouch, then pressed their backs against the cooling metal of the truck. They pulled out their knives almost as one

Torsten pointed to himself, then to the back of the truck, and Meredith nodded. Meredith moved around the front, her feet silent as she crouched below the level of the metal.

They pounced, their attackers on the ground in a flash, arms pinned behind their backs. But these were not members of a Zorro raiding party. These men were novices by comparison, without the benefit of hundreds of years' combat experience.

'Slayers,' said Meredith, urgently. 'Get something in his mouth, or knock him out.'

Meredith rammed the hilt of her dagger between her man's teeth, but a third attacker slammed into her as she tried ... and this was no human. Torsten watched as Meredith went down, then heard a crack, his man going limp beneath him. Cursing, he dumped the body and rushed to aid Meredith.

Meredith's Slayer ran, but Torsten was on him in a second, pinning him to the ground. The telltale crack sounded again.

'No, you fucker,' said Torsten. But it was too late.

'Great,' said Meredith, as she tied up her demon attacker with cable ties. Her anger flared white hot.

'I'm sorry,' said Torsten, facing Meredith.

'You said you'd like this …' she said, then punched him hard in the face … so hard he went down. Then she returned to her captive. 'Instead of pining after me, maybe you should pay attention to your own shit. You just cost us a chance to find out how the Slayers and Templars are working together.' She pointed to her captive's Templar wrist band.

'We've still got the Templar …' said Torsten. 'My love … '

Meredith fumed. 'We could have had them all if you hadn't got distracted … And this isn't a holiday movie, Torsten. I've told you no, so would you finally take a fucking hint and find someone else.'

Leila moved nervously around Jon's palatial suite. 'This isn't too shabby,' she said, eyeing the closing elevator door nervously. She knew logically she shouldn't be here, but she didn't want to leave—Jon was the only person who'd been nice to her in weeks. And for some reason, despite his infuriating cockiness, and all evidence pointing to his involvement in a terrifying cult, she liked him … trusted him. Apparently she'd hit rock bottom.

'Drink?' said Jon, pointing to the fully stocked bar in the corner.

'Maybe just a sparkling water,' she said, moving to look through the window. New York's lights dazzled. It was overpowering, intimidating, and for some reason brought tears to her eyes once more. How did she have any left? She brushed them away.

'Here you go,' said Jon, holding out a bottle. 'Oh … Leila? What is it?'

She hugged herself tightly, the loss of Amari flooding her anew. She shuddered as a sob wracked her body.

Jon put the water on a side table, then stretched out his arms in invitation. He waited for her to move, and after a moment's pause, she rushed to him, holding him tight.

My God, the contact felt good. He was hard, and warm, and smelled like a summer's night. As he closed his arms around her, she sobbed in relief.

'Hey,' said Jon. 'Sushhh.'

He rested his cheek against her head and stoked her hair. She held tighter, never wanting it to end.

Jon didn't pull away. He just held her, stroked her, soothed her.

She eventually put space between them … they couldn't stand by the window all night … 'I think maybe I should sleep,' she said.

'Sounds good,' said Jon. 'You take the bed …'

'We can share,' said Leila too quickly; she couldn't face being alone. 'I mean, in a plutonic way … I'm sure there's space for two …'

Jon nodded, seeming to understand.

Leila lay on her side of the colossal bed, wearing a t-shirt Jon had leant her, her face puffy and red. She didn't even care anymore.

Jon rolled over, Leila suddenly aware of his proximity, his warmth. 'Would a cuddle help?' he said. 'A fully plutonic one.'

She should say no. She shouldn't let this strange, delusional man get any closer. 'Yes,' she whispered.

The viselike pain around her organs eased as his naked chest came flush against her back. He cocooned her, the fronts of his thighs pressed against the backs of hers, and some deep, tense part of her unspooled. Her body relaxed, her mind unclenched, and she fell into the welcome oblivion of sleep.

Leila woke the following morning to find Jon asleep on his back, her hand under his, pressed to his chest. He woke as she shifted, opened his blue eyes, and looked deep into hers. It was intimate, but neither of them looked away.

'How are you feeling?' he said.

'Wrung out ... but ... better.'

'Good,' said Jon, 'because we have a big day of planning ahead.'

He made to get up, but she stopped him. 'Jon,' she said tentatively.

He rolled back to look at her. 'Uh huh?'

'Can you prove the reincarnation stuff? I ... it's all so cult-like ... I need proof before I agree to help.'

'What proof do you want?'

'I don't know … just … *something*.'

Jon leaned over to the nightstand and pulled a gold bangle from the drawer. 'When you speak to Raina, ask her where this came from … what it means to her. If her answer matches mine, you'll know it's true. And if one object isn't enough, we can play this game with as many as you'd like until you believe me.'

'One object isn't nearly enough,' said Leila. 'One object could easily be part of some sick game.'

'Okay,' said Jon, searching around. He picked up a set of cufflinks, ridiculously large, ostentatious things. 'I stole these from Nelson's dress uniform after the Battle of Trafalgar. They're my most prized possession. That man was a legend, and not even a demon …'

Jon pulled out a phone and dialed.

'Hey,' said a man's voice through the speakerphone.

'Elliot,' said Jon. 'Leila needs proof we're not a cult … that we genuinely reincarnate.'

'You told her?' said Elliot's soft tone.

'You're on speakerphone,' said Jon. 'Just tell her where I got my cufflinks.'

'The big ones? From Nelson?'

'Thank you,' said Jon, then hung up.

'Do you require more?' said Jon.

Leila smiled. This was fun. 'Yes,' she said resolutely.

Jon huffed out an exasperated breath as he got out of bed, wearing nothing but a pair of boxer briefs. Leila didn't look … not much anyway.

Jon scouted around. 'I'm really not a hoarder … I don't keep much stuff …' He pulled out a laptop, loaded up a picture, then put it on the bed in front of Leila. 'That is treasure Meredith just dug up in Israel.

How would she have known where it was unless she had knowledge from the past?'

'How do I know the picture's recent, or that you know those people?' said Leila.

'Jesus Christ …' He video called Meredith.

'Yes?' said Meredith.

'Show Leila the treasure,' he said.

'What the … you told her? I'm going to have to …'

'She's right here,' said Jon. 'Just show her already.'

Meredith opened a chest and displayed the treasure.

'It could be fake,' said Leila, although it looked authentic enough, all mismatched and ancient, just like the treasure they showed on the news when some enthusiast with a metal detector struck gold.

'You want me to bite it?' said Meredith, her features furious.

'No,' said Leila, apologetically, feeling the hostility all the way from wherever Meredith was. 'Thank you.'

'She's scary, huh?' said Jon, after hanging up.

Leila nodded.

'Enough proof? Do you believe me now?'

Leila wasn't sure what to believe, but she had to admit, they were convincing.

'What's the bangle about?' said Leila. 'The one you want me to give to Raina …'

'She should be the one to tell you, and afterwards, I'll confirm it's true.'

Jon opened the package from Ira, finding a memory stick and instructions inside. They spent the rest of the day creating a plan to get it to Raina without arousing suspicion. They settled on Leila approaching Raina in the park, while Ira monitored the whereabouts of key Templars. Ira would set up alerts to tell them when Raina headed out. All they could do now was wait for an opening.

110

Chapter 8

Elliot and Gemma entered a private garden in an unknown part of San Francisco. They'd been blindfolded, so didn't know the exact whereabouts of the headquarters of the new West Coast nation. Rose had sent them to infiltrate, to assess the threat, but it had taken weeks to locate a single member, and several more to secure this meeting.

The rest of the Pagan leadership—and all their allies—had been breathing down their necks, pressing for updates every two minutes, but Elliot and Gemma had refused to push. They knew the new nation would back off if pressed too hard, shrouded in secrecy as they were. They obviously had no interest in being part of the status quo …

A man and a woman sat on garden chairs, lounging back in their seats, holding hands as they chatted. The woman was glamourous, with long dark hair, big green eyes, and full, pouty lips. The man looked middle eastern, with dark eyes and blond curls that were out of place on his head. He was short and pudgy, carrying many excess pounds.

In the human world, they'd wonder what a woman like this saw in a man like that ... they'd assume he had money. But this wasn't the human world, and Elliot knew both were formidable creatures, or neither would be sitting in these seats. They had somehow formed a powerful and fully fledged new nation, under the noses of the whole demon world, and no one had been any the wiser until it was too late. Underestimating them would be fatal.

'Elliot and Gemma,' said the man. 'It is a pleasure to meet you.'

'The pleasure's all ours,' said Elliot. 'Forgive me, but I don't know your names.'

The woman smiled then got to her feet, her flimsy silk dress pulling tight across her extreme curves, her nipples pushing through the almost sheer fabric.

'I am Aphrodite,' she said, in a buttery tone. She went to a table with a pitcher of liquid the color of burnt orange, poured, then handed a glass to each of them.

'And I'm Ares,' said the man.

Oh, Jesus ... did they actually believe they were Greek gods?

'Yes,' said Aphrodite, handing them their drinks, 'as in the God of War, and the Goddess of Love.'

She poured two more glasses for her and Ares, then sat back in her chair. 'Please, sit,' she said.

Elliot and Gemma did as she said, sipping tentatively. The usually delicious flavors of orange, mango, and papaya fell flat on Elliot's tongue as he tried to make sense of his hosts.

'You're reincarnated Gods?' said Gemma. 'Or you pay homage to them within your nation?'

'All in good time,' said Aphrodite, placing her hand on Ares'.

112

'We'd like you to stay awhile,' said Ares. 'Get to know us … see firsthand what we stand for and how we live … what kind of world we want to create.'

'Take refuge within our walls,' said Aphrodite, her smile seductive … or was that her normal smile? 'War is in the air …'

'We feel it more than most,' said Ares.

'Let us help you disconnect from the hostility … to find peace … at least for the time you're with us.'

'Thank you,' said Gemma. 'We appreciate your hospitality.'

'You must know why we're here?' said Elliot.

Ares laughed. 'Your nation is at war, and you want allies … or at least to be sure we won't ally with your enemies. Believe me, war is my game. But this war is futile … petty … we have no interest in the Templars' ambitions.'

'You'll see,' said Aphrodite, with a secret smile that promised they'd see that, and so much more …

Raina stared at the stone before her, which sat on top of a hill, in the center of a clearing, surrounded by other standing stones. They were in the middle of nowhere. Raina hadn't been told where, and wasn't allowed to know. All she could see were trees. Trees, trees, and more trees. And her knowledge of stone locations was patchy …

Alerac and Callie stepped up beside her, friction irritating the air between them. Alerac didn't appreciate

Callie's modern-day entitlement, and Callie didn't appreciate Alerac's uncompromising approach. Raina was tired of it … maybe Alerac wasn't the best teacher for her daughter after all …

'Is this it?' said Callie, eyeing the stone suspiciously. Alerac nodded.

'I want to go home,' said Callie.

'Well, do what you're told, and then you can,' said Raina, although she felt for the child; they'd been in the car for hours. Raina was angsty after the ride, so it wasn't surprising Callie was too.

Callie crossed her arms. 'What do I have to do?'

'Touch the stone, and see if you feel anything,' said Alerac. 'Do not push towards it. Just touch it, and don't let it suck you in.'

'Fine,' said Callie, stomping towards the stone.

'Wait,' said Raina, her heart leaping in her chest. 'Could anyone be here? Observing? Could anyone take hold of her soul? The way you did with the Pagan girl?'

'If they try, they won't succeed,' said Alerac, with such calm certainty she believed him.

Raina paused a beat, trying to get her heart under control, giving Callie a moment to slow down, willing her not to do anything stupid. 'Okay,' said Raina, and Callie approached the stone, Alerac just behind her.

Callie reached for it, touched it, and Raina held her breath, bracing herself.

Nothing happened.

'Well?' said Alerac. 'What do you feel?'

Callie shrugged, then looked back over her shoulder, confused. 'It's cold …?'

'Do you feel magic?' said Raina.

'No,' said Callie, and dropped her hand.

'I can feel it from here,' said Alerac.

Raina stepped forward and touched the stone. 'I can hardly feel it,' she said.

'Strange,' said Alerac, touching the stone himself. 'It's there, just ... different ...'

'Different how?' said Raina.

'Less potent ... or more like ... fluctuating?'

'How can that be?' said Raina.

Alerac's brow creased the smallest bit. 'I don't know,' he said, placing both hands on the stone. 'I need time. Go for a walk if you like ... the child could do with a run.'

Raina nodded, then took Callie's hand and headed back to the SUV. There was no sign of the driver, or the henchmen Jamie had sent to keep tabs on them.

A shot of adrenaline spiked through Raina's blood. Were the keys inside? Surely they wouldn't have left them ... She climbed into the back and picked up Callie's water bottle, casting her eyes over the front for the keys. There they were, in a cup holder between the two front seats.

This was as good a chance as she might ever get ... they could drive into the wilderness, ditch the car—which probably had a tracker—and go on foot. Raina could survive anything, and in this kind of terrain, it wouldn't be hard to disappear. They could be back with Caspar in a few short days.

'Mum?' said Callie. 'Come. On.'

Raina took a breath. This was too good to be true ... too tempting. Jamie was meticulous with security; there was no way his henchmen would be so careless. If she was wrong, this could be the only opportunity to escape she'd ever get ... but if she was right, and this was a trap—a test ... if she tried to run, they'd be waiting, and then Jamie would never trust her. Ever.

Raina left the keys, climbed out of the car, and handed Callie her water bottle. 'Come on,' she said. 'Let's explore.'

Zahora and the other magiks sat in a circle around the standing stone, having collectively probed the magic of the Registerium. They'd been doing it for days and Zahorah was tired of the monotony.

'Debrief,' said Marla, who stood in the middle, next to the stone. She pointed to a man in front of her. 'Start here, and circle clockwise.'

Zahora listened to their words. They sounded much like hers would: *Came up against the Registerium's defenses. Did not find a way through. All seems normal. Nothing to report.*

Except no one else had noticed one small detail. 'It's fluctuating,' said Zahora, when it was her turn.

Marla's piercing eyes bored into hers. It was unnerving ... so much authority radiating from the body of a child. Maybe she'd get used to it when she, too, had lived for millennia ...

'Go on,' said Marla.

'It's faint, but it's there ... the magic's pulsing up and down.'

'What could this mean?' said Marla, like a schoolteacher.

'None of us felt it,' said a woman two down from Zahora. 'Maybe it's not actually there ...'

Zahora told herself the woman wasn't being a bitch ... but her tone made it hard to believe.

'That is one possibility,' said Marla, inclining her head. 'Others?'

116

'Something about the Registerium's recent activities is causing the pulsing?' called out a man.

'Someone else is doing something in the Nexus ... something big that's putting strain on the whole system?'

'The Registerium's magical protections could be weakening, because of their recent activities,' said Zahora.

The room went silent.

'Others?' said Marla again.

'Zahora has a higher sensitivity than anyone else?' said a timid girl from the front who didn't look older than eighteen. 'So it's been there for some time ... or forever ... but no one's ever noticed before?'

'The magic's getting old,' said another man. 'It could be deteriorating due to age?'

Marla raised an eyebrow. 'The Registerium's magic is renewed once a decade,' said Marla. 'There's a ceremony with all member nations.'

'Oh,' said the man.

He must be a baby ... even Zahora knew that.

'We're approaching a renewal,' said Marla. 'It is unlikely to be the cause, but not beyond the realm of possibility.'

'More people are using the Nexus now we're at war?' said another. 'So it could be strain from many users, not one big use?'

The room quietened again.

'We will pursue all theories,' said Marla. 'Each of you who came up with a theory will research it. Others will join you at their discretion.'

Zahora beat a hasty retreat before anyone could volunteer to help her test her theory. She made it back to her room without being caught, closing the door hurriedly behind her.

With a start, she realized she wasn't alone; Noah sprawled sleeping on her bed.

Zahora's heart lurched. She hadn't seen him in days … had had no time. She crept to his side and crouched, reaching a hand towards his face. She brushed her thumb across his lips, traced his eyebrows, cheekbones, jaw.

His lips turned upward in a smile, and his eyes slowly opened, dilating under the assault of the light. They watched each other for a beat, two, then she leaned in and kissed him. He swung his legs over the side of the bed, and she climbed onto his lap, wrapping herself around him. His hand went to her hair, the other on her waist, holding onto her like she might disappear. Their lips parted, bodies pressed together as tightly as they could get.

'I missed you,' said Noah, pulling back.

'Me too,' she said, burying her hands in his hair. 'And this.' She rocked her hips back and forth.

'We don't have to,' he said.

'You don't want to?'

'Believe me, I do … it's just … that's not why I'm here. I wanted to see you … I brought food,' he said, stroking her hair as she nuzzled his chest. 'When do you eat?'

'They bring us food,' she said, although in truth she couldn't remember the last time anything but water had passed her lips.

'How much longer will it go on like this?' he asked.

She had no idea. 'A while at least.'

'Is this a regular thing?'

'No.'

He'd asked before what they were doing, but since she'd told him she couldn't discuss it, he hadn't asked again, even though curiosity radiated from him.

'I wish I could help,' he said.

'Me too, but ... actually ... maybe there's a way you can ...'

Zahora and Noah snuck into the caves. They passed the standing stone, then the pool, and went deeper, to the most sacred place in the caves. Or at least, the most sacred place Zahora had discovered. She wasn't meant to know it existed, let alone be here ...

'Wow,' said Noah, as he took in the enormous pool of water extending into the blackness as far as their eyes could see. Flame torches lined the entrance and a small beach of coarse sand, but it was impossible to tell what lay beyond.

'This place feels ... wrong,' said Noah.

Zahora knew what he meant, but she wasn't sure if it was wrongness, or just ... strangeness that tingled her senses.

'I'm going to meditate, lying on the beach, partly in the water. Can you watch me, like you did before? And bring me back if I look like I'm in trouble?'

Zahora had brought a sound bowl and candles, and Noah had his guitar.

'Can you play the whole time?' she said. 'That way, I'll always have something to follow …'

'It won't be too distracting?'

'No, I don't think so.'

She kissed him, then stripped off her clothes and lay naked at the water's edge.

The frigid water hit, and she had to force herself to take long, deep breaths. She made her shoulders relax, closed her eyes, and felt for the Nexus.

It was there, but different … blacker … more potent.

She pushed all thoughts away, feeling for her Dara Knot, making sure it was still intact; she had a feeling she would need its strength.

Zahora had to test her idea that the Registerium's magical protections were weakening, but there was only one way she could think to do it … using force. Rubbing up against the shields would do no good. How could she tell if they were about to give way without actually making them do so? It wasn't like she could see them. She could only feel them … sense them. But to prove the pulsing in the magic was an indicator of its weakness, she had to make it break.

She felt for the Triskelion on her other hand; the symbol for momentum … the one that had got her into trouble. She couldn't think about that now … she needed all the force she could get. She put all thoughts out of her mind, except for one, and flew for the Registerium.

New recruits filed through the warehouse doors. Jamie watched approvingly as Tamsin gave them directions.

'From Janet?' said Raina, referring to the Templars' representative at the Registerium.

'She's done a good job, don't you think?' said Jamie.

'She's been convincing the best of the best to join the Templars?' said Raina. 'That's why she's been combing the Registerium's records? To find people to join us?'

Her use of the word "us" was purposeful, and delight danced in Jamie's eyes.

'Yes,' said Jamie. 'We're at war, and wartime calls for extreme measures.'

'We are?' said Raina. 'I thought we only might be soon …?'

'Semantics,' said Jamie. 'But the Pagans are acting as though we are, so we may as well give them what they want.'

Raina's blood boiled, but she held her tongue. This was a test, just like the chance of escape had been, and she wasn't about to fail.

Jamie led her into a boardroom with Janet's face plastered across an enormous television screen. Janet turned on a megawatt smile at the site of Jamie. 'Hello, Sir,' she said, but her smile became fixed as she spotted Raina.

'Hi Janet,' said Raina.

Janet nodded as Tamsin joined them.

'Let's get to it,' said Jamie, sitting next to Raina. 'As you all know, Raina has joined the Templar nation. She's proven her loyalty, and I'd like to bring her up to speed on our relationships.'

'If I could express my concern ...' said Tamsin fervently.

Jamie cut her off. 'No, you may not. You may do what you're told.'

Tamsin's cheeks flushed and she sat back in her seat. She arranged her features in a neutral expression, but her eyes glowed hot.

'Where would you like to start?' said Janet, a little too brightly.

'Our strategy,' said Jamie, looking directly at Raina, 'is aggressive. We believe demons have become soft ... that we lack purpose. Gone are the days of wielding swords and sacking cities, of feast and famine, of being beholden to the seasons. We all have enough ... want for nothing ... and so, what is the point of so many nations? Why do we continue to live separately? Ineffective and inefficient?

'Why spend so much time around tables at the Registerium, discussing petty issues, to achieve bland results? Results that lack in ambition, or worse, are detrimental to our species? Why should the Templars be beholden to those who—intentionally or otherwise—do us harm? Should not the best of us, the strongest of our species, rightfully rule? Why do we insist on stifling evolution—the most fundamental of forces for good?'

Raina wasn't surprised, per se. She'd encountered this kind of rambling, illogical mess many times before, and she took it seriously. The impassioned misinformation Jamie was spouting could easily capture a person's imagination, could make them do all kinds of terrible things ...

'How?' said Raina. 'I'm assuming not by ending the Registerium, and fighting it out until one nation reigns supreme?'

Jamie laughed. 'Fun as that would be my little war monger, that's not the plan. Tamsin ...' he said, handing the floor to her.

'The plan,' said Tamsin, refusing to look Jamie in the eye, 'is to infiltrate and manipulate the Registerium to the point of Templar control. We will ally with those who share our aspirations, and use our control to remove those who stand in our way, by any means necessary.'

'Snappy,' said Raina. 'Janet is, I assume, on Registerium infiltration duty ... and doing a good job from what I've seen so far ...'

Janet's lips twitched as she fought a smile. She nodded.

'The relationship with the Slayers is part of how we're removing nations by any means necessary?' said Raina. 'And our potential allies are the Aztecs, Egyptians, Persian Zorros, Animists of Africa, and the Pacific Nations?'

'And that's why we're delighted to have you on our side,' said Jamie, beaming.

Raina held his gaze until it was uncomfortable for Tamsin and Janet, then said, 'Have you actually secured any allies, aside from the Aztecs?'

'Why don't I tell you about our work at the Registerium ...' said Janet.

Evidently Tamsin wasn't alone in her concerns about Raina's trustworthiness ...

She could make a fuss ... make Jamie tell her ... force his hand in front of the others ... but there was more than one way to skin a cat ... She smiled sweetly. 'Please, go ahead.'

Jamie, Raina, and Callie ate a dinner of smoked ribs in Jamie's warehouse. Callie was being fussy—unusual for her—and it was making Jamie irritable.

'Time for bed,' said Raina. No good would come from sitting here any longer, and she couldn't stand it when Jamie snapped at Callie. She was only five years old and had been thrust into a strange house with strange people who endlessly ordered her about.

Callie was testing boundaries—like any kid would—but understanding this, or allowing her to be a kid, was alien to the Templar demons ... then again, they'd most likely never had that luxury themselves ... it had been so different back when they were all young.

'Come on,' said Raina, standing and holding out her hand to Callie. She smiled at her daughter ... *her daughter* ... would she ever get used to that?

'She can put herself to bed,' said Jamie, in a tone that made Raina's spine stiffen. 'She's five years old ... you baby her.'

Raina hugged Callie tightly. 'Go on,' she said. 'I'll tuck you in later ... don't forget to brush your teeth.'

Callie gave her one last squeeze then went, Raina breathing a sigh of relief that she left willingly, not putting up a fight.

'I do not baby her,' said Raina, sinking back into her seat. 'But I am parenting her in a way less barbaric than most demons experienced.'

'It didn't do us any harm,' said Jamie, swirling the wine in his glass.

Raina raised an eyebrow. 'That's a matter of opinion … and times have changed.'

'For the worse, if you ask me.'

'So I gather from your war plans.'

'Our war plans,' said Jamie.

'They're not ours until I've thoroughly assessed and agreed to them,' countered Raina. 'Which I can't do until you share details of our alliances.'

Jamie took a sip of wine. 'The Aztecs are our primary ally,' he said. 'They're well aligned with our goals.'

Raina nodded and took a sip too.

'We're in talks with the Egyptians and Pacific Nations. I'm expecting to have both on side imminently. The Persian Zorros and Animists of Africa have also expressed interest in supporting our cause, but their fragmented nature means it takes time—a long time—to gain agreement about anything.'

And because of that fragmented nature, neither the Zorros nor Animists had ever been that useful in a war. 'You want them as allies just so they don't work with the Pagans?' said Raina.

'Yes. They're difficult partners to manage, but the more nations we have, the less for the Pagans. If we can keep them out of the game, that will be enough.'

'Confident …' said Raina.

'As Janet said, we have Registerium backing, so the small nations will side with us. And we have the Slayers …'

'What about the new nation on the West Coast?' said Raina. Tamsin had returned with alarming speed, which meant she'd either had outlandish success or failed spectacularly.

'We have more work to do there, although I doubt a nation so new has any interest in war …'

It was a relief the Templars hadn't made headway with the new nation. Maybe the West Coast could help cause turbulence in Jamie's own back yard …

'What next?' said Raina. 'What's the plan of attack?'

Jamie flicked his eyes over her, then put down his wine glass and leaned forward in his seat. 'We'll continue running sorties with the Slayers, test out their capabilities, and determine next steps from there. The Registerium is already ours … we plan to issue a statement to all nations.'

'Saying what?'

'To be determined.'

Raina held his gaze for a beat, then switched course. 'When's the first out-and-out attack?' she asked, giving Jamie a sultry look, like she lusted for battle.

'To be determined,' he said again slowly, holding her gaze.

Raina wanted to ask about magic … did the Templars plan to use it? Did they have any aces up their sleeve? But to do so might arouse Jamie's interest, and if he was currently underestimating magic, it would be better to keep it that way.

'Jamie, we need you,' said Tamsin from the doorway.

Jamie nodded, then stood.

'Do you need me?' said Raina.

Jamie faltered. 'You wanted to tuck Callie in …' he said, a smirk on his face.

Raina reached out a hand as he passed, taking hold of his arm. 'Thank you for telling me,' she said, looking up at him from under her lashes.

'You're welcome,' he said, then strode away.

She was making progress, but there was still something holding him back …

Zahora hurtled through the Nexus, every conscious thought focused on the Registerium. And then, just as she got close to the Registerium's standing stone—the epicenter of their magic—she slammed into something solid which did not give way. It hurt, her bones jarring, her soul shaking. And then she was moving again, pulled back the way she'd come by some invisible force.

Zahora struggled against it. She clawed and scraped, setting every ounce of her intention on getting free. But it was no use.

She realized with a jolt that Noah's music had stopped. Had someone attacked him? Was someone attacking her body in the cave?

Zahora changed her intention, applying all her energy to returning to the cave. The Triskelion burned brightly on her soul as she sped, faster and faster, back to her body.

She collided with herself with such force that she convulsed, her back arching clean off the ground. And then she vomited, the pain in her head so crushing her body needed an outlet.

She looked around, but Noah nowhere to be seen. She was alone … but he wouldn't just leave her … not when she needed him … She washed her mouth, sensing for threats with every part of her being.

The water splashed up and hit her in the face, and she recoiled, shocked, terrified. But a force pushed her from behind, tipping her forward into the water. She surfaced to see Marla sitting on a rock thirty paces away.

'I'd get out of there if I were you,' said Marla.

Zahora didn't hang around to ask why. Now she thought about it, any kind of magic—or creature—could reside in the lake. They'd performed magic here since ancient times, and water had memory ...

'It was you?' said Zahora, shaking from both the shock and the cold.

Marla sent her a quizzical look.

'You pulled me back from the Nexus?'

'Yes.'

'Why? I was doing what you told me ... testing my theory that the Registerium's magic is weak.'

'No,' said Marla.

'Yes, I ...'

'You were being a spoiled, petulant, impulsive, reckless little girl.'

This was almost laughable coming from a teenager ... or at least someone who looked like one. But Marla was not a teenager. She was the most formidable magik the Pagans had. One of the best in the world.

'I thought I was helping.'

'That's why you snuck out in the middle of the night? And brought with you someone who isn't supposed to know what we do here?'

'He doesn't know what we're doing,' said Zahora, hotly. 'He just helps bring me back ... he thinks I'm meditating.'

'I'm sure ...' said Marla, scathingly.

'And I don't like other people. I don't want to work with the others ... they waste so much time ...'

'Then you shall work with me.'

'But ...' But what could she say? Marla was unequivocally in charge. 'Why did you pull me back?'

'Because you've already caused one shock-wave through the system, I couldn't let you cause another.'

'How would assaulting the Registerium's magic cause a shock-wave?'

'It might, or it might not. We don't know the repercussions, and you planned to attack them anyway, without thought or backup.'

Zahora shook her head.

'And,' said Marla, 'did you stop to consider that the pulsing magic could be a result of you touching the Sphere? Maybe the entire system is unstable.'

No, she hadn't stopped to consider that ... 'Is that possible?'

'Anything is possible. We must test our theories before hurtling into the unknown.'

'How?'

'We must probe the Registerium's magic subtly ... less like a bull in a china shop ...' Marla walked to the water's edge and crouched. 'You don't know what this place is, do you?'

'Other than a lake in a cave?'

Marla gave her a withering look. 'This place is as close as most will ever get to magic. Look,' she said, as she placed a palm flat on the water.

Five distinct strands of light rippled out from Marla's ink-covered fingers. They meandered across the gloom until they hit something on the water. The light travelled two ways, then met the far side, forming a ring across the lake, travelling faster now as it traced the edges of an eight-pointed star inside the ring.

'The wheel,' said Zahora.

'The source of Pagan power,' said Marla, with a nod. 'Each nation has a different way of accessing the Sphere ... has a different interpretation of magic.

Pagans use the eight-pointed star, each spoke signifying a key time in our year. To learn to use magic, as a Pagan, is distinctly different to learning as a Buddhist, or Egyptian, or as a member of any other nation. The Registerium has their own interpretation of magic, their own practice, their own means of pulling power.'

'But I've never known of this eight-spoked wheel,' said Zahora, 'and I can still use magic.'

'One can practice magic any which way you like, if you have sufficient power. But to understand the magic of a nation, to comprehend its protections, you must first understand the approach ... the ideology ... the design ...'

'And you think I should understand the Registerium's magic before attacking it?' said Zahora.

Marla nodded. 'If we must attack at all.'

'How?' said Zahora.

'Through research ...'

Zahora groaned.

'... careful exploration, and asking those who constructed it.'

'Who did construct it?'

'A group of independent magiks. They were ancient, and most of them have died.'

'That's who Christa and Talli are trying to find?'

Marla inclined her head.

'But how does any of this help me? I can already access the Nexus without the wheel.'

'You'll be stronger if you learn to use it, and its protections. I plucked you from the Nexus as though you were a gnat. Anyone could have, and you did nothing ... could do nothing ... except panic.'

A protest rose to Zahora's lips, but her near death at the hands of Alerac came to mind ... Marla was right. Zahora had things to learn, but she wanted to learn, had been asking the Pagans to teach her for two lifetimes!

'What do we know about the Registerium's magic?' said Zahora, tramping down her frustration. 'If we can understand it, then we know where to attack, right?'

'We have some information, which I will share only once you've learned to use the wheel. Until then, we'll concentrate on basic skills.'

Zahora wanted to rage about how no one had ever taught her ... how they'd refused to teach her anything useful ... had gone at a snail's pace ... done nothing but frustrate her efforts. But for possibly the first time in her life, she exercised restraint. 'Where do we start?' she said.

'Sit, and I'll show you.'

Chapter 9

Marla and Zahora worked for days by the pool. They barely slept, rarely ate, and spoke to no one.

'The wheel represents the year and its key moments—equinoxes and the like. The Pagan nation has been attuned to the workings of our planet from the beginning. We worship and respect the natural way of things, and our magic reflects this,' Marla had said on the first day.

Zahora had nodded, but not understood. She knew of the eight calendar celebrations the Pagans held dear—Midsummer the pinnacle—but had never stopped to think about them deeply.

On the second day, Marla's topic had been the magic itself. 'Energy moves across the magma of the Earth—what we call the Sphere. There are no boundaries and obstructions there, no politics. It's pure, unadulterated, liquid magic. The Nexus gives us access, but also acts as a filter, to keep it pure. That you touched the Sphere is troubling. That you came back is something else entirely ... something I have never seen in my lifetime. The shock you sent across the world ...

well, we have no way of telling what that was, or what damage it caused.'

Zahora felt abashed, ashamed ... she looked down at her hands.

'We connect to the Nexus primarily through stones—our gates. They grant us access to the Nexus, and are tethered to the energy of the Sphere. The gate is your access, and your protector. A powerful gate, with a strong connection to the Sphere, can shield you from harm and warn you when others draw near. This is why we maintain our stones. Used correctly, they are an invaluable asset.

'The symbols we ink on our skin—different for each nation—are part of our contract with the magic. They help to guide and protect us ... allow us to find our way home. We must find symbols that work for us, but also for our gate.'

'The symbols form part of our contract? What contract?'

'Nothing comes without a cost,' said Marla, 'and magic is no different. Each nation has their own terms of use ... their own price.'

'What's ours?'

'Sacrifice,' said Marla.

'What?' said Zahora, paling.

'You'll see soon enough ... now, what symbols have you tried already?'

Zahora shook off her surprise and told her. They spent days trying new ones. She should have committed herself to the task before ... she'd wasted so much time ...

'You're an earth child,' said Marla, as they reviewed the symbols that most called to Zahora. 'An encircled Pentagram—like the center of an apple—and the Dara Knot, for the great oak tree.'

'What about the other two …?' said Zahora. 'The Serch Bythol and the Triskelion?' Zahora silently noted only the Pentagram was an addition to her arsenal; she'd already identified the other three. Maybe she hadn't been too far off the mark after all …

'Those are eternal symbols,' said Marla. 'The Triskelion is as much a representation of an ongoing cycle as it is about speed or motion. You're interested in the future, impatient to get there, have a desire to make a mark on the world. Whether you do so through love or other action … that is your choice to make.'

'Should I use them all at once?'

'First, we paint you with the Pagan wheel, then we add your symbols. After that, you must learn to use them, and not let them use you.'

Zahora sat stone still as Marla painted her hands with first the wheel, and then her four chosen symbols.

'You may wish to add more in time,' said Marla, holding out her arms, inked top to bottom. It looked so strange on one so young … barbaric even. 'Your skin becomes your history, plane for all to see.'

'What should I see when I look at yours?' said Zahora, studying Marla's hands, picking out elements she recognized, noticing many she did not.

'Someone old and wizened, with many scars.'

The Serch Bythol caught Zahora's eye, almost hidden in the crease between Marla's thumb and finger. It was struck through with a line of missing ink, obliterating the meaning.

'What happened?' asked Zahora, without thinking, her eyes still locked on the symbol of broken love.

'Life isn't a fairytale,' said Marla, finishing Zahora's symbols. 'And people aren't always who you think they are … that's a lesson worth remembering.'

Zahora shuddered. Marla's words, demeanor, and avoidance all pointed to something terrible …

unspeakable. Any semblance of joy had scurried from the room, a yawning pit of black replacing it.

'Stop it,' said Marla.

'Stop what?' said Zahora.

'You're using magic.'

'I am?'

'Intention, emotion, desire … they all affect the way we access magic. You're projecting your thoughts about my broken Serch Bythol out into the world, dreading a day when it may happen to you, and sucking all the energy from the room as you do so. Stop it.'

'I … I didn't realize.'

'You have power. Using it has consequences, and not only for you.'

'Then what should I do?'

'Pay attention to what I tell you, and be more careful with your actions.'

'I'm trying to learn. I want to learn, but I can't always do things the way you want me to.'

'Why not?' said Marla. 'It's worked for hundreds of years.'

'Because it doesn't work for me. And I know I'm young and inexperienced, but that doesn't mean I don't know my own mind, or that I shouldn't take responsibility for my progression. I've tried to tell you, the way you teach me isn't the best way for me. It might work for you, and others like you, but not for me. I've been trying to find my own way, but I'll happily admit that hasn't worked either. I don't know what I'm doing …

'Please, can't we compromise? Meet in the middle? Even these last few days—where we've moved faster than ever before—have left me itching to *do* something. To push myself. I may not be the pupil you wanted, but I am the one you have … we need to work together.'

Marla assessed Zahora for long moments. 'Very well,' she said eventually. 'What do you propose?'

'Seriously?'

'Change is the only constant,' said Marla. 'I suppose that means occasionally I should change my ways too. But you have to promise to listen to me, especially when I tell you not to do something. There is always a reason for my hesitation, even if you don't immediately understand, and by increasing the pace of your education, you increase the danger too.'

'Okay,' she said, going cold as she thought of her encounter with Alerac. She told Marla about it. 'How did he have protections in the Nexus without a stone?' asked Zahora.

Marla exhaled. 'It's possible to become your own gate if you're very powerful. It's dangerous, as you're not tethered to the Sphere ... the magic could suck you in, or an enemy could find you, your only protection that which you're able to provide for yourself ... It sounds like Alerac was using Raina as an anchor, and maybe an amplifier too.'

'He was using her energy?'

'Probably.'

Zahora's mind almost exploded ... she hadn't known that was possible.

'You've been accessing the Sphere without an external gate too,' said Marla.

'What?'

'You said yourself, you didn't know about the wheel, or how to use it.'

'But I've always touched the stone ...'

'Which helped you feel the Nexus, but you didn't use it as a gateway ... how could you have?'

Zahora's heart thumped. That meant she was powerful ... Marla had just told her that. 'Then I'll need my own protections ...'

'First, I'll show you how to use the stone, then I'll teach you to create your own. But remember, everything we do comes at a cost.'

Leila headed for the park near the Templar headquarters where she'd spoken to Raina before. She and Jon had received word from Ira, of the Holy Star, that Raina and Callie were heading there, along with their usual security detail.

Jon was following at a discrete distance as Leila hurried along the sidewalk, nervously fingering the bangle in her pocket. Both she and Jon had a surveillance device—Ira had sent another—given they had no choice but to be opportunistic about getting it to Raina.

Leila entered the park to find Raina already there, pushing Callie on a swing. Raina's security team leaned against the railing, looking bored.

'Leila!' squealed Callie, jumping off the swing and running to give her a hug.

Leila dropped to her knees and wrapped Callie in a bear hug. 'Callie! It's so nice to see you! What have you been up to?'

'Urgh, we went on a stupid trip to a stupid stone, and …'

'Callie, I'm sure Leila doesn't want to hear about that,' said Raina, coming up behind the girl. 'Do you, Leila?'

'I'm just happy to see you,' said Leila, giving Callie one last squeeze before standing. 'And you,' she said to Raina.

'Go play on the slide,' said Raina, pushing Callie forcefully away.

'Mum!' said Callie angrily, shaking herself free of Raina's grip. She stomped towards the swings in protest.

'You need to leave,' said Raina. 'I told you before, it's not safe. Please, just leave New York and never contact me again.'

'I … just wanted to give you something,' said Leila, pulling the bangle out of her pocket.

Raina's eyes went wide, the only sign she was rattled. 'Where did you get that?'

'A friend gave it to me.'

'Why?'

'As a cover,' said Leila, 'for the real reason I need to talk to you.'

'What the fuck, Leila? Do you have any idea how dangerous this is?'

'The Holy Star can't hack the Templars' systems. They need your help. We have a USB device. It's small, taped to the bangle. All you have to do is put it in one of their computers, leave it for five minutes, then get rid of it. Just take it … tell them the bracelet was something sentimental between us.'

'They weren't born yesterday,' said Raina. 'If I take something from you, they'll search me and destroy it … and that's not something I want destroyed …'

'Then take it, remove the USB device, and give it back to me.'

'Back again?' said Tamsin's voice, approaching from behind.

Leila closed her eyes and exhaled slowly, putting the bracelet back in her pocket before facing the threat.

'I'm here to see my cousin. I know she won't come with me, but I came to check she's okay ... that Callie's okay.'

'Mission accomplished,' said Tamsin. 'Unless you'd like to come home with us ...? See how we party ...?'

'She was just leaving,' said Raina. 'Leila, never contact me again.'

Fuck. Fuck. Fuck. Leila silently repeated the swear word all the way back to Jon's apartment. She took a meandering route full of loops, through markets, and via pit stops at cafes. She was impatient to see Jon, to regroup and work out how to fix the mess she'd made. She should have forced the bangle into Raina's hand ... should have been quicker to explain her purpose ... shouldn't have wasted time hugging Callie ... *FUCK!*

Jon eventually made it back to the apartment, his features unreadable.

'I know, I screwed up ... I'm sorry.'

'We were followed,' he said. 'We need to leave ... now.'

'Shit.'

They had a car waiting in the basement, their belongings already inside. They'd known this could happen, had planned for it, but Leila had never considered they might have to act on that plan ... not really ... it had seemed like a paranoid contingency, nothing more.

Jon took her hand and pulled her to the elevator. He seemed calm as he pressed the button and waited.

'You know what to do?' he said, squeezing her fingers.

Leila nodded. She couldn't speak over the thundering of her heart.

The doors opened, and they stepped in, Jon not letting go of her hand. Leila watched the numbers count slowly down as Jon checked his phone. 'Ira says no one's been near the car, and the basement's clear.'

Someone might be lying in wait …? Her stomach roiled.

They approached the basement and Jon pushed Leila to one side—so she'd be out of view when the doors opened—then positioned himself on the other side. He let the doors open fully before peeking round the edge.

'Go,' he mouthed, grabbing Leila's hand and pulling her in his wake. They crouched below the level of the car windows, just in case.

They reached their car, and Jon eased the passenger door open. Leila got in and donned the waiting wig and sunglasses. It had felt ridiculous when they'd prepared all this, but now she wished they'd done more … although, what more could they have done? She didn't know … she'd never been involved in anything like this … would be happy never to be again.

Jon slid into the driver's seat of their nondescript hatchback, slipping a baseball cap over his blonde hair, then fired up the engine.

'Look bored,' said Jon. 'Stare out of the window, or … just act natural.'

'Are they outside?'

'Ira's not sure. He hasn't spotted anyone, but that doesn't mean no one's there.'

Leila wanted to be sick, but she did her best to look like this was just a regular car ride.

Jon pulled out of the carpark, and Leila's eyes darted around frantically behind the shield of her sunglasses. She searched for Tamsin, or leather cuffs, or anything that looked odd. But demons looked exactly like humans ... it was impossible.

'Fuck,' said Jon, as they pulled away.

'What?' said Leila, trying not to let her terror show as her heart leapt in her chest and adrenaline ripped through her blood.

'Tamsin's in the doorway over there. She's on her phone and looking right at us.'

'What does that mean?'

'She's probably calling in our number plate so they can track us. The Templars probably own the police.'

'Oh, Jesus ... what do we do?'

'Two options ... we try to get to the airport in this car, or we ditch it and flag down a cab.'

'Will they follow us?'

'I don't know ... keep watch while I drive. It would be better to ditch the car, just in case, but not if they're following us. They might just be making sure we leave ...'

'Maybe the disguises worked, and Tamsin doesn't know it's us.'

'Maybe,' said Jon, skeptically, 'but we can't rely on that.'

Leila watched in the mirrors for any sign of pursuit, but it was difficult without turning around. She told herself not to panic, that it would be alright, but she didn't really believe that. They were in Templar territory ...

Jon reached for her hand. 'It's going to be okay,' he said, then dialed Ira.

'The good thing about New York is their police department's cyber security is terrible,' said Ira. 'I have access to the entire network.'

'Can you turn it off?' said Leila.

'If they're looking for your number plate, I can stop the cameras from finding you, but not the cops on the ground.'

'Does it look like anyone's following us?' said Jon, having to stop at a red light.

'Nothing obvious,' said Ira.

As they crossed the Hudson, Leila looked down at the water traffic, trying to calm her nerves.

'If there's no change by the time we get to the other side,' said Jon, 'I'm going to ditch the car. Leila, can you hail a cab while I get our bags?'

'Yes,' she said numbly. She could do that.

They made it across, and Jon turned onto a side street, found a parking slot, and pulled in.

'Any change?' Jon asked the phone.

'None. You're good to go,' said Ira.

Leila jumped out and flagged a cab. It ignored her. Maybe she'd waved too hard …? What if she couldn't get anyone to stop? She eased up a bit as she flagged the next one, and relief flooded her as it slowed.

She helped Jon grab their bags, her heart hammering louder than it ever had before.

'Anything?' Jon said in a low voice into his phone.

Jon smiled at Leila, and she relaxed the smallest bit.

The ride to Newark felt like an eternity … why hadn't she listened to Jon in the first place and left New York? Why was she such a stubborn fool?

They reached the airport, but the Templars probably had surveillance here too … she kept her head down, unsure of Ira's capabilities inside the building.

She barely noticed their progress through the airport until they were being ushered through a private security line and heading for a private jet.

'Um ...' said Leila, her mouth falling open.

Jon grabbed her hand again, squeezing hard enough to make her gasp. *Right ... play it cool.*

By the time they were in their seats, Leila was a wreck. She'd conjured all manner of scenarios where they didn't make it out, but eventually the place took off. She turned to Jon, who took one look at her face and pulled her to him.

'Sush,' he said, stroking her hair. 'It's okay ... we're out.'

'But we failed ... I failed ... it was all for nothing ...'

'Speak for yourself,' said Jon, pulling back to look in her eyes.

'What?'

'While you were distracting them, I put my device in Callie's backpack. We just have to hope Raina finds it before anyone else does ...'

Raina slipped into Jamie's office—the only room she was confident didn't have security cameras. Although, if security were paying attention, they would have seen her enter, so she didn't have long.

She went to his desk, not hesitating before pushing the USB device into his desktop stack. Five minutes ... she just needed five minutes.

The seconds ticked by slowly … unbelievably so. Raina cast around for anything else that might be helpful, but Jamie's office was minimalist to the point of sterility. No shelves, no books, hardly any furniture, modern art, a single curved computer screen, no desk drawers. A safe probably sat behind one of the pictures, but she didn't have time to look, and he'd have alarms.

She sat in his chair and waited. And waited. With ten seconds left, she heard approaching footsteps. She held her breath, her pulse pounding in her ears. She willed them to keep going, but they didn't. They stopped. Eight, seven … the handle turned. Damn … she had to get away from the desk.

'Jamie,' said Tamsin's voice from the corridor.

Thank the Gods. Three, two, one. Raina pulled out the device and hid it in her bra, then picked up the phone and dialed Jamie's room, listening to the conversation outside.

'Leila came again,' said Tamsin. 'She tried to give something to Raina.'

'What?' said Jamie.

'A bracelet.'

'Did Raina take it?'

'No.'

'Did she touch it?'

'No.'

'Where's Leila now?'

'She flew out … used her passport at Newark and got on a plane with a man.'

'A human, or a demon?'

'Impossible to say, but we found their abandoned car, so they must have at least suspected they were being followed. And it was a private plane, so if not a demon, then a human with means …'

'Monitor both passports,' said Jamie. 'If either of them return, I want to know about it.'

Leila and Jon had made it out ... that was something ... even if the close call made her shudder. Raina replaced the receiver, then travelled on silent feet to the door. She stood to the side, her back flat against the wall.

The door opened, and Jamie stepped through. He scanned the office, obviously looking for her.

'Behind you, darling,' said Raina, laughing as he jumped and spun. She pushed the door closed in case Tamsin was loitering. 'You're getting sloppy.'

'I'm in my own home ... I don't need to be vigilant, and I knew you were in here.' The security team must have tipped him off ...

'Took you long enough to get here ... I tried calling your room ... thought you might be napping like the old man you are.'

Jamie stepped forward. He placed a hand on her abdomen, pushing her back against the door. She met his angry gaze with flirtatious eyes.

'Why are you in my office?'

'I want to discuss our next move.'

'Tamsin says you saw Leila.'

'She sought me out ... I told her to leave.'

'What was she trying to give you?'

'A bracelet.'

'Why?'

'Because she's sentimental, and the jewelry means something to her. She has no one left. She's sad ... grieving ... but I sent her away. I have no need for human company.'

Jamie seemed unconvinced, so she picked an imaginary piece of lint from his t-shirt, then smoothed her hand across his shoulder. He was all masculine muscle, and sensation stirred low in her belly. She loved Caspar ... as a life partner, had only ever wanted him, but lust was an old companion ... a traitorous, dangerous impulse that would lead to nothing good.

Raina broke away. 'So,' she said, 'what is our next move?'

Jamie caught her hand. 'I told you, we're running sorties with the Slayers.'

She turned back to face him. 'Who have we attacked so far? What were the results? How are we planning to improve?'

'It's too early for any meaningful data,' he said, pulling the back of her hand to his lips.

He kissed her skin, and she shivered, his eyes locked on hers, watching with interest.

She lifted her head, acknowledging his words. 'Well, tell me as soon as we know more.'

She left, rubbing the back of her hand against the fabric of her jeans, trying to obliterate the feel of Jamie's lips. She thought of all the times Caspar had kissed her hand ... the back, the palm, her fingertips ... of their hands tied together during their many marriages. She couldn't wait to tie herself to him again, for Callie to meet him properly ... for them to start their lives together. But as she returned to her daughter, a bubble of panic rose in her chest, because she couldn't rub the feel of Jamie's kiss off her skin.

Chapter 10

Rose and Malcolm—the Pagans' representative at the Registerium—walked side by side into the Registerium's circular stone chamber used for official meetings and ceremonial occasions. It filled the whole of one of the castle's four turrets, from the ground to the roof.

A spiral staircase wound around the perimeter, the steps set into the wall, with no railing, and void space between each one ... stairs not for the faint of heart. The place was dimly lit by slit windows and candles hanging from the underside of the stone stairs.

A circle of stone shelves protruded from the wall near the bottom, on which sat representatives from each demon nation. A man—the Registrar—awaited them in the circle's center.

Malcolm went to find his seat, leaving Rose to face the man alone.

'Registrar,' said Rose, inclining her head.

The Registrar mirrored her movement then said to the room, 'We all know why we're here: for the outcome of the official complaint made by the Pagan nation regarding the transfer of the demon Raina Halabi from their own ranks to the Templars.'

'The lawful transfer,' shouted Janet—the Templars' representative—from her seat.

'Lawful?' said Malcolm, mockingly. 'Did the laws change?'

'Thank you,' said the Registrar sternly. 'We have heard the evidence, have debated, and have come to the decision that Raina's transfer was lawful ...'

An explosion of sound erupted from the Pagans' supporters, led by the Vikings' boisterous representative. They booed and stamped and called their disapproval.

'Thank you,' the Registrar boomed. 'The Templars acted in good faith and in full collaboration with the Registerium. They consulted us regarding their concerns that the Pagans would kidnap Raina if she came to Scotland, and we believed their claims to have solid foundation.'

'What of the claims that the Registerium is the Templars' lapdog? Eh?' said the shaggy-haired Viking. 'What of the evidence supporting that claim?'

'Furthermore,' said the Registrar, 'the Registerium stands behind the Templar nation in the coming war, and would urge other nations to do the same.'

More shouts rang out until Rose held up her hand for silence. 'And what of the evidence that the Templars are working with the Slayers?' she said, her voice like iron. 'Or that the Registerium is corrupt? There is only one way the Templars' actions can be considered legal, and that is that those holding the reins of power cannot read.'

The laughs and jeers came again, the Registrar's features turning to ice.

'Furthermore,' said Rose, mimicking the Registrar, 'the Pagan nation seeks a full investigation into these allegations by a separate, independent committee. And, in case anyone wishes to fight this,' she held a document aloft, 'I have here a copy of the original bylaws, and I quote, *If such situation arises that any nation has reason to question the integrity of the sanctity of the Registerium's ability to act in an independent manner, a nation, by simple majority vote of member representatives, may force an independent inquiry.* And so, Registrar, I call a vote.'

'You can't,' said the Registrar. 'It says ...'

'All those in favor of an independent inquiry into the Registerium, say *aye.*'

'Aye,' said the Viking. 'Fuck aye!'

'Nay,' said Janet, looking furiously at her allies.

'Aye,' said the representatives for the Buddhists, Shindu Council, Holy Star, and Wakans.

'Nay,' said the Aztecs, the Persian Zorros, the Aboriginals, and the Pacific Nations.

'We abstain,' said the Russian Spirituals.

Five each, and the Egyptians held the deciding vote ...

'Did it work?' said Caspar. 'Did the vote go our way?'

'I don't know what you promised the Egyptians, but whatever it was, they must really want it.'

'They haven't even got it yet ...'

'Well, either way, they gave us our inquiry.'

'Thank the Gods,' said Caspar. 'Have the Registerium given open access to the records?'

'Not yet, although Pablo—the record keeper—is working with us.'

'He's a friend of Raina's,' said Caspar, his relief palpable. 'At least we have one friend there.'

'I heard the Holy Star has access to the Templars' systems?' said Rose.

'Ira's not sure how far they can maneuver inside the network—it might take a while to find a path to any decent information—but they have a foot in the door at least.'

'And the disruption here should keep the Registerium busy for a while,' said Rose.

'One can only hope. Now, tell me, who voted against us, and what information do we have on them?'

Raina and Alerac sat in Alerac's teaching room with Callie asleep between them. Their relationship was strained, and Raina worried about Alerac and Jamie's developing rapport. Would Alerac sell her out? She didn't think he had so far, otherwise Jamie would have said something … done something, but the possibility loomed large.

Raina stroked Callie's hair, the silence becoming unbearable.

'She's leaning,' said Alerac. 'She'll never be a great magik, but she'll be able to defend herself at least …'

Raina prickled at his prophetic words. How could anyone pretend to understand the potential of another? Especially of one so young …

'Have you thought more about the Pagan magik?' asked Raina. 'She had potential, did she not?'

'That she did. I have pondered her awhile ... and the pulsing energy.'

'You feel the pulsing here too?'

'I do.'

Silence settled again.

'A demon like the Pagan woman would be a worthy pupil. She'd no doubt appreciate your teaching talents ... unlike my daughter,' Raina said with a smile, both hoping and dreading that he would understand her meaning.

Alerac gave her a long look. 'Of course,' he said. 'What teacher wouldn't want a pupil like her? Although I fear her power would outstrip my own.'

'Really?'

'Certainly. As I said, she did something I've never seen, and would never in a million years attempt.'

'Why?'

'Because she left herself open to death.'

'Of but one life ...'

'No; eternal death.'

Raina flinched. 'How?'

'The usual way of administering the true death— removing and destroying a demon's eyes while they still live—is effective, because it prevents our souls escaping our bodies. When the body dies, the soul has no way out, so it dies too.

'When she traveled here, the Pagan removed her soul from her body and put it wholly in the Nexus. She offered it on a plate for anyone with the skill to catch it ... no physical body to protect her ... and no magical defenses either.'

'Gods,' said Raina.

'What she's doing is dangerous, and she doesn't even know it.'

'She needs a teacher,' said Raina.

'She does …'

'Would you do it? Teach her, I mean?'

Alerac's eyes widened. 'In another life maybe … if she lasts that long. In this life, you know that's impossible. I'm Aztec, and I love my nation. Would you train your nation's enemy to satisfy your own curiosity?'

'I just …'

'You are a Templar now …'

He paused, daring her to contradict him.

'I take my nation's allegiances seriously,' he said. 'Maybe you should too.'

'Alerac, I'm sorry, I didn't mean …'

'Don't ask me to compromise myself again. Our session is over …' Alerac's eyes flicked to the door.

Raina nodded. She picked up Callie's sleeping form and awkwardly exited the room.

'Hello darling,' said Jamie, coming up the corridor.

'Jamie,' said Raina, rearranging Callie so she could see over her shoulder.

'How's our little angel?'

'Alerac says she's coming along, although she'll never be a great magik.'

Jamie laughed. 'Good! She'll never need to be … she'll have a new world at her feet. Magic is of the old … out with it!'

Raina smiled but inwardly cringed. How could Jamie be so naïve? 'Have a good session,' she said.

152

Jamie entered Alerac's room. It depressed him how the curtains were so often drawn, the lights low, relics of the past scattered around. Half the point of a loft apartment was the light … but he couldn't deny the man had magic hands …

Jamie lay face down on the massage table.

'Clear your mind,' said Alerac, approaching with an ancient-looking bottle of oil.

'Callie's education is coming along?' said Jamie.

Alerac breathed an audible sigh—a sign of his irritation—and Jamie chuckled inside. The man was so composed, Jamie made it his mission to ruffle his feathers.

'She is, yes. Now if you would …'

'Is Raina practicing magic too?' said Jamie.

'Barely,' said Alerac with a scoff.

'She can't …?'

'Who knows that woman's reasons …' he said.

Was that irritation in his tone? Heavens above … an emotion! 'Have you two had a disagreement?' said Jamie, lifting his head to look Alerac in the eye.

'No.'

'What's put you in a bad mood then?'

'A lack of respect for magic,' he said pointedly. 'Now, if you would close your eyes and clear your mind?'

'Why do you care if people respect magic? I won't deny it's a God-send for massage, but … it's outdated.'

Alerac put down the bottle with an audible click … definitely ruffled. A thrill travelled down Jamie's spine.

'Magic goes to the very heart of who we are: agreements forged, allegiances made, nations … it's what makes us reincarnate … underestimate that at your own peril. And if I were you, I'd magically transfer Raina to the Templars as a matter of priority.'

'What? Why?'

'Because I have respect for ancient and powerful things.'

Jamie was formulating his next question when Tamsin burst in.

'News from Janet,' she said without preamble.

He rolled his eyes. 'What is it now?'

'The Registerium deemed Raina's nation transfer lawful, but the Pagans have forced an independent inquiry into the Registerium's conduct.'

'Shit,' said Jamie. 'Who voted against us? Actually, fuck it, I'm having a massage. Arrange the strike. I'll find you when I'm done.'

'Respect for old and powerful things …' said Alerac, then he put his magic hands to work.

Torsten rapped on the glass door of a house built into a cave overlooking the sea. Marvelous as it was, it seemed perilous to Meredith … like the whole thing was teetering … waiting to topple over the edge into the water. But that might have been because the walkway to reach the house was a bridge suspended over the frothing surf.

'Hello?' said a glamorous woman with grey hair and enormous pearl earrings.

She had the look of a person ready to sit in the Royal Box at Wimbledon. What was she doing living here? Their research had been inconclusive …

'Good afternoon, Mrs Smythe-Brown,' said Torsten, flashing her his most charming smile. 'I'm so sorry to disturb you, but my fiancé and I are collectors of art. A friend told us you were of a mind to sell several pieces in your collection?'

'Well ... yes ... but ...'

'I told you,' said Meredith, smacking Torsten on the arm. 'We can't just knock on some poor lady's door ...' Meredith put on an American accent, sinking into the role of a spoiled heiress. She'd even worn a dress and makeup, her long dark hair twisted into an elegant up do. Stilettos completed the getup, and she was glad Torsten was tall and broad, so at least she didn't look out of proportion.

'Honey ...' said Torsten, rolling his eyes at Mrs Smythe-Brown, as though he were a long-suffering husband-to-be. Then he gave Meredith an indulgent look, as though her insufferable behavior wasn't so bad after all, because, of course, he was totally in love.

For a second, Meredith let herself pretend she loved him back ... it wasn't so unpleasant.

'I just want to give you the world,' he said.

Meredith beamed, trying not to be sick in her mouth ... he'd taken it too far. She put a hand on his arm, and he leaned down to kiss her.

She had no choice but to let him, and she was big enough to admit he had good lips. The kiss was short and chaste—given their audience—and it was nice to be kissed ... it hadn't happened in a while.

He pulled back, and she looked up into his eyes, softening the smallest bit. Torsten put his arm around her, and she fit herself into his side. He dropped a kiss on her hair.

'I'm sorry,' said Torsten, 'we can go through your agent if you give us their details.'

The woman hesitated, then backed up. 'Don't be silly,' she said. 'Come in. I've only got one piece here, but there's no harm in you taking a look.'

155

'Thank you,' they said together, grabbing each other as though excited beyond measure.

Mrs Blythe-Smith showed them into the cave, which was small but cozy and surprisingly well-lit due to strategically placed lamps.

She stopped in front of a picture hanging against the jagged stone wall. 'Here it is,' she said.

Meredith cast her eyes over the yellow and red of Van Gogh's *Poppy Flowers*. It had been stolen from a museum a decade ago, only those with ties to the underground art market aware of its current whereabouts.

It was brazen of the woman to let them in. Although, the only way they could know about the painting was to be part of the illicit market themselves … and owners of paintings like these had so few opportunities to show them off. They longed to display to the world how clever they were, how rich and powerful, so it wasn't too great a surprise when they seized moments like these. And anyway, Mrs Blythe-Smith would use her CCTV footage and have the two of them killed if they ever started making trouble … or at least, she'd try …

'Stunning,' said Torsten, pulling Meredith to him. 'Don't you think, sweetie?'

'I do,' said Meredith, with wonder. In reality, there were few pieces of art Meredith could give two hoots about, and this was not one of them. It wasn't her style at all … so fussy and floral.

'Oh my God,' said Torsten, his eyes dipping to Mrs Blythe-Smith's necklace, with which she was absently playing. 'That's … surely that's not …'

'A Sa Amulet from Ancient Egyptian,' said Mrs Blythe-Smith. 'Believed to have belonged to Nefertiti herself.'

'Oh my word!' said Meredith. 'We've been searching for so long for something just like that ... for our wedding.'

'Would you consider selling?' said Torsten. 'We'd pay top dollar.'

The woman laughed. 'Money doesn't get you far in my circles ...'

'We're open to barter,' said Meredith. 'Is there something you want?'

'No,' she said. 'There is nothing I want. I'm reducing the size of my collection, not adding new pieces.'

'Access?' said Torsten. 'Somewhere you'd like to go? Some influence you'd like to have?'

'You are an audacious one,' said Mrs Blythe-Smith. 'I'm afraid there's nothing I want I don't already have.'

'Is there anything that might change your mind?' said Torsten.

'No,' she said.

'We'll buy all the paintings you're selling too, to sweeten the deal,' said Meredith. She was selling for a reason ... whether because the strain of owning incriminating, ill-begotten pieces had become too much, or because she needed the money. If they could only find the button they needed to press.

Mrs Blythe-Smith perked up. 'All of them? The four together will go for over four hundred million dollars ...'

'And they could take a long time to sell,' said Meredith. 'The market's small ... I should know ... Daddy's been in it forever ...'

The woman eyed Meredith speculatively then raised an eyebrow. 'Then I'm sure I know him ... Who is your father?'

Meredith smiled. 'He taught me better than that,' she said.

'Ha!' laughed Mrs Blythe-Smith. 'Very well; let me think on it. Tell me how to reach you, and I'll call when I've made a decision.'

Meredith handed over a card with her number. 'I also have the inside line on a lost Monet ... the one of Charing Cross Bridge,' she said.

Mrs Blythe-Smith's eyes went wide. 'Impossible.'

'I assure you it's not.'

'A friend of mine owns that painting ...'

'They're lying,' said Meredith. 'Have you ever seen it?'

The woman went still, then showed them to the door. 'I'll call you.'

Torsten and Meredith sat in a secluded restaurant later that night, full on linguine and savoring Camparis.

'It's a good painting,' said Torsten, leaning back in his chair.

Meredith brought herself back from the sound of lapping waves. 'I can't say it does much for me.'

'Are you blind?'

She gave him a withering look.

'Van Gogh was an odd chap, but I liked him,' said Torsten.

'I don't think we ever crossed paths ... he wasn't a demon?'

'No.'

She sighed. She'd had enough of treasure hunting and wanted to go home. Others liked to travel ...

maybe Meredith had once too, but she missed England … couldn't wait to return.

'Do you think she'll give us the necklace?' said Meredith.

'She was tempted, and I hope so … I'm too old for petty theft.'

It was a joke, but Meredith couldn't bring herself to laugh. She gave a small nod of agreement then sipped her drink.

It was beautiful here, truly, and the tourists had mostly gone home, leaving the place more like she remembered it from the old days. It made her nostalgic—a rarity—and she wondered what on earth had come over her …

Meredith's phone rang. 'Good evening, Mrs Blythe-Smith.' The only person with this number.

'I'll sell you the paintings and exchange the necklace for the Monet,' said Mrs Blythe-Smith's uncompromising voice, 'on two conditions. First, the Monet must be verified. Second, I want to come to your wedding.'

'You want to come to our wedding?' said Meredith, for Torsten's benefit.

His face split into a wide smile, and Meredith's stomach lurched.

'Of course,' said Meredith. 'We'd be delighted for you to join us, although it will be a small, exclusive affair. Very traditional. No photographs. No big party.'

'I can tell the two of you are the real deal, and I wish to be a part of your celebration,' she said. 'The only things in life that interest me now are those that money cannot buy.'

'In which case,' said Meredith, 'we have a deal.'

'Good. I'll send you the details of my expert.'

'Thank you,' said Meredith, as the woman hung up. Moments later, a text message lit the screen—details of the art expert who would inspect the Monet.

Torsten took hold of Meredith's hand. 'Our wedding! I can't wait to start planning.'

Meredith pulled back and shook her head at him, reaching for a second phone. She hoped Caspar was awake, wherever in the world he was currently located.

'Hey,' said Casper, after only one ring.

'She'll give us the necklace if we swap your Monet.'

The line went quiet. 'That's Raina's painting, not mine …'

'Would you like me to phone her and ask if she's okay with swapping some fucking painting in exchange for securing an alliance that might help us rescue her and her daughter?' said Meredith quietly, so none of the other patrons could hear. 'Some old painting, or freedom? A tough call …'

'I didn't mean …'

'I'll send you the assessor's details to arrange an inspection. She won't hand over the necklace until she's sure the painting's real.'

'Of course,' said Caspar. 'Rose is back in London; I'll get her to deal with it.'

'Don't forget to tell him about the wedding!' said Torsten, downing the rest of his drink.

'The what?' said Caspar.

'The old bat wants to come to Torsten's and my wedding … we pretended to be engaged as a cover, and she's decided we're the real deal …'

'Oh … sorry, Meredith. Look, why don't you come home for Mabon? The next assignment's easy … we need to convince Jon to give over a cufflink, and he's back in the UK.'

'What?' she said, running a hand through her hair. 'Who wants those?'

'Just one,' said Caspar, 'at the request of the leader of a tiny tribe of the Wakan nation.'

'Why are we pissing about running errands for them?'

'I have reasons,' said Caspar.

Meredith sighed again. 'Fine. I'll be on a flight as soon as I can.'

'*We* will be,' said Torsten, with a smile.

Meredith hung up and looked away. 'Check please,' she said to a passing server.

They walked back to their hotel in silence, all fight having gone out of Meredith. She'd never been like this … flat … depressed … homesick, but she didn't have the will to shake it off. She focused on the thought that she was going home to her friends … her family.

'Hey,' said Torsten gently, as they reached Meredith's door.

'Night, Torsten.'

'Wait,' he said, stopping her with a hand on her arm.

'What?'

'I … I'm sorry. I'll back off. I thought we were having fun, but …'

'All the times I told you to fuck off weren't clear enough?'

'I'm Viking … telling each other to fuck off is like an invitation to jump into bed.'

Meredith turned away.

'I'm sorry,' he said to her retreating back.

She closed the door, then slumped back against it, sliding to the ground, leaning her head against the wood. She'd rarely felt so alone, so isolated, so powerless, not in all her time alive.

She'd have to marry Torsten—there was no getting around it—but it was too much. She didn't know why a fake marriage was breaking her, but out of everything she'd had to endure, across all her lifetimes, this was somehow the worst.

Chapter 11

Zahora returned to her hut to find Noah pacing.

'Hey,' she said, going to him, 'what's wrong?'

'Dad wants me to move on or go home. He says I've been here long enough, and if I don't do either of those things, he'll come and get me.'

'He can't!' said Zahora. 'You're an adult ... he can't order you around like that ...'

'He seems to think he can.'

'What will you do?'

Noah grabbed his hair, then sat on the bed. 'I don't know. I don't want to go ... I don't want to leave you, but ...'

'What?' she said, sitting next to him, taking his hand.

'My dad isn't a forgiving man. If I don't do what he says, our relationship will never be the same ...'

'But he's manipulating you ... forcing you to be something you're not.'

'But I am!'

She faltered. 'I don't understand.'

'I'm both what he wants me to be, and a musician. I don't want to choose between two lives ... I want one life with both things in it.'

'And your dad doesn't want you to do that?' Zahora was rapidly losing the thread. 'I thought you wanted to be a full-time musician?'

Noah got to his feet in frustration. 'I don't know what I want ...'

'Do you want me?'

His eyes flashed as he faced her. 'Yes,' he said firmly. 'More than anything ... but ...'

'But?' she said, anger stirring in her veins.

'This place is fucking weird ... I mean, what are you even doing here? I haven't seen you in days, you're exhausted, and these people have some kind of hold over you ... it's fucked up.'

'They're teaching me,' she said defensively.

'About what? Meditation? Because I've looked into it, and no meditation I can find causes what happens to you ...'

'It's ... complicated.'

'What is? What's going on here?'

Zahora looked at him blankly, not sure what to say. She didn't lie well ... didn't know how to cover her tracks ...

'And I heard ...' Noah's words cut off abruptly and he turned to face the wall.

'You heard what?'

'People talking about multiple lives ... and about you being special ...'

Zahora laughed, although it sounded false even to her own ears. 'That's ridiculous ...' Everyone here was so discrete, almost to the point of paranoia ... had he really heard someone talking, or had he been snooping around?

He turned back to face her. 'What is this place?'

164

Zahora met his gaze, but didn't know what to say. 'I ...'

'Why won't you tell me the truth?'

'Noah ...'

'Do you believe you've had multiple lives?'

Zahora shook her head, attempting to clear the fog. She tried to swallow, but her mouth was dry.

He crossed the floor and knelt in front of her. 'Zahora, come with me. We could travel the world together. I miss you ... love you ... I don't want to leave, but I don't think I can stay ...'

'You're leaving then?' *He loved her?*

He looked away, and a heavy silence filled the air.

'What caused all this?' she said eventually. 'Is it just about your dad?'

Noah took her hands and pulled her into his arms.

'I can't leave, Noah ...'

'Why not?'

'Because I want to be here.'

'*Why?*'

'I have to go.'

'Zahora ... he'll kill you ...'

The words didn't register until she was on the other side of the door. What? Who would kill her? He loved her. She loved him. But relationships with humans were impossible, and this was exactly why ... relationships without truth were based on sand, and everyone knew what happened to things built there ...

165

Raina entered the underground room, her escort peeling off at the door. She'd never been to this part of the warehouse, and it was all very dramatic, reminding her of the US President's war bunker.

She paused at the entrance and looked around at the gathered crowd: Jamie, Tamsin, Janet, and the leader of the Slayers. They watched TV screens with real-time footage of soldiers carrying out a mission. It was night wherever the soldiers were, the images from night-vision cameras.

'You called?' said Raina, trying to find something on the screen that would tell her where they were.

'Ah, darling,' said Jamie. 'Come.' He patted the seat next to his.

She walked to it, but remained standing, leaning her weight on the chair's tall back. 'What are we watching?'

'Our first full joint strike,' said Jamie.

Raina swung her head to look at the Slayer. The so-called Grand Master. He didn't look grand to her; he looked like prejudice and death.

'We already had men on the ground in Egypt,' said the Grand Master, 'completing their individual missions, so it made sense for us to join forces.'

'You all go on a mission? As part of your initiation process?' said Raina. She knew of other organizations who followed similar practices.

'Indeed. My son is on a mission as we speak.'

'In Egypt?' said Raina, her head swinging back to the screen.

'On the West Coast,' he said. 'Monitoring the new nation there.'

'Has he found anything?' said Raina.

'More than she did,' he said, his eyes on Tamsin. 'But I suppose that's not surprising ...'

Tamsin visibly bristled, her back snapping straight, but she didn't give him the satisfaction of rising to his bait.

'Not surprising because Slayers are superior to our kind?' said Raina.

'That, but also, she's a woman.'

'Women have no place in your organization?' said Raina.

'On the contrary, they have a most important place … in the home … breeding, and tending to our next generation.'

'Do they go on missions?' said Raina.

'Heavens no!' said the Grand Master. 'That would benefit no one, and inconvenience everyone.'

'You realize you're in a room with three women?' said Raina, keeping her features blank.

'And two men,' he said, as though this proved some point.

'Darling,' said Jamie, putting his hand on Raina's, 'don't antagonize our allies. We all have our differences. Let us celebrate our similarities … our shared goals.'

'Like attacking the Egyptians,' said Raina.

'I must say, I was surprised,' said the Grand Master. 'I thought this lot was on your side.'

'They were,' said Tamsin, 'until a man came along and screwed it all up.'

'What man?' said Raina.

'Your husband,' said Tamsin, with a malicious smile.

'Tamsin …' Jamie warned.

'Her what?' said the Grand Master, but a dull thud snapped their attention back to the screen.

'Guard one down,' said a soldier. It was impossible to tell if the voice belonged to a Templar or a Slayer.

'Guard two down,' said another.

'Guard three down,' said a third voice.

167

'Proceeding to the primary target,' said the first voice.

'I thought the plan was to start with weaker nations,' said Raina. 'To test the waters?'

'That was before they betrayed us,' said Jamie, 'and it would be wasteful to squander this opportunity. We believe a high value target's inside. '

'Who?' said Raina, her insides turning cold.

Jamie smiled. 'You'll see …'

Raina's focus tore back to the screen. Was Caspar there? He'd turned the Egyptians against the Templars … Gods only knew what he'd done to achieve that. Jamie had been sure of Egyptian support, which meant whatever Caspar had done, it had been costly … Not that it mattered; they could rebuild from scratch if they had to. Any cost would be worth it, to stop the Templars, to be back together … any cost aside from Caspar's life. Please, not that.

Jamie watched her as she watched the screen. He would be recording this too, so he could watch it back later … watch her reaction the moment he killed her soulmate. He was sick and twisted, and Raina wondered what she'd ever seen in him … why did animal attraction have to pull her to him? Him, of all the despicable people? Surely now, even her most base self would despise him …

'Entering the main building. Radio silence until mission complete,' said another male voice.

Raina's eyes were glued to the screen, although she kept her body loose, her face neutral. *Please don't be there. Please don't be there. Please don't be there.* She repeated the mantra over and over in her head. Then, *if you're there, escape. Run.*

She put every ounce of magical ability she still possessed into making a sending, her intention rock solid … single minded. *Run. Run. Run.*

The soldiers stormed through the building, wherever it was. There were too many screens to follow everything at once, but the soldiers were entering bedrooms, pulling people from their beds. Most resisted. More than one was killed. It was better that way … better than death at the hands of the Slayers … true death.

Her eyes flicked frantically from screen to screen, praying she didn't see Caspar's tall, dark-skinned form. More than once, her stomach lurched, only for relief to flood her seconds later.

It ended with a series of voice confirmations from the soldiers. Raina barely heard them. It was a struggle to remain standing after the effort of the sending, not to mention the emotional cost of preparing to lose her soulmate forever.

The soldiers turned on the lights, lining up their captives on their knees, their hands bound behind their backs. Raina didn't recognize anyone in the lineup.

'That one,' said Janet, 'is the demon son of the Egyptian leader, Heba.'

'Good,' said Jamie.

'He's ours,' said the Grand Master. 'They're all ours … that was the agreement.'

'Of course,' said Jamie. 'I merely meant it's good he will experience his end … suitable vengeance for their recent betrayal at the Registerium.'

'It will push the Egyptians more firmly into the bosom of the Pagans,' said Janet.

'Oh, they're already in a solid embrace,' said Jamie, looking at Raina.

Raina kept her features impassive. This was war. People died. There would be many more deaths before they were through. It made her sick in a way it never had when she'd been young and ambitious. She felt for Heba, her empathy genuine … she imagined losing

169

Callie in the way Heba had lost her son tonight. But this was the way of things, and she'd seen far worse in her time.

Raina looked back at Jamie with contempt in her eyes. 'Sloppy,' she said. 'Look at the state of that place. You captured a pampered prince after a party, and couldn't even manage to take everyone alive.'

'Hang on …' said the Grand Master.

'You don't think there's room for improvement?' said Raina.

'Well … I …'

'If you'd tried that on the Pagans, or the Vikings, you would have lost an entire unit of soldiers. Had that mission been to take the Egyptians' leader, Heba, you most likely would have failed. The mission was a success solely because you picked an easy target who had little protection. However, I'm assuming that was the point … to learn?'

'Yes,' said Jamie. 'Start easy and work our way up, remember?'

Raina breathed an inward sigh of relief … at least that meant the Pagans—one of the biggest and most powerful nations—should be safe for now.

'They need better training,' she said.

Jamie sent her a self-satisfied look. 'What would you suggest?'

Raina laid out a plan. She pretended to share everything, but kept the best stuff back. She told them things about the defenses of other nations that weren't strictly true … or, more accurately, had once been true, but weren't any longer. And she made the Grand Master give up a few secrets of his own … secrets she hoped would come in useful before the war was done …

Caspar awoke with a start, Raina's voice pounding through his head. *Run. Run. Run.* He looked frantically around his sparsely furnished room, calling on each of his senses to reveal the threat, but he found none.

He jumped out of bed and rushed to Talli and Christa's hut. 'Did you feel it?' he asked their groggy forms.

'Feel what?' they said, sitting bolt upright and throwing back the covers. 'What's going on?'

'I got a sending from Raina telling me to run.'

'Ring the bell,' said Talli.

Christa rushed from the room to rouse the rest of the magik compound. Talli and Caspar ran to Rose's hut, but she wasn't there. They ran to Marla's, and found her drinking tea with Rose, the two women talking intently.

'What is it?' said Rose, rising to her feet just as the bell began to toll.

'Sending from Raina, telling me to run,' said Caspar.

'How does she know where you are?' said Talli.

'I don't think she does,' he said. 'How could she?'

Caspar's phone buzzed. Ira. 'Hello?' he said, picking up the call and putting it on speakerphone.

'There's been an attack on the Egyptians,' said Ira. 'Seemed to be a joint mission between the Templars and Slayers.'

'How do you know?' said Caspar.

'The Egyptians already gave us access to some of their security cameras, and two of their demons escaped the attack ... they sounded the alarm. Egyptian reinforcements are on their way, hoping to prevent exfiltration ... they took Heba's son.'

Caspar inhaled sharply. 'Fuck ... what can we do?'

'I've sent a link to our joint communications,' said Ira

'I'll join now,' said Caspar, hanging up. 'Is Meredith back yet?'

'I'm here,' she said, entering the room. 'Just got here. What's happening?'

'Let's get to my laptop ... I'll explain on the way, but there's a possibility they're going to attack here too ... Raina sent a warning to run ...'

'I'm coming too,' said Torsten, following in their wake.

'Rose, get everyone to the tunnels,' said Meredith. 'Just in case.'

Hours later, the community of magiks returned to their usual tasks. Meredith and her soldiers could find no imminent threat, and nor could Ira. Caspar reflected that a shock like this was good ... it would put everyone on their toes.

The Templar-Slayer alliance had successfully exfiltrated themselves along with seven demons, including Heba's son. They all knew he would likely never be seen again, unless he could find a way to kill himself before the Slayers did ... It was a grim prospect, and Caspar assured Heba the Pagans would do everything they could to help retrieve him. But the Templars had no reason to keep him alive, and they all knew it ...

'Should we change our Mabon plans?' asked Talli.

'I don't think so,' said Meredith. 'But we should remain vigilant.'

172

'We've warned all our allies?' said Rose.

'Yes,' said Caspar, 'as well as those we're still wooing.'

'What about Gemma and Elliot?' said Rose. 'Still no word?'

'We've tried to contact them many times,' said Caspar, 'but to no avail.'

'Hopefully no news is good news,' said Rose, but a shadow crossed her features.

'I'd rather not have to hope,' said Meredith. 'We should ask Ira to double down. It worries me we've heard nothing in all this time ...'

Chapter 12

Aphrodite led Gemma and Elliot into an amphitheater next to the sea. They'd stretched a sail across half of the circle, providing shade against the beating sun, and sun loungers and daybeds sat in a ring around the edge of the space, both in and out of the shade. In the center lay a single enormous slab of perfectly round granite.

'What is this place?' said Gemma, looking around in awe. The scale was impressive.

'A place where we relax and seek entertainment in the presence of the sun, moon, and stars,' said Aphrodite, with a knowing smile.

'What kind of entertainment?' asked Elliot.

'It's a surprise,' she replied.

A pang of apprehension gripped Gemma's organs as she tried to glean clues from their surroundings. Opera? Song and dance? Something more sinister? It was impossible to tell, but the persistent smile playing around Aphrodite's lips made her nervous.

They'd moved from the building in San Francisco to somewhere else along the coast, although Gemma and Elliot hadn't been allowed to know where. The days since they'd arrived had been filled with eating, drinking, and talking well into the night with Ares and Aphrodite.

They were a strange couple … volatility sitting just beneath the surface. Gemma couldn't help but wonder about their history, and how they'd ended up here, acquiring a formidable stronghold right under the Templars' noses, and so far from their alleged European beginnings … beginnings that should have put them squarely on the Pagans' radar …

'I'll show you to your rooms,' said Aphrodite.

Their rooms were a slice of paradise: billowing fabric, doors folded back to reveal an infinity pool above the sea, steps down to the sand, the sounds of waves crashing and palm trees swishing. It was heaven, and Gemma's shoulders dropped an inch as she took it all in.

'It's breathtaking,' she said, turning to look at Aphrodite, who was watching them.

'A dream come true,' she agreed. 'You'll find a fully stocked wardrobe in the Greco-modern style. We like to embrace our origins, and would appreciate your participation.'

'Wow,' said Elliot, apparently unable to manage anything more.

'Thank you,' said Gemma. 'This is wonderful.'

'If you need anything, your private butler will help, and your masseuses will arrive shortly. There are tables down on the sand. Dinner's at eight. Until then … enjoy.'

Aphrodite left with a flourish of fabric, leaving Gemma and Elliot dumbstruck.

'This is unexpected,' said Gemma.

Elliot took Gemma's hand and led her down onto the beach, to the water's edge. He pulled her into his arms and kissed her. 'Why are they trying so hard to woo us?'

'I don't know,' said Gemma, enjoying the feel of Elliot against her while the sun was on her back and her feet were in the sand. She ran her hands through his hair. 'But I like it. It's such a welcome break from everything.'

'We're still at work,' he reminded her, kissing her neck.

'Mmm ... it doesn't feel like work.'

He looked into her eyes. 'I wish we had a way of communicating with the others,' he said. 'The world could be going to shit, and we'd have no idea.'

'I know I shouldn't say this, but I can't find the will to care. I'm happy to have a break from it all ... the politics and stress and constant vigilance.'

'We can't let them fool us,' said Elliot. 'We have to be vigilant here too ... we don't know what these people want ... what they might be planning.'

Gemma sighed. 'I know, but I want to pretend for a while. Pretend we live a life where all we have to care about is massages and lying on daybeds.'

'We can pretend,' said Elliot, drawing her to his chest. 'So long as we don't forget the truth ...'

Zahora woke with a start, covered in sweat. She was relieved to find Noah in bed beside her and reached for him. He woke, groggily rubbing his eyes.

'What is it?' he said, cradling her to him. 'Bad dream?'

'I'm ... not sure. It seemed nice ... a couple cuddling on the beach, but there was a sinister edge ... and something was chasing me ... and then I woke up.'

Noah rubbed soothing circles across her back. 'It was just a dream,' he said. 'It's over.'

She pressed herself into him, nuzzling his neck, drinking in his scent. What would she do without him? Love was like a drug ... now she'd had it, its absence would drive her crazy ... she was half crazed already.

She kissed him, wanted to crawl inside his skin, restless and wild. Maybe it was the adrenaline from the dream ... but he responded without hesitation, on top of her in a heartbeat, pressing inside her, matching her frantic tone. It was feral and uninhibited, frantic, but even her climax couldn't still her disquiet.

She pushed him off and got to her feet, barely noticing her nakedness. 'Are you leaving?' she said. 'Have you made up your mind?'

Noah rolled onto his back, looking up at the ceiling, still panting. He was probably struggling to keep up with her erratic mood ... Zahora knew she was ...

'I have to at some stage,' he said, when he'd got his breathing under control. 'I can't live here forever ... and I can only stall Dad for so long ...'

'You could stay ...'

'He'll come for me.'

'Tell him you don't want to go.'

'He won't give me a choice.'

'Fight!' she said, waving her arms.

Noah went still and so did she. Silence stretched taught in the air between them.

'You don't want to ...' she whispered.

'I do ... I just ... I ...'

Zahora grabbed a dress from the floor, slipped it over her head, and fled.

'Zahora,' he called after her, but he didn't follow.

Zahora ran to the caves, the sun just peaking over the horizon, and to her surprise, the cave with the standing stone was occupied. Talli and Christa stood in white robes, wearing autumnal crowns, presiding over a ceremony. Mabon ... it was today ... Zahora had totally forgotten ...

'You're late,' said Marla. 'I was about to send someone to get you.'

'Sorry,' she murmured, unable to tear her eyes from the four withered figures kneeling around the stone. 'What's happening?'

'Harvest sacrifice,' said Marla. 'If we want to use magic, we must give something in return.'

'You're sacrificing people?' she said, shocked.

'They're demons ... this is but one life, and they have all lived to a great age.'

'What?' said Zahora, finally looking at Marla's face.

Marla was smirking. 'It's not as bad as you think,' she said. 'They sacrifice a single lifetime to the magic. Instead of reincarnating soon after death, they'll be gone longer ... every magik does it at some point.'

'Will I have to?' she said, her eyes wide.

'If you want to be a true magik, then yes. Maybe more than once.'

'Have you?'

'Of course ... several times.'

'What ... what's it like?'

'Killing oneself is never pleasant, but after that, you feel nothing until you're born again. It's not a hardship.'

'But everyone else will have had another life in the time you're away ...'

'Yes. But what is one life when we get so many? Some even appreciate the time ... it gives us space, eases tension ...'

Talli's voice cut across them. 'As we descend towards Winter, when the dark outweighs the light, we thank the Gods for all they have given us this harvest. And in return, we present our offerings, one for each season: Spring, Summer, Autumn, and Winter.'

Daggers appeared in the hands of the four kneeling souls, and Christa set four sound bowls singing. The hairs on Zahora's arms stood on end. As one, the four sacrifices turned the daggers on themselves.

Zahora looked away; she didn't have the stomach for this. Maybe Noah was right ... this place was fucked up. Human sacrifices? Willing ones ... but still ...

The sound bowls almost covered the thuds as the four bodies hit the ground ... almost, but not quite. Zahora felt sick, only then noticing the other Pagan leaders against the edge of the cave. They moved forward together, pushing the bodies into the water, the lifeblood of the sacrifices turning it red.

'This is more important now than ever,' said Marla, placing an uncharacteristically gentle hand on Zahora's arm. 'You took something from the Sphere, and you must give something in return. If magic were to fail us now ...'

Guilt seeped through her, but she reminded herself they would have done this anyway, regardless of her actions. Either way, she had to make sure their sacrifice

179

was worth it … that their faith in her and the other magiks was worthwhile … that they weren't giving up a precious life for nothing.

The sun was setting, and the feasting and music had begun. The mood was more somber than usual, Raina's absence palpable, but Talli was determined to make the rest of the Pagan leaders enjoy themselves. They'd come together for Mabon … just for being able to, they should be thankful.

'Moping helps no one,' said Talli. 'Caspar gets a pass, but everyone else, buck up. Jon, you can start … tell us what's going on with Leila …'

Talli's eyes followed his to where Leila was helping herself to food, chatting to Torsten. Jon had been assigned to protect her in New York, and he hadn't given it up now they were back.

'Nothing's going on,' he said.

They laughed.

'What? We haven't even kissed. I'm protecting her, that's all.'

'You're protecting her?' said Meredith, raising an eyebrow. 'Does she know you're still in combat kindergarten?'

Jon threw an apple core at her. 'Want to teach me some tricks? Or are you too busy play-fighting with Torsten?'

The quip even got Caspar laughing.

'There has never been, and will never be, any play-fighting with him,' said Meredith menacingly. 'And I've finally made him understand that.'

'Not judging by the way he was eyeing you earlier,' said Talli. 'Can't say I'd mind him looking at me that way.'

Christa hit Talli on the arm.

'What? I can't help it if I miss your male form from time to time ... and he's not an unappealing hunk of man flesh.'

'You're not wrong there,' said Christa, eyeing Torsten appreciatively.

'Careful,' said Jon. 'Meredith might get protective over her man.'

'Please ... take him off my hands,' she said.

'Someone else you'd rather tussle with?' said Jon.

'Alas, no,' said Meredith, although a part of her wished there was. It always happened when the others coupled up. Flings could only go so far to fill the ache in her chest. Maybe the Gods hadn't created a soulmate for her. Did she even believe in soulmates? She missed Gemma ... she'd always understood. But even Gemma was lost to true love now ...

'Who's the new guy?' said Jon, nodding to where Noah sat, singing and playing his guitar. 'He's good.'

'Noah,' said Rose, joining them with Marla in tow. 'We're pretty sure he's a baby demon.'

'You don't know who he is?' said Meredith, sitting up straighter in her seat. 'Where did he come from?'

'He's the son of an American businessman,' said Rose. 'We checked him out, and we've been monitoring him, but you know how difficult it is to tell with baby demons ... they have virtually no metal in their eyes, and we don't have a hunter on hand ...'

'And it's not like we have any magiks about the place ...' said Meredith sarcastically.

Marla scowled. 'Hold this,' she said, handing her drink to Rose.

Zahora watched as Marla interrupted Noah's song and pulled him down from the stage. Dread gripped her. She hurried to his side, ready to intervene.

'Give me your hand and look into my eyes,' said Marla, just as Zahora got there.

'What are you doing?' said Noah.

'Testing,' said Marla.

'Marla …'

'This is Marla?' said Noah, snatching back his hand and rounding on Zahora. 'The leader of this place is a child?'

'Said the baby demon,' said Marla, taking back his hand.

Zahora's head swam. Did she mean …? She couldn't … Noah was a demon? He couldn't be … she hadn't felt anything from him … but then, she hadn't a clue what to look for.

Marla faltered, her knees buckling. Zahora caught her. 'Yep, he's one of us,' she said, 'and now I have to sleep for twelve hours … I hope Rose is happy …'

Marla summoned another demon to help her, then left the party, presumably to sleep off the drain of the test.

'What the fuck?' said Noah. 'What did she mean? And you're being taught by a *kid*? That's why you can't leave?'

'Sush,' said Zahora. 'Everyone's watching; please don't make a scene.'

'I don't give a flying fuck! I'm leaving … I'm going back to the states.'

Zahora looked up at him, searching his ferocious eyes. He turned away. 'You're one of us.'

Noah stopped in his tracks, then spun back to face her. 'I sure as hell am not.'

'Why would she lie?'

'Because she's a *kid*, and she's obviously crazy.'

'You think I'm crazy too?'

'I didn't … but … you can't seriously believe her? She's what … fourteen years old?'

'Would it be so bad? To be one of us? To be part of something?'

Noah grabbed his hair. 'I'm already part of something in America. I don't belong here …'

She turned away, not wanting him to see the sting of tears in her eyes.

She stood there for what seemed like an eternity, and then warm breath caressed her neck. 'I love you,' he said in a low voice. 'That's why I'm here. That's why I'm torn. That's why I'm defying my father. I want us to be together, but I've racked my brains … I don't see how … and you can't expect me to follow Marla?'

'Marla isn't a kid,' Zahora said firmly, 'despite how she looks … and we don't follow Marla, we follow Rose … who you'll probably say is too old …'

'Zahora …' he said, in a censoring tone.

She ignored it. 'And anyway, you're one of us,' she said. 'That means you belong here, regardless of what your dad wants, or your internal conflict. You're a demon …'

'I am not,' he said so forcefully she turned to face him.

'Why's it so bad? It means we can be together …'

183

'I'm loyal to my family.'

'We're your family ...'

'No.'

Zahora took a step back. 'What does he have over you? What control? This isn't normal ...'

'Zaha ... I ...' He reached for her, but an urgent bell cut through the night, and the place turned to chaos.

'Come with me,' said Noah. 'We have to hide ... you have to hide.'

'It's the Templars,' said Zahora.

'It's the Slayers,' said Noah.

Zahora froze, her feet like balls of lead. 'How do you know about Slayers?'

'People talk.'

'Noah ...'

'Zaha, we need to hide.'

Meredith and the other leaders snapped to action. Lifetimes of experience gave their feet wings and stomped on their fear as they rushed to the gates.

Caspar handed round earpieces, connecting them to each other and to Ira. Ira had access to the security cameras on the approach to the compound, but there was only so much he could do ... and there were no cameras inside.

'They're coming from all sides,' said Ira. 'Most are storming the front gates, but a few have slipped around the side. They're nearly on you.'

'Caspar, Marla, take some guards and find the ones round the side,' said Meredith. 'Jon, hide Leila. The rest of you, with me.'

The front gate was just a five-bar gate to keep animals in or out. The walls on either side were designed for the same purpose; they provided little deterrent for attackers. The only blessing was that the approach was steep and rocky, forcing most of their attackers up the main path. They had to hold them there … prevent them from fanning out.

Meredith, Torsten, Talli, Christa, and Rose formed a line in front of the gate, just where the path opened up. They drew hastily grabbed weapons, and one of Meredith's guards beat on a drum he must have grabbed from the celebration.

Torsten's deep voice cut across the din, working in time with the drum. He sang a harrowing Viking war song, terrifying, chilling. The others knew it and joined in, their enemy visibly faltering.

Meredith threw a dagger into the approaching mass. A man went down, and the enemy slowed.

'Charge!' shouted Meredith, and they surged as one.

Half of the attackers turned and fled.

Zahora ran with Noah into the caves.
'Is there another way out?' he said.

Zahora came up short. What was she doing? She had magic ... felt it stir in her bones at the sound of the war drum. Why was she running? She could help ...

She spun around, but Noah caught her. 'What are you doing?'

'They need me.'

'To do what?'

'Help.'

'They'll kill you ...'

'I can't run when everyone else is fighting.'

'Zahora ... we'll get out and sound the alarm ...'

'What is wrong with you? Run and hide if you must, but I'm going to help!'

She pulled out of his grip and ran back the way they'd come. She emerged from the caves to find the place quiet, deserted. The absence of sound and movement grasped at her senses, and she shivered. This wasn't what she'd expected. She'd thought there would be noise, fighting, screaming. Her insides turned to ice ... this was a mistake.

She spun around, but strong hands caught her, a hand over her mouth, silencing her scream. She kicked and struggled, but an urgent whisper cut through her terror. 'It's Caspar ... it's okay ... calm down.'

She stilled, and Caspar removed his hands.

'Are you hurt?' he mouthed, drawing them back into the shadow of a hut.

'I ... I'm fine. Where are they? What can I do?'

'We're looking for them. We think a smaller group came round the side ... we don't know what they want.'

Three men stepped around the side of the hut, and wasted no time before launching their attack. Caspar had one down in no time, and Zahora backed up, calling on the wheel inked on her hand. Mabon, sacrifice, power. The magic leapt to answer her call, but as she made to use it, a voice ... Noah's voice ... rang out behind her.

'Noooooo!' he screamed, and she spun to see Noah throwing a rock at a fourth man, who was running towards her.

The rock hit the man's back, and bounced off ... he barely seemed to notice, but he changed course, rushing to where Noah stood. The man grabbed Noah, flipped him to the ground, and pinned his arms.

Zahora could only watch. She tried to pull magic to her, but panic flooded every part of her being. She was muddled, couldn't focus. 'Caspar,' she breathed, hearing something hit the ground behind her. She turned to see him standing over the bodies of all three men. Her stomach roiled at the sight of blood—so much blood—visible in the moonlight.

'They've got Noah,' she said. But when she turned back, Noah was gone.

The sun was rising by the time the compound was once again secure. The Pagans had been working flat out, dealing with dead bodies, communicating with their allies, ensuring everyone was accounted for. Jon had done little but look after Leila, and he found, to his surprise, he was content to do so.

He cradled her shivering form to his chest, stroking her hair, muttering soothing words. It was one thing for a demon to undergo an attack like this—they knew it was par for the course, and it rattled them still—it was quite another for a human. Things like this just didn't happen in the normal course of western society.

'I'm sorry,' said Leila. 'I'll be okay in a minute.'

She'd said similar things off and on since the attack had finished. He doubted she would be okay for a while …

'It's just so … strange … I'm not prepared … never thought …'

'It's okay,' he said. 'It's normal to feel this way … I'm shaken too.'

Leila eventually drifted off to sleep, and Jon eased out from under her, covered her with a blanket, and ventured outside to help. He immediately felt the loss of her.

'Is she okay?' said Meredith, handing him a steaming cup of hot chocolate. She perched on a wall, watching the clean-up effort.

He drank gratefully as he sat beside her. 'She will be, but not yet.'

Meredith nodded, sipping her drink. 'They were all Slayers. Not a single demon,' she said.

'Is that surprising?'

'Only because the Templars and Slayers have been working together … their chances of success would have been higher if they'd had Templar help.'

'Did we lose anyone?'

'No,' said Meredith. 'Aside from the baby—Noah.'

Jon looked at Meredith, bewildered. 'Why would they take him?'

'No idea. He was defending Zahora. Caspar was there too, but by the time he'd dealt with his own attackers, the one with Noah had fled.'

'Random abduction?'

'Maybe ... Zahora's pretty cut up about it ... thinks it's her fault, but she said Noah knew the attackers were Slayers.'

'Did Zahora tell him that?' said Jon, furrowing his brow in annoyance.

'She says not. Apparently, he implied he'd overheard the term here ...'

'Unlikely,' said Jon.

'Possible,' said Meredith.

Silence settled over them as Jon lifted his mug to his lips once more. 'Hot chocolate's much nicer than what we used to get the morning after a battle,' he said with a chuckle.

'You're not wrong,' said Meredith. 'And while you're in a good mood ...'

'Uh oh ...'

'The Pagan nation needs something from you ... something for the good of the cause.'

Joh huffed. 'What now?'

Meredith turned her head and looked him directly in the eye. She seemed unusually empathetic. 'A cufflink.'

'No,' said Jon. 'You can't be serious?'

'I'm afraid I am.'

'Who?'

'You don't want to know ...'

'Who even knows about them?'

Meredith gave him an incredulous look.

'Okay ...' he said, 'I'm proud of them!'

'On the upside, they only want one.'

'What? That makes no ...' Jon came up short, the puzzle pieces fitting into place.

Meredith laughed.

'Ex-fucking-lovers ...' he said. It could only be one person.

'Ooh, do tell ...'

'Don't make me bring up Torsten,' said Jon.

'You can; I don't care. I think I've finally got through to him. And I've told Rose and Caspar, I'm done treasure hunting. I'm needed here, now more than ever. I don't enjoy being away from the nation, from our people ... it's not the life for me, out on my own ... especially with Torsten ...'

Meredith was rarely this open with her feelings. Jon took her hand and squeezed it. 'I'm sorry it was so tough. If you need to talk, I've recently discovered I'm a surprisingly good listener.'

Meredith didn't meet his eyes, but she gave a little squeeze in return.

'Where is he?' said Zahora, storming into Rose's hut, interrupting Caspar and Rose, who looked deep in conversation. She didn't care. 'Where do you think they've taken him?'

'I should think to America,' said Rose, eying Zahora in a way that made her shrink back, knocking some of the wind from her sails.

'What are we going to do?' she said.

'Nothing,' said Rose. 'He's not one of us.'

'But ... he ... *I* can't do nothing. I have to help him.'

'Girl, there's nothing you can do,' said Rose, the word *girl* stinging, for it was an insult.

'You've seen everything we're doing to get Raina back,' said Caspar. 'It's no simple thing.'

'And we should do the same for Noah,' said Zahora, her anger flaring.

Caspar shook his head in disbelief.

'From what I've heard,' said Rose, 'Noah knew the attackers were Slayers before anyone else did … which implies he may have been a spy all along.'

'No … he wanted to travel the world … to be a musician …'

Rose shrugged. 'And yet he did neither of those things. Zahora, there are four options. One: Noah is dead already. Two: Noah is on the way to his death. Three: Noah is being kept alive because he's already working with the Slayers. Four: Noah is being kept alive because the Slayers think they can turn him. Raina is an ancient demon with skills and relationships that would be an asset to any nation; she's worth fighting for. Noah is not.'

'But you said he's a demon … and we want new recruits … we need them!'

'If you ever see Noah again,' said Rose, 'make no mistake, he's working with our enemies.'

Zahora left in a rage, shrieking as she slammed the door.

'Young demons …' said Rose.

'Young powerful demons,' said Caspar. 'We need her, even if we don't need Noah.'

'I know. But she's so irritating.'

'She's young and ambitious … Raina was a lot like that.'

'Well, fortunately I was younger then … more tolerant of theatrics.'

Caspar laughed. 'You've never been tolerant of anything, let alone theatrics.'

Rose scowled.

'Jon's agreed to hand over the cufflink,' said Caspar. 'We'll hold Meredith and Torsten's wedding tomorrow, then I'll take the cufflink to the Wakan.'

'No,' said Rose.

'Rose …'

'Don't even try it,' she said. 'It's too dangerous for you so close to Aztec territory—they're the Templars' closest ally, and you are likely their highest value target. Talli and Christa will go, and you will stay put.'

Chapter 13

The sun was shining as Meredith prepared for her wedding day in a large country house in Shropshire. She'd deemed the venue suitable, given its cove of standing stones and close proximity to the magical compound.

It would be her first wedding, in all her lifetimes. She'd never wanted to marry anyone … and had never been forced to. She struggled to make sense of her feelings as she looked in the mirror, finishing her makeup, because amid the dread and embarrassment at having to marry someone like Torsten—no matter that it was a sham—a strange flutter of anticipation kindled.

Maybe it was because it was her first wedding, the first time she would be the center of attention, everyone's eyes on her as she said vows she didn't mean. If only it were real …

'Ready?' said Christa. Talli and the others already waiting at the stones. According to Christa, Mrs Blythe-Smith had arrived alone, driving a vintage, bottle green sports car, and wearing a fur coat. The necklace was apparently on full display around her neck, so at least that was something.

'No,' said Meredith, 'I'm not ready.'

'Sorry,' said Christa. 'Stupid question.'

'But I want to get it over with.'

'You look lovely, if that's any consolation. And Talli made you this,' said Christa, holding up a bottle.

'Perfume?' said Meredith, a lump in her throat.

'You don't have to wear it … Talls just didn't want you to feel left out, and she wanted to say thank you … we all know this is a sacrifice.'

Meredith took the bottle and pulled out the stopper. The scent of earthy spice hit her, and her shoulders dropped just a fraction.

'Thank you,' she said, applying the perfume. 'I think this will help.'

Christa and Meredith walked slowly to the stone cove—one large flat stone flanked by two mighty uprights that fanned out like wings on either side. Torsten and Talli were already standing on the flat stone, and Christa sat as they passed where the others were seated, giving Meredith space to walk the last few steps alone.

Meredith clutched her small autumnal posy, the weight of her leaf headpiece strangely comforting, grounding, keeping her mind connected to her body amid the bizarre charade. She wore a traditional white shift dress, covered with a long green cape to keep out the cold which was sealed at the front with a weighty silver brooch.

Torsten stared as she approached. They all stared. Her friends … her chosen family.

Talli hummed with energy as Meredith stepped up to join them, and it made her want to cry. This wasn't how this was supposed to happen. If it ever happened, she'd wanted it to be with someone she truly loved … and who loved her in return.

Torsten reached for her hand, and Meredith had no choice but to place her hand in his. It was strangely comforting ... his strength and size.

Meredith was detached during the ceremony—a mix of the Pagan and Viking traditions—where they exchanged swords and rings, and then had their hands bound. She had so many emotions raging inside, she had no choice but to shut them down, to stop herself from thinking.

When it was done, Torsten leaned in to kiss her. Meredith kissed him back, to an eruption of wolf whistles, claps, and stamps from the crowd. Mrs Blythe-Smith seemed particularly delighted with the show.

Torsten led Meredith to the reception barn, which Talli had decked out in elaborate autumnal fashion, filled with chrysanthemums, helichrysums, rosehips, and towering grasses in shades of the setting sun.

Torsten blocked the entryway with his sword, then lifted Meredith over the threshold, dropping another kiss on her lips as he put her down, presumably for Mrs Blythe-Smith's benefit.

They took their places at the middle of the central table, the others taking their own seats, and drank the honey mead the Viking nation had provided. They'd sent enough for the whole month—for their honeymoon—but Meredith hated the stuff, so would be damned if she would drink it ... she didn't want the wedding officially recognized anyway.

The speeches were brief, and music filled the air as they feasted on roasted venison with redcurrant jelly, mashed squash, buttered carrots, and braised red cabbage.

Torsten leaned in as they ate. 'I know this isn't a wedding you wanted, and for that, I'm sorry,' he said, his breath on her ear. 'But for what it's worth, I'm glad my first wedding was with you.'

This was his first too? Meredith took his hand and squeezed. He kissed her cheek, then withdrew.

Mrs Blythe-Smith approached as they pulled apart, the amulet in her hand. She held it out by the chain, offering it to Meredith, who carefully took it.

'Thank you,' said Meredith.

'I have to say,' said Mrs Blythe-Smith, 'it surprised me to hear your marriage would be in England of all places ... but I suppose, for an American and an Irish man, the peculiarity is fitting.'

Meredith chuckled; she liked the woman. 'We told you we wanted a traditional wedding,' she said.

'It wasn't this tradition I had imagined ...'

'Well,' said Torsten, taking the necklace and hanging it around Meredith's neck, 'nothing could be worse than being a foregone conclusion, now could it?'

Mrs Blythe-Smith gave a small nod of acquiescence. 'Congratulations,' she said, 'and thank you for a truly entertaining day.'

Meredith looked down at the necklace as Mrs Blythe-Smith retreated. It sat on top of her white dress, cold and weighty, a reminder of what this was all for ... for Raina and their nation.

'What happened?' said Jamie, thundering into the underground command room. Tamsin and Janet looked nervous, and so they should.

'The Slayers staged their own attack on the Pagans the night of Mabon,' said Tamsin.

'Why?' said Jamie, his features dark.

'We're not sure … they're being evasive,' said Janet.

'They're showing us we're not in charge,' said Tamsin.

'Possibly …' said Janet.

'I'll speak to the Grand Master,' said Jamie. Jamie didn't trust the man, but had thought he understood the precarious position the Slayers were in. 'What was the outcome?'

'Unclear,' said Tamsin. 'We think the Slayers had casualties—many of them—but we got that through chatter at the lower levels … it's not verified. A contingent of our youngest members—those not easily identifiable as demon—infiltrated their ranks.'

'And became soldiers?' said Jamie. He'd been preoccupied with the top-level strategy … didn't know all the tactics Tamsin had employed. It was good work.

'Soldiers and romantic partners,' said Tamsin. 'The Sayers are a homophobic organization—a weakness we've been able to exploit—and of course, they don't believe in sex before marriage, so a few strategically placed women offering forbidden fruits have been good sources for us too.'

'It's been successful,' said Janet, 'but most of the soldiers know nothing useful … their information control is excellent.'

'Keep at it,' said Jamie. 'Any news from the Registerium?'

'They're stalling where they can,' said Janet. 'And …'

She seemed to be searching for a tactical way to say whatever it was. 'Spit it out,' snapped Jamie. He couldn't stand being handled.

'The chaos might present an opportunity for us to quietly transfer Raina. I could fly back to Scotland … make it look like I'm returning to my post … and take her with me. By the time the Pagans realize what's going on, it'll be too late.'

'Things are never that simple,' said Jamie. 'We'd have to send a small army for Raina's protection, and we have no reason to rush the transfer.'

'The longer we delay, the longer we leave ourselves open to losing her,' said Janet heatedly.

'She'll never leave Callie,' said Jamie.

'She might kill Callie, and hope to find her first in their next lives,' said Janet. 'Raina knows you'll never kill your own daughter ... at least not in the final way.'

Jamie stood very still, thinking.

'If Raina's magically ours, there are ways to control her,' said Janet. 'I read about it at the Registerium. But we'd need magiks to help us ... someone with knowledge of such things.'

Every fiber of Jamie's being rejected the use of magic. He neither understood nor respected it, and visceral hatred bubbled in his guts at the thought of having to rely on something so archaic ... something threadbare and fickle. But if it could give them an edge, keep Raina loyal ...

'Come up with options,' he said, 'then war game everything that could go wrong.'

Zahora's chest was set to explode. No one could care less that Noah—her boyfriend—had been abducted. They'd written him off as dead, or worse ... a spy. She couldn't concentrate, couldn't think, couldn't breathe.

The others had carried on as normal, had hosted a fucking *wedding*, hadn't given her or Noah a second thought. How could they treat people like that? Like only demons like them—those who'd lived for hundreds of years—were worth saving ...? Were worth anything ...

It brought it home in stark relief ... she was an outsider ... why was she even here? She'd been clawing at their door, asking for entry, but they wouldn't let her in. She didn't know them ... why had she trusted them? Because of old legends? They didn't trust her ... didn't care what she wanted.

She wanted Noah ... she knew that now. And she would find him.

She sank to the ground in front of the standing stone and reached out a hand, feeling the familiar pull of the pulsing magic. She used the wheel inked on her hand to unlock the Pagan gate, called on it to protect her as she cast herself around the Nexus, searching for her love.

She headed west, to America, looking for the Slayers' headquarters. She searched and searched, thinking of Noah, trying to feel him, casting in every direction, but it was no use. No matter how hard she looked, how frantic she became, she could find no trace.

She returned to the gate—simple now she knew how—and reunited with her body. She stood, turning to leave, but found Caspar in the entrance, watching her.

'Hey,' he said. 'Are you okay?'

'I ...' She faltered. No, of course she wasn't fucking okay ... but she wasn't going to tell him that.

'Sorry, stupid question,' he said.

She looked at him, trying to work out what he wanted.

'We do care, you know, even if it seems like we don't. Ignore Rose ... she's just like that. She has to worry about the bigger picture, which makes her harsh and unfeeling. It's why the rest of us don't want her job ... we don't have the backbone for it ... don't want to force our spines ramrod straight like hers.'

Why was he telling her this? 'She's a coldhearted bitch,' she heard herself say.

Caspar laughed loudly. 'That's one way to put it.'

'None of you could give a damn about me.'

Caspar nodded sympathetically. 'That's not true, but I understand why you feel that way.'

'None of you care about Noah ... you won't help me find him!'

Caspar raised his eyebrows, then moved from the entryway, running a hand along the wall as he circled the cave. 'I know you don't want to admit this to yourself, but what Rose said is true.'

'For fuck's sake ...'

She headed for the exit. She could feel Caspar watching her progress, letting her almost reach the tunnel before saying, 'There is, however, one other option Rose didn't mention ...'

Zahora stopped dead, whirling to face him head on. 'What?'

'It's possible Noah's working with our enemies, but also fell in love with you. If that were the case, you would still have hope.'

Zahora swallowed. 'Of getting him back?'

'Yes. But you'd need to turn him ...'

Zahora's pulse rocketed. 'How?'

'That depends on Noah, and what he wants ... you told him he's a demon?'

'Yes.'

'Did he already know?'

'I ... don't think so,' said Zahora. She returned to the memory anew, but everything about that night was blurry and confused.

'Then if he's still alive, he's most likely working with the Slayers, and they most likely think he's human ... they would have killed him otherwise.'

'You think he'll question his loyalty to them? Now he knows he's a demon?'

'It's certainly possible ...'

'But there must be something I can do? Other than sit around and wait ...'

'Believe me,' said Caspar with a sigh, 'as someone currently sitting in wait, sometimes it's the best thing one can do.'

Zahora eyes roamed the cave, looking for answers it couldn't give her. 'I met Raina ... through the Nexus.'

'I heard.'

'She seemed nice ... said she'd help find me a teacher.'

'Alerac?'

Zahora nodded. 'I think so.'

'He's one of the best ...'

A heavy silence stretched between them.

'How did she seem?' asked Caspar.

'Fiery and fierce,' said Zahora, with a half laugh, 'but kind. She didn't seem hurt, if that's what you mean. Strained maybe ... but then, I don't know her well enough to say for sure. Maybe she always looks that way ...'

Caspar nodded. 'Does he really love you?'

The question was like a punch in the gut ... a question she kept asking herself. She'd never been in love—just like Noah—so she had little experience, but, 'Yes,' she said. 'He loves me. I'm sure of it.' Maybe if she said that to herself enough times with absolute confidence, the universe would make sure it was so.

He nodded again. 'Then you still have hope,' he said, heading for the exit, 'so don't do anything reckless ... I hear you've got form ...'

Zahora couldn't help but smile. She rolled her eyes, but the friendly insult made her feel more like she belonged here than ever before.

Aphrodite stood atop the perfect circle of granite in the center of the Amphitheatre. The place was lit by flames and starlight, those on the beds around the edge mostly in shadow. The atmosphere was intimate ... full of possibility.

'Friends,' said Aphrodite, turning in a slow circle, 'welcome. At this time in Earth's unfaltering cycle, where other nations celebrate the harvest, or the dead, *we*,' she completed her turn, then paused, holding space, creating a sense of occasion. 'We gather to celebrate my love—Ares—the God of War.

'For where others have been celebrated for generations, Ares was not, and we shall put to rights that which was wrong. People wonder about our match—love and war—but make no mistake, love is a weapon ... ours a union of perfect harmony ... of balance ...' Aphrodite looked to Ares, who sprawled on a bed, propped against cushions, watching her every curvaceous move. 'My love, on this most precious of days, I offer myself to you.'

Handmaidens approached Aphrodite. She held out her arms, and they removed her robes and took down her hair. They washed her with scented water, then draped flowers around her shoulders. They took her hands and guided her to the bed where Ares lay. Her long hair swayed as she walked, obscuring her nakedness just enough to keep all eyes glued on her.

Gemma gripped Elliot's hand with white knuckles. Whatever would come next, she wasn't sure she wanted any part.

Aphrodite reached Ares, the handmaidens wafting incense as she sank to her knees on the bed, then straddled his legs. She leaned forward, resting her head on the rolls of fat of his naked torso, prostrating herself.

Ares stroked Aphrodite's hair in possessive fashion. 'Let the celebration begin,' he said.

Gemma shut her eyes tight as drumbeats filled the air, trying to hide, her flight or fight response triggered, but Elliot urged her to look, and when she did, she saw dancers cavorting, spinning, leaping. They were phenomenal—the perfect mix of art and edge, their moves executed with fluid perfection.

Gemma gripped Elliot's arm in relief, although her heart still hammered in her chest. He kissed her hair, and she turned her head and kissed his mouth, buoyed by the music and dancers. When they broke apart, it surprised Gemma to find Aphrodite's head—still resting on Ares—turned towards them, watching with interest.

Gemma ignored the icy chill that ran down her spine, turning her attention back to the performers. They were acting out stories of heroic battles, along with the celebrations that came after ... representing both Ares and Aphrodite.

They watched singers, musicians, dancers, and poets while drinking endless glasses of wine. The servers seemed to appear out of thin air the very second they were needed.

Gemma was lightheaded by the end, when the performers gave way to a DJ, the stage now a dance floor for all. Elliot pulled her to her feet, and they cavorted alongside the others, a thrill running through her at every new song, high on the music.

Aphrodite and Ares joined the dancing, and the mood turned hot, perhaps because she was still naked, and Ares did nothing to hide his appreciation of her curves. They devoured each other in plain view, and other couples followed suit, the dance floor tipping from something almost safe to something treacherous.

Gemma fled, pulling Elliot behind her. She didn't stop until they were back in their room, under the covers of their bed.

'Hey,' said Elliot, holding her tight. 'What is it?'

Pagan festivals often ended this way, although not usually in quite such brazen fashion, but this had reminded her of times she'd rather forget ... of times she'd buried so deep it physically hurt, memories forcing their way to the surface.

'It's okay,' said Elliot. 'I've got you.'

Gemma turned in his arms and pressed her face to his chest, hiding in the darkness. She didn't want to tell him, even though she'd always known she'd have to, eventually, but not like this, not here ... she just ... couldn't.

Caspar had nothing to do, so like a caged animal, he prowled. Talli and Christa had gone to South America, and Torsten had gone too, much to Meredith's relief.

Caspar had flown to the Egyptians and handed over the necklace earlier that evening. Heba—the Egyptian leader—had received no word about her son and feared the worst, so it had been a somber affair. He'd offered his condolences, then escaped back to his plane as soon as he was able.

But his flight was delayed, and now he wanted to punch something, or run a marathon, or do *anything* other than sit around and wait.

Caspar's phone vibrated, and he rushed to pick up the call ... any distraction was welcome.

'Patching you into the feed,' said Ira.

'What feed?'

His phone screen displayed video footage of Talli and Torsten approaching an old Wakan woman, who sat cross-legged in front of a fire inside a teepee. She had white skin and white hair, her green eyes aged, her face a sea of sagging skin.

'It's an honor to meet you,' said Talli with a bow.

'Pfff,' said the Wakan, waving her wrinkled hand, 'stop with all that and sit down. You have what I want?'

'I do,' said Talli, sitting cross-legged, her skirt billowing around her. 'I would love to hear the story, if you're open to sharing ...'

'Why?' said the old woman, with an intrigued smile, her head cocked to one side, displaying remarkably good teeth. 'You have an interest in Jon?'

Talli laughed. 'No. But I, and the rest of our leadership, are very fond of winding him up, and this story has all the hallmarks of gold.'

'Ah,' said the Wakan, rocking back and forth to get comfortable. 'I see. Well, if I am to tell you a story, then first we must eat.'

Talli would never refuse the hospitality of a friend, nor would Caspar want her to, but the delay did nothing to improve his mood. He watched them eat, pacing around the private plane, willing them to get a move on.

After what seemed like an eternity, and with nothing to do but watch the others, the woman finally got to it. Caspar sat, picking up the beer the flight attendant had served him when he'd first boarded. It was warm, but he didn't care, his attention on the Wakan leader.

'Well,' she said, 'Jon and I had a liaison some years ago. He was young ... full of the frenetic energy of youth ... very good looking ... a fast, clever mouth ... in demand.'

'After we'd been seeing each other for a few weeks, my sister took a liking to him ... not uncommon ... she takes a liking to most men of that sort. But she swore nothing was going on, despite the flirting and the dancing ...

'I asked Jon about her, and he told me the same thing, but I knew there was something ... so I followed him one night when he'd told me he couldn't see me ...'

'Uh oh,' said Talli, leaning forward, hanging on her every word.

'He left the village and headed into the hills, to a hut I'd built ... that I'd shown him ...'

Talli sucked air through her teeth.

'Now, my husband had asked if I had plans for my hut earlier in the night, and I'd told him I did not.'

'No!' said Torsten.

'When I pushed open the door, they were fucking over the table.'

Talli clamped a hand over her mouth.

'I swore that day I would take something he held dear, as he had done to me.'

'Did your husband know about your liaison with Jon?' said Torsten.

'Yes,' she said. 'That was what angered me most ... we were free to pursue pleasure wherever we desired, but we never hid our dalliances from one another ... not until Jon.'

'Well, I am pleased to give you what Jon holds most dear,' said Talli, retrieving a jewelry box from her pocket.

The woman took the box with strong but withered hands, smiling when she saw the contents. 'And every time he looks at the one he has left, it will remind him of me,' she said, satisfaction laced through her words.

Talli giggled.

'And in return,' said the Wakan, handing over an envelope.

'Thank you,' said Talli.

Caspar's heart gave a leap as Talli retreated. The keys to the kingdom. Did the woman know what she'd just done? Not that it mattered. The Pagans were one step closer to getting Raina back. He was one step closer to holding Raina and his daughter in his arms. But that made his frustration worse. His guts clenched ... he needed to *do* something, or these feelings would consume him.

He'd racked his brains for anyone else to treat with, but he was out of ideas ... out of options until Gemma and Elliot came back on grid ...

'Ira,' said Caspar, before the call dropped.

'No, Caspar, for the millionth time, there is no news on Raina ... I'll let you know as soon as we have something ...'

'If it's okay with you, I'm going to come to Tel Aviv. I want to help.' It was the only place he could think of where he might be useful.

'Oh. Okay. Yeah ... sounds good.'

Chapter 14

Callie's Halloween party was unbelievably grand, demonstrating that the party wasn't, in fact, for Callie, but for Jamie.

Jamie had spared no expense, decorating his loft in spectacular style with balloons, lights, flowers, and candles hung to look as though they floated. The result was breathtaking, sinister, intimate, and Raina shivered as she entered, gripping Callie's hand just a little too tight.

Jamie had vetoed trick or treating, which Raina wasn't unhappy about; it wasn't a Pagan tradition. But Callie had desperately wanted to go, so Jamie had ordered the demons living in his warehouse to buy candy and wait patiently in their rooms for Callie to come knocking. Callie had been delighted, and Raina's heart had almost burst.

Callie ran off to explore the table filled with food, and Raina smiled indulgently. She'd probably be sick by the end of the night from gorging on sweet things, but Raina didn't care … it was exactly the kind of experience every kid should have at least once.

'Raina, darling,' said Jamie, approaching her with a glint in his eye. 'You remember the Grand Master?'

Raina nodded. 'I do.'

The Grand Master assessed her, taking in her black witch's outfit that stopped mid-thigh, with streams of fabric flitting down her legs.

Scandalous, said the Grand Master's eyes, before they dipped to the swell of cleavage on display at the top.

Jamie wrapped a possessive arm around Raina's waist, pinning her to his side, bristling at the Grand Master's blatant appraisal.

'This is my son, Noah,' said the Grand Master, ushering the young man behind him forward.

Noah moved stiffly, then politely shook first Jamie's and then Raina's hand. He winced almost imperceptibly at the movement.

'It's a pleasure to meet you both,' said Noah. 'Dad's told me a lot about you.'

'Noah recently returned from the West Coast,' said the Grand Master. 'He was on a mission there.'

'To infiltrate the new demon nation?' said Jamie, his eyes fixed on Noah in an intimidating fashion.

'Ah, yes, Sir,' said Noah, looking uncomfortable. Raina wondered why.

'What did you find?' said Jamie. 'Were you successful?'

'Not as successful as we would have liked, Sir.'

'You must have learned *something*,' said Jamie, irritated.

'I'd say we learned about as much as you did,' said the Grand Master. 'But you sent a woman, so your failure wasn't so surprising …'

Raina smiled as though he'd cracked a great joke. 'We are all just air-headed bimbos, good for nothing but breeding,' she said sweetly, her eyes promising fire.

Jamie chuckled and dropped a kiss on her hair, stroking her waist. 'Personally, I like my women feisty,' he said. 'Keeps things interesting.'

The Grand Master looked away in disgust, but Noah's attention was raptly focused on them.

'What do you think, Noah?' said Raina.

Noah blushed. 'I ... think everyone has their place in the world.'

Raina laughed. 'How very diplomatic you are ...'

Noah gave a half-hearted smile.

'Stop playing with the poor boy,' said Jamie, 'and let the Grand Master tell us about his attack on the Pagans ...'

Raina's blood stilled in her veins, but she refused to give any outward sign ... not when Jamie was monitoring her so closely.

Noah flinched, and the Grand Master looked as though he'd swallowed a wasp.

'There's nothing to share,' said the Grand Master.

'What was the mission's purpose?' said Jamie. 'I've been trying to speak with you for a while now ... I get the impression you're avoiding me ...'

'I'm a busy man,' said the Grand Master. 'We were testing their defenses, and our troops. We received intelligence of a mass gathering, had men in the area, and executed without delay.'

'Did you?' said Jamie. 'Execute, I mean ...? How many Pagans did you kill or capture?'

Noah was looking increasingly uncomfortable, casting furtive glances his father's way. The Grand Master was steadfast. 'None,' he said. 'But we learned a lot.'

'I hope it wasn't those pesky women who sent you on your way,' said Raina, unable to help herself.

A glint shone in Noah's eyes.

'I need a drink,' said the Grand Master.

211

'Right this way,' said Jamie.

Raina and Noah were suddenly alone, eyeing each other suspiciously. 'Why do you wince every time you move?' asked Raina.

'Training,' said Noah, too quickly.

'You mean punishment?'

'Are they different?'

'In my experience, yes.'

'Then your experience is different from mine.' Raina nodded. 'Why are you lying?'

'I'm not ...'

Raina raised an eyebrow, cutting him off.

Noah looked away and took a long breath. 'You were a Pagan, weren't you?'

Raina nodded.

'Why did you leave?'

'It's complicated.'

'Are they good people? The Pagans? Or is everything they say a lie?'

'They're the best people ... although don't tell Jamie I said that ...' she said, attempting to soften him up. There was obviously something he wanted to get off his chest ...

'Then why are you here?'

'Because I have a daughter with Jamie, and she's more important to me than anything.'

Noah nodded, still uncomfortable.

'Do you know any Pagans?' said Raina. 'Were you part of the attack?'

'I ...'

'Noah, come,' said the Grand Master.

Noah deflated. He threw Raina an indecipherable look, then did as his father bade.

Jamie and the Grand Master accepted drinks from the bartender, then watched Raina interact with Noah. The Grand Master soon got nervous and called his son away, which made Jamie even more curious. What did they have to hide?

'She's not loyal to you, you know that ...' said Janet, sidling up next to Jamie, standing so close her perfume choked him.

'I've forced her hand, and she doesn't like it,' he said. 'She needs time to be angry.'

'Well, she's certainly that,' said Janet.

'She caught me fucking Tamsin ... that set us back a few weeks,' he said defensively.

'You really think she'll desert the Pagan nation for you? That you'll ever be able to trust her?'

Yes, he wanted to say, but Alerac's words rang in his ears: *Magically transfer Raina to the Templars as a matter of priority.* The words had gone round and round. Did Alerac know something? Had Raina said something?

Raina couldn't still love Caspar ... not after what he'd done. Raina had refused to see Caspar for over a hundred years, and when she'd awoken this time, she'd rejected him in spectacularly public fashion. But Jamie had Callie ... had given Raina no choice. She'd registered as a Pagan and hated that he'd forced her to become a Templar. But she said she was loyal ... that their daughter was all that mattered ... How could he ever know the truth?

Jamie left Janet and found Raina. She was draping a blanket over Callie, who'd passed out on a sofa, surrounded by candy wrappers.

'Look at her,' said Raina, brushing a strand of hair off Callie's face.

She did look adorable, but Jamie couldn't care less right now. He took Raina's hand and led her to an armchair, pulling her down onto his lap.

'Jamie ...' said Raina, 'what are you doing?'

'We haven't spent time together in a while ...'

'We see each other every day.'

'That's not the same ... and you always act like you hate me.'

'Then maybe you should stop doing things to make me hate you,' she said.

He ran a finger up her side, across the tantalizing swell of her breast.

She looked at him from under hooded eyes.

'I could make it up to you,' he said.

She leaned into his neck, huffed out a breath as his thumb ghosted across her nipple, then nipped his ear.

'I like the way this is going,' he growled, so only she could hear.

Jamie knew every eye in the room was on them ... he was sure he could feel Tamsin's hostile energy, like daggers against his skin. He loved every second, demonstrating to the world that *the* Raina Halabi wanted him. *Keep watching ... the show's only just begun ...*

Raina pulled back, a hand on his cheek, her nail scraping his jaw. He pushed her more firmly into his lap and looked up into her eyes, and then she kissed him. Their lips met in a collision of pent-up frustration, their movements fast and deep and wild. She tugged on his bottom lip, and he growled, tilting his hips as much as he was able. Their mouths found a sensual rhythm, a rhythm that promised more, and Jamie lost himself in it.

Raina broke away, breathing heavily, shattering their blissful, lustful cocoon. She got to her feet, and Jamie could do nothing but watch as she receded, wanting to chase her like some rabid dog. The Grand Master and his son left in disgust, but Jamie didn't care … all that mattered was that she'd kissed him in front of everyone, and he needed her to do it again, and again, forever more.

Raina left the party. On the outside, she was the picture of composure, but on the inside, she was vacant … numb. Her mind played visions of Caspar … his lips, his deep brown eyes, his fingers on her skin. The kiss had cast open the box she'd carefully built to cage all thoughts of him inside. And now they were free, clamping on her heart … stealing her breath.

Caspar would understand; the kiss was part of her getting back to him. And it had only been a kiss, a purposefully public display, a feather in Jamie's cap, giving him reason to drown out the doubts she knew he harbored.

She knew it had worked. Jamie wanted to believe the lie, wanted to prove the sceptics wrong ... to become a kingpin with a worthy queen by his side.

She'd held him off for so long, he'd been getting nervous, might have done something stupid ... She'd had to give him something ... some hope. But now the genie was out, and Jamie would want all the wishes ... Raina's time was running out.

'Tell me the plan,' said Jamie. He had to tie Raina to him in every possible way ... would do whatever it took. His demons had looked at him differently since the kiss, their faces filled with pride ... with respect. Those who had doubted Raina's intentions, her loyalty, had been proven wrong, with every senior demon in their nation bearing witness.

'We'll travel directly to Scotland, telling no one we're coming,' said Janet. 'We'll dispatch a team to retrieve the Registerium's record keeper as soon as we arrive at the castle, while team two escorts Raina directly to the stone. We'll complete the transfer without delay, inform the record keeper, and leave immediately.'

'The mission will take place under the cover of darkness,' said Tamsin. 'We hope to be in and out before anyone even realizes we're there.'

'Good,' said Jamie.

'The team we're taking is big,' said Tamsin. 'It will leave our headquarters vulnerable to attack, either by hostile demons, or by the Slayers ...'

'You think they would do that?' said Jamie. 'Given what we have over them?'

'We know they're withholding information,' said Tamsin. 'And they're zealots ... anything's possible ...'

'The Grand Master wasn't happy about your display at Halloween,' said Janet, with a smirk.

Tamsin scowled.

'Our cultures differ in places ...' said Jamie.

'Aside from sharing a God,' said Janet, 'and a love of swords, there are few similarities.'

'And their mission is to wipe out the demon race,' said Tamsin.

'Then what about Callie, if we can't leave her here?' said Jamie. 'There's no way she's coming with us.'

'Of course,' said Tamsin. 'She'll go on an educational trip to the south with Alerac. Raina's been badgering us to let Callie out more, so she should be happy about it.'

'She won't be happy to let Callie out of her sight,' said Jamie.

'I'm sure a trip with her lover will sweeten the blow,' said Janet.

It was a challenge, but Jamie didn't give her the reaction she sought.

'Fine,' he said, 'but Tamsin will go with Callie.'

'No,' said Tamsin. 'We need our best team with you and Raina.'

Jamie whirled towards her, crowding her. 'Callie's my daughter. Janet and I will handle Raina. You make sure Callie comes to no harm.'

Chapter 15

Ira and Caspar watched on the screens in Ira's nerve center as four black SUVs drove out from under Jamie's warehouse. Caspar's heart hurt as he watched the cars, Ira logging the license plates and setting members of his team to the task of tracking them. The room's reclined seats were full, Ira having called everyone in at the first whiff of action.

The SUVs headed in four different directions.

'They're up to something,' said Caspar.

'They are ...' said Ira, 'but, what ...?'

'Three of the cars have women in the back, matching Raina's size,' said one of Ira's team. 'The fourth has a little girl. We can't see clearly through the glass but ... wait ... visual confirmation ...'

A video appeared on the screens of Callie and Alerac in the back of one of the cars. Callie had rolled her window down, and Alerac was leaning over, his features urgent as he pulled her away. The window rolled back up and Caspar's heart gave a thud.

'Do you think Raina's really in one of the other cars?' said Caspar. 'Or are they decoys?'

'Who knows?' said Ira, then, to his team, 'Check all flight records. We're looking for private jets leaving any airport easily accessible from Manhattan ... go back twenty-four hours, and scan all the CCTV we have in the area from the last forty-eight. You're looking for Raina, Jamie, or any of his top brass.'

'It could be a diversion,' said Caspar. 'They could already be in Scotland, or nearly there.'

'Call your rep. I'll call mine.'

Caspar group-called Rose, Meredith, and Malcolm. They all picked up straight away, and Caspar filled them in.

'We'll head straight to the Registerium,' said Meredith.

'It could be a trap,' said Rose.

'Or a trick,' said Caspar. 'What if they're drawing us out so they can attack our headquarters? Or the magic compound?'

'It's unlikely,' said Rose. 'They stand to gain little that way.'

'I'll quietly alert our trusted allies,' said Rose, 'and ask them to tip off their Registerium representatives.'

'What's our plan if that is where they're headed?' said Caspar. 'Raina will never leave Callie ...'

'We can kidnap Raina,' said Rose. 'Jamie believes Callie's his daughter ... he won't harm her. And it's easier to extract one person than two ...'

'We can't...' said Caspar. He wouldn't leave Callie in danger. 'We've just forced an inquiry into the Registerium. If we kidnap Raina, what will our allies think? I've spent a huge amount of time and effort counteracting the rumor we kidnapped Raina before she awoke ... we'll lose their support if we do it for real.'

'And Raina won't like it,' said Meredith.

'Have the Holy Star found anything from the malware on Jamie's computer?' asked Malcolm.

'No,' said Caspar. 'Turns out Jamie rarely uses it; he leaves working to others. Ira's made some progress, but it's slow going.'

'Then we have to retrieve Callie now,' said Rose, 'while their leadership's playing some other game.'

'We don't know where they're taking her,' said Caspar, 'or if they're taking her anywhere at all. It would be reckless ... dangerous.'

Silence sounded down the line as they contemplated.

'Alerac,' said Caspar. 'He's with Callie ...'

'The Aztecs ...' said Rose. 'It's a long shot ... we haven't fully planned that either.'

'And we need to locate Raina first,' said Meredith. 'This whole thing could be a trap. They could be playing with us ... flushing us out.'

'But Talli and Christa are already doing reconnaissance ... I'll call them,' said Caspar. 'It's the only hope we have.'

Caspar hung up the phone, looking at the vast surveillance screens. 'Anything?' he said.

'Nothing yet,' said Ira.

'Wait,' said Caspar. 'Zoom in ... there.'

'Oh man,' said Ira, zooming in on the two men walking down a street near Jamie's warehouse. 'Isn't that ...'

'Noah. The demon stolen from our compound ...'

'And we believe that man to be a senior Slayer,' said Ira.

'Fuck.'

Zahora put down the pestle she was using to crush herbs and picked up her buzzing phone. 'Caspar, hi,' she said, clamping the phone to her ear with her shoulder as she washed her hands. 'What's up?'

'I have news about Noah,' said Caspar, his voice sounding strained.

Zahora stilled. 'And?'

'We've just seen him on CCTV in New York, walking down the street with a senior Slayer.'

'Oh …'

The line went silent for several moments.

'Is it as bad as it sounds?' she said. 'Were there other Slayers? Were they forcing him?'

'We have no way to tell if he's there willingly. He didn't appear to be under duress, but neither does Raina in the images we have of her.'

That popped the bubble of fear and uncertainty that had formed around her. She dried her hands, getting a glimpse of what Caspar had been going through for weeks. It made her feel closer to him … like they were in this together … although Caspar knew who Raina really was. With Noah, she had no such luxury.

'Thank you for telling me,' she said.

'We'll monitor his movements. The Slayers have been difficult to pin down, and maybe Noah will help us find them. I have to go, but I'll let you know as soon as I have more.'

'Thank you.'

Caspar hung up, and Zahora clutched her phone to her chest. It was both a relief and a burden to know Noah was in New York. She thanked the universe because he was alive, but maybe he'd been a Slayer all along ... maybe it had all been a lie ... maybe he didn't love her.

But Caspar's words came back to her. Raina looked like a free woman, and that was far from the truth ... maybe the same was true for Noah.

'Man ... jackpot!' said Ira, excitedly watching his screen. He flicked it over to the big screen so Caspar could see too.

'Looks like a man in front of a computer to me,' said Caspar, watching intently. They'd been here for eight straight hours, eliminating SUV by SUV, and there was a pounding behind his eyes, reminding him he hadn't slept properly for days.

'That man is a member of the Templar nation. We hacked a load of private jet firms, then sent out fake emails to their clients, including the Templars. This guy just clicked. I sent him an email entitled *Urgent news about your booking.*'

'Nice,' said Caspar.

'I'm in his email account,' said Ira. 'They have two bookings with a company called LetJet. One plane is to Miami, the other to Inverness.'

Caspar's heart jumped in excitement. 'When do they land?'

'The one to Miami is already there. They just landed. The one to Scotland is in the air.'

'That's got to be them,' said Caspar. 'I can make it if I go now.'

'That's a terrible idea,' said Ira. 'The last thing everyone needs is your irrational ass hanging around, just itching to do something stupid.'

'I'll call the others on the way.'

'Caspar, if you fuck this up, I'm gonna be pissed,' Ira called after his retreating form.

Chapter 16

Talli took step after upward step toward the top of the temple of the Aztecs. Torsten and Christa flanked her, and she drew quiet strength from their presence. *You can do this. You can do this. You can do this. You have to do this. The fate of our nation, the fate of our friend, is hanging in the balance.*

She repeated the mantra again and again as she trudged upwards, happy the documents they'd swapped for Jon's cufflink were safely tucked inside Christa's clothes.

Caspar's carefully laid plans, his and Meredith's travels, their many sacrifices—the extent of which they'd likely never know—all came down to this moment. And diplomacy wasn't Talli's greatest strength ...

Talli reached the top, where a man sat waiting, clad in brightly colored swathes of fabric secured with a large, elaborate gold pin. He wore a feathered headdress and a stern expression that made him doubly intimidating, just in case sitting at the top of a mountainous pyramid wasn't enough ...

Terrifying warriors flanked him on both sides, also wearing tunics and feathered headdresses, and carrying spears or bows.

Talli bowed deeply. 'Supreme Leader,' she said.

The Supreme Leader inclined his head as she straightened.

'I know why you're here,' said the Aztec.

'You do?' said Talli.

'You want my nation to be your friend in this war. I'm sorry for your wasted journey, but we are friends to the Templars. As a curtesy, I will let the three of you go unharmed, but for your own safety, do not set foot in my territory again.'

The ruler lifted his hand, about to dismiss them, but Talli got in first. 'Ah,' she said, halting him in his tracks. 'That's not exactly why we're here.'

He dropped his hand, using his head to indicate she should continue. His brow furrowed.

'It is true, we Pagans would be honored to call the great Aztec nation our friend. However, if that is not possible through other means, I am sorry to say we have it within our power to compel you.'

The Aztec laughed. 'I am all ears, Pagan, but I am skeptical of your possession of such an ability, make no mistake.'

Talli nodded her head, taking a steadying breath. 'The Pagans have many friends, including trading partners of the Aztec nation. The Shindu Council and the Egyptians are your biggest partners, and we are honored to call them our friends as well. Should you remain allies to the Templars, those trading relationships will cease.'

The Aztec laughed again. 'That would hurt them as much as it would hurt us, and trade wars are temporary things. If that is all ...'

'It's not,' said Talli. 'We have uncovered records of your financial dealings, and have discovered your current ... predicament.'

The leader's eyes darted sideways, his hands gripping the arms of his throne a little too tight. 'Leave,' he said, waving his arm at his warriors. They faltered, but he was insistent. They retreated inside the pyramid, probably lurking nearby, waiting for the slightest sign of foul play.

'We are experiencing financial difficulty,' said the leader, 'but we are working with our partners to rebuild our resources.'

'Yes,' said Talli, 'but reckless mismanagement aside, your problem is that you do not own the land we stand on.'

'Neither do you own the land you call yours,' he said.

'True,' said Talli. 'But Europe is so populated, so fragmented in its ownership, that to us, it hardly poses a threat. But to you ... your lands are a commodity, cut down and destroyed by powerful companies for financial gain.'

'Our lands do not belong to some disgusting human company,' he said.

'You're correct,' said Talli. 'They belong to us.'

The Aztec became statue still. 'Pagans would never condone the destruction of our forests,' he said. 'So your ownership is no different to the Waken ownership before you.'

'Not quite,' said Talli. 'The Wakans charged you a crippling rent, but we will turn your lands into a tourist attraction ... the conservation of this place for future generations is of utmost importance ... I'm sure you agree. Humans will crawl over your temples, your sacred spaces, considering them quaint or exotic, and they will pay us for the privilege.'

The Aztec balled his fists atop the arms of his throne. 'Or?' he said, through gritted teeth.

'Or you could be a friend to the Pagans. You could publicly withdraw your support for the Templar cause and throw your weight behind us. In return, we'll charge you no rent, which will ease your financial woes, and leave you to live long and happy lives.'

The leader's shoulders sagged in defeat. 'Fine, although I need time to call my people back before we make the announcement. I won't put them in danger.'

'Very well,' said Talli, 'but here's the kicker ... Your magik, Alerac, is currently travelling with our demon, Callie. If the Aztec nation were to assist us in retrieving her, upon her safe return, we would give you the deed to your land. You'd be masters of your own domain once more.'

'Consider it done,' said the Aztec.

Talli nodded, then said sincerely, 'The Pagans are delighted to call the Aztec nation a friend.'

Raina and Jamie sat sipping cocktails in the spacious jet Jamie had hired to take them to Scotland. Jamie had relegated the rest of his team to another section of the cabin, including Janet, much to her annoyance.

They'd left New York shortly after Callie, hiding in the trunk of a beaten-up old car that belonged to Jamie's janitor. Jamie was delighted by his deception, convinced no one would realize the truth. He'd sent three other cars to decoy planes, one of the women travelling on Raina's passport. Not that it made any difference … as long as the Templars had Callie, Raina wasn't going anywhere.

Raina had taken a plush leather seat as far from Jamie as she could, but Jamie moved to sit opposite, leaning forward, encroaching on her space.

'You can't trust the Slayers,' said Raina, abruptly.

Jamie pulled back a little. 'I know.'

'That kid—Noah—there's something weird going on with him. It's like he's hand shy.'

'His dad probably beats him … or makes him beat himself; it's a strict sect.'

'Their goals aren't the same as ours … never leave Callie alone with them.'

'I know,' he said again, his tone soothing. He leaned forward and took her hand. 'Nothing's going to happen to her. She's safe.'

Raina looked away. 'And we need more structure behind our sorties. If the Slayers are running missions without us, then we should do the same. Keep them on their toes … show them two can play at their game.'

'Where would you attack next?' said Jamie, rubbing his thumb across her skin, making her stomach churn.

'The West Coast, before they become a menace. You need to own North America, or you'll always have a threat at your back.'

'They're a tiny new nation … they're not a threat.'

'They are a threat,' she said adamantly. 'They've set up a stronghold right under your nose, and no one can get in …'

'The Wakan live right under my nose too … you think I should attack them?' He scoffed.

'The Wakan have been here forever. They are not generally hostile, and you know their intentions … you understand them. The West Coast is a different beast entirely.'

Jamie raised his eyebrows, considering her words.

'And you need leverage on the Slayers,' she continued.

'I have leverage.'

'It had better be watertight ... Where are we going?'

'You'll find out soon enough.'

'Given that's the Atlantic, I'm assuming we're headed to Scotland ...?'

'Yes,' he said, lifting her palm to his lips.

So she would be tethered to the Templars magically ... this life was lost. The Templars owned their people ... did not allow them to come and go as they pleased ... did not allow them to leave and join another nation. It was written into their founding laws, so anyone joining knew what they were getting themselves into.

'And I want us to marry,' said Jamie, snapping Raina's full attention back to him. She fought to keep her features neutral.

'How romantic,' she said.

'I'm merely floating the topic ... that wasn't a proposal.'

'I'm glad to hear it.'

'I want to be a proper family.'

'We already are.'

'Templars believe in the sanctity of marriage.'

Marriage ... Raina had had other relationships— flings mainly—but she'd only ever married one man ... at least when her demon memories were intact.

'It's a big step,' she said.

'It is,' he agreed, kneeling before her, running his hands up the outsides of her thighs. 'I love you. I want

229

our lives to be joined in front of God. I pushed you too hard in our last life … but we have a daughter now.'

Raina had to suppress a shudder. She didn't believe in God … at least not his one.

'I need more time,' she hedged, leaning forward to soften the blow, running a hand through his hair.

He kissed her, his lips soft and needy, and Raina leaned into the kiss, made him believe it.

A cough sounded from the door, and Jamie pulled back lazily.

'What?' he said, flicking fiery eyes towards the intruder.

'I need a word,' said Janet.

'It can wait,' said Jamie.

'No, it can't.'

Janet's tone made Jamie tense. He placed an unhurried kiss on Raina's lips, then followed Janet out of the cabin.

Raina slumped heavily against her seat.

'What is it?' said Jamie, barely suppressing his frustration.

'A call from Tamsin … Callie's gone … most likely Alerac took her … he's gone too, and we're getting reports from other teams saying the Aztecs working with us have disappeared.'

'Fuck,' said Jamie, his eyes turning to the door behind which Raina sat. 'It goes without saying, Raina can know nothing of this …'

'I thought she was loyal to you ...' said Janet, a challenging glint in her eye.

Jamie wrapped a hand around her throat and pushed her back against the wall. 'She is,' he said. 'But she doesn't need to know our daughter is missing ... at least not until we've got her back.'

Janet cocked an eyebrow. 'Your wish is my command.'

Jamie released her and turned away. 'What are you doing about the Aztecs? Who's got to them? What can we do to bring them back in line?'

'We're working on it. I'll update you as soon as we know more.'

'Detain any Aztecs we still have,' said Jamie.

'Tamsin's already on it.'

'Good. And don't barge in on me again. Knock, then wait outside like everyone else.'

Talli hopped around nervously, while Torsten and Christa sat on the beds in their flimsy, communal hut. The call had gone out, and Aztecs had begun to arrive, but there was no sign of Alerac and Callie yet, and they were all on edge.

'Why are you even here?' said Christa, as Talli eyed Torsten's naked torso. 'And why are you half naked?'

'It's hot,' said Torsten, with a shrug, 'and I like you two. You've got a grumpy-meets-sunshine kinda vibe.'

'I am not grumpy,' said Christa.

'Thank you,' said Talli, with a smile. She took Christa's hand and kissed the back.

Christa relaxed a little.

'And anyway, where else do I have to be? We live these endless lives ... what's the point if we stay in our homelands all the time? We used to battle ... on fields ... with swords, our blood hammering in our hearts. That made us feel alive! What do we have now? Politics and paperwork?' He practically spat the words.

'I'm personally hoping we don't have to fight anyone,' said Talli.

'Prissy Pagan,' he said.

'Hey, I thought you liked my sunny disposition.'

'Not if you begrudge me my fun.'

'I thought you'd had your fill of fighting, fending off the Zorros with Meredith,' said Talli.

'Meredith is a true fighter,' he said wistfully.

Talli and Christa sat up a little straighter at the promise of gossip, because Torsten was right ... they had to live for something. Where he sought entertainment in battle, they passed the time with tales of heartbreak and scandal.

'She's a closed book, that one,' said Talli.

'We could have been great warriors together ...'

'She doesn't see herself that way,' said Christa.

'She's philosophical,' said Talli. 'Doesn't enjoy killing.'

'Even though she's really good at it,' said Christa.

'She's one of the finest warriors I've ever met,' said Torsten. 'She would be an asset to any nation.'

'True,' said Talli. 'But she's ours, so don't get any ideas.'

'Hey, she's my wife!'

'Do actors consider themselves married when they wed on stage?' said Talli.

Torsten scowled. 'I love her.'

Talli's heart gave a little squeeze. Was there anything worse than unrequited love?

The door to their hut banged open, and Alerac stood in the doorway, Callie in tow.

'The Templars have reported Callie's kidnapping to the Registerium,' said Alerac, without preamble. 'She's tied magically to the Templars ...'

'She's a child,' said Talli, holding out her arms to the trembling girl. Callie rushed into her embrace, even though they'd never met. 'She never had a chance to make a proper choice.'

Callie shook uncontrollably as Talli held her tight.

'Yes, well, that's not how the system works,' said Alerac.

'And yet,' said Christa, 'you brought her here, to us.'

'The Aztecs are no longer allied with the Templars. We have an agreement with the Pagans. I will honor that agreement, and let the Pagans and the Registerium fight over the details. For what it's worth, my view is the girl belongs with Raina.'

'Let's move,' said Talli, gathering their possessions. 'We have to get her out of here.'

The others were already moving, and they were out of the hut in a heartbeat.

'Do the Aztecs know she's here?' said Torsten.

'Yes,' said Alerac, his tone grim. 'I'm supposed to take her to our leader, but he's ... unreliable.'

'Won't they punish you?' said Talli.

'Not if I come with you.'

'But you're magically tied to the Aztecs,' said Christa.

'And I'm the only magik they have who knows how to enforce the connection. If they want me back, they too will have to go through the Registerium.'

'And you're assuming they won't do that ... the embarrassment of losing you too great to make it public?' said Christa.

'Yes,' said Alerac.

Alerac loaded them into a jeep, then jumped into the driver's seat, heading for the makeshift runway the Aztecs had cleared from the forest.

They got as far as the gates to the airstrip ... could see their plane waiting, but between them and escape stood twenty fearsome warriors covered in war-paint and wielding spears.

Chapter 17

'This way,' said Janet. 'The car's over there.'

Raina's senses tingled. Janet rarely talked to her if she could help it ... her words a departure from her usual stern silence ... maybe Jamie had told her to be nice ...

Jamie and Raina sat in the back of the unassuming Volkswagen, and Jamie took Raina's hand. He entwined their fingers as she looked out of the window, the first rays of dawn peeking over the horizon.

Raina fought the urge to pull away. She was here for Callie ... this life was lost ... she would live as a Templar. But in their next lives, Raina would find Callie first ... then everything would be different.

They reached the castle as it basked in the golden light of dawn. Frost crunched underfoot and there was a bite in the air, reminding them winter was almost here.

A second car pulled up, and four demons emerged, sprinting for the castle, presumably to find Pablo, the record keeper.

'Let's go,' said Jamie, taking Raina's hand and pulling her behind him.

Raina had little choice but to follow, the urgency unsettling. Was she really going to do this? She'd never been a member of any nation other than the Pagans ...

They hurried her around the side of the castle, down the stairs, Raina's feet dragging, doing what she could to slow everything down, to put off the inevitable.

They reached the stone, and Jamie took her hand, pressing it to the freezing surface. 'Say the words,' he said, kissing her cheek before stepping back.

'After all,' said Janet maliciously, 'you never hesitate at moments like these ...'

That's what Raina had told Janet when she'd registered as a Pagan only two months before. When Janet had rushed to the stone but failed to stop her.

Raina swung her head to stare Janet down, happy to seize any opportunity to delay.

'Janet,' said Jamie. 'Leave.'

Janet looked furious, but turned on her heel.

'Darling ...' said Jamie, expectantly.

Raina inhaled. There was no other choice she could make ... 'I, Raina, of the Pagan nation ...'

'WAIT!' came a cry from the path.

Raina yanked her hand away and turned towards the voice.

'Rose?' said Raina.

'Janet, stop her!' shouted Jamie.

'We have Callie!' said Rose.

Raina spun to face Jamie, even as she made sense of Rose's words.

'It's a lie,' he said. 'We have Callie. You know we do.'

'Then call her, right now.'

'No electronic devices, remember?'

'Call her from the car.'

'I will, as soon as you transfer … unless there's some reason not to.'

'Where is my daughter?'

'*Our* daughter is safe … with Alerac,' said Jamie.

'The Aztecs have switched their allegiance,' said Rose. She tripped Janet, following it up with a kick to her face. 'We own the deed to their land. We offered it in exchange for their help retrieving Callie.'

'She's lying,' said Jamie. 'They want you back … they don't care about Callie. They know she's my daughter … they only want you.'

'He's lying,' said Rose, pinning Janet to the ground.

'If they had her, they would have shown us,' said Jamie. 'But they can't, because they don't. And anyway, Callie's a Templar … registered magically to *my* nation … she belongs to me.'

'Give us the document and the girl,' said a warrior with a thick accent.

'Ram them,' said Torsten.

'That would be an act of war against our ally …' said Talli in a singsong voice. She had a terrible habit of making light during high-stress situations.

'They're trying to hold us hostage,' said Torsten. 'That's an act of war.'

'Maybe they just want the deed before we leave,' said Christa.

'They're hostile,' said Alerac, 'make no mistake.'

'Ram them,' said Torsten again.

Alerac huffed. He put his foot to the floor and the jeep shot forward.

'Get down,' Christa said to Callie, pushing her down onto the floor, covering her as best she could.

The warriors jumped out of the way, but tried to spear them as they passed. Luckily the spears only found metal ... Talli couldn't face telling Raina she'd let her daughter die ...

The Jeep crashed through the flimsy gates and screeched to their waiting plane, the warriors in hot pursuit.

They jumped from the vehicle and ran for the steps. Torsten picked up Callie, practically throwing her onto the plane before turning to fight. 'Go!' he screamed to the others. 'I'll hold them off!'

'We can't leave you,' said Talli. Alerac boarded the plane with not even an apologetic glance over his shoulder.

'There are too many,' said Torsten. 'Go, before it's too late. Give me the deed and let me die in battle, as I have longed to do for lifetimes.'

Talli knew she couldn't change his mind ... and they probably wouldn't make it out unless he covered their exit. She gave him the deed, then ran, glad to see Christa a few paces ahead.

The prop plane was already moving as they jumped onboard. By the time they shut the door, warriors had engulfed Torsten. Some chased the plane, throwing their spears at the engines, but Torsten had held off the front runners, giving them time to get out of range.

Torsten was screaming, and ... laughing, wielding a knife and a spear he must have taken from one of his attackers. And then they were in the sky, and Torsten disappeared in the mass of trees.

'I can't believe we left him,' said Talli, her breathing staccato, her heart hammering from the rollercoaster of emotions.

'It's what he wanted,' said Christa, wrapping her arms around Talli. 'To die in battle ... an honorable death.'

Talli nodded, shook off the melancholy, then moved to sit next to a trembling Callie. She hugged the girl close. 'You're safe now,' she said as she pulled out her phone.

Meredith ran around the side of the castle and held her phone aloft. 'We have her!' she shouted.

'Mum?' said Callie through the speaker.

'Oh my Gods,' said Raina, shrugging off Jamie and sprinting for the phone. 'Are you okay?'

'Yes,' said Callie. 'We're ... ' Raina couldn't hear most of what Callie said, the noise of the plane drowning out her words.

'I love you,' said Raina.

'Give me the phone,' said Jamie, standing over Raina's shoulder.

Raina held it away.

'I'd like to see my daughter.'

'You lied to me,' said Raina.

'Don't be dramatic.'

Raina punched him in the face. Jamie went down like a sack of bricks, screaming.

'Don't be dramatic,' said Raina, walking calmly up the steps.

'Get back here,' said Jamie. 'I'm the leader of your nation.'

'No, you are not,' said Raina. 'Rose is my leader.'

'But I am Callie's leader,' said Jamie, 'and I command ...'

Raina terminated the call. 'She can't hear you,' she said.

'She's my daughter ... I demand to see her.'

'No, she's not,' said a deep male voice.

The place went still, like a dome had descended over the castle and its grounds, and someone had sucked out all the air. Raina couldn't move, her heart thudding almost painfully in her chest.

Footfall approached, the group of Templar demons halting when they saw the scene. They had Pablo tucked between them, his face pale, clothing disheveled.

The air whooshed back in ... too much air ... so strong it propelled the Templars forward.

'On me,' said Meredith, pulling out a knife.

Caspar, Rose, and Raina formed up around her. Rose had bound Janet's hands and feet, so they left her on the gravel.

Jamie stood, his eye already swollen. He approached the Pagans slowly, his hands out to the side, showing he had no weapons. 'Come with us, Raina,' he said, 'and no one will be harmed. The Registerium has no choice but to rule that Callie lawfully belongs to me; she's a Templar—on paper, and through the cursed magic.'

'Callie isn't an object to be owned,' said Raina. 'And certainly not by you.' She clawed at her Templar cuff and ripped it from her arm. She held it aloft, then threw it to the ground.

The Templars didn't wait for an order to attack, and the world descended into chaos. Raina made swift work of two men, but the third was more of a challenge. She lost sight of Jamie … lost sight of everything but the danger before her.

The fighting lasted for what seemed like hours. Every time a Templar went down, another got back to their feet. In the end, the Pagans had no choice but to kill them.

The last of them ran, as Jamie must have, because he was nowhere to be seen. Janet cowered by the wall, and every other Templar lay dead, the scene a horrific mural painted in blood.

'Shall we kill her?' said Meredith, panting as she pointed to Janet's quivering form.

'No,' said Rose, her breathing labored. 'We'll hand her over to the Registerium and ask them to charge her for breaching nation transfer rules. I shouldn't think our challenge will be successful, given their recent ruling, but I won't have it said the Pagans don't follow the law …'

Caspar threw down his knife and watched Raina watch him. Meredith and Rose took Janet inside, but he didn't spare them a look. Pablo went too, to provide his own independent testimony.

Caspar's pulse thudded, the effects of the exertion overshadowed by Raina's grip on his heart. He almost put a hand to his chest, only the thought of her mocking him keeping him still. She was all that mattered, along with their daughter. He'd torn the world apart to get her back, had manipulated, sacrificed, and used resources he shouldn't have, all for this moment.

And now it was here, he could scarcely believe it was true. She was alive. She was here. And their daughter was on her way …

Raina discarded her weapon and moved towards him. She slid her arms around him without hesitation, and he exhaled as her warmth seeped through his shirt. He clung to her, as though if he held on with enough force no one could ever pry them apart.

'I love you,' said Raina, burying her head in his neck, kissing his pulse.

Caspar squeezed tighter. 'I love you too,' he said, looking down into her eyes.

He had no words to convey his feelings, so he willed his soul to show what she meant to him.

She reached up and kissed him, a chaste, simple kiss, then pressed her face to his chest, gripping him as tightly as he did her.

They stood, lost in the rise and fall of their breaths, until Meredith's voice punctured the air. 'I hate to break up the reunion, but we should get out of here, in case Jamie has any tricks up his sleeve.'

Caspar caressed Raina's cheek, kissed her, then took her hand and followed Meredith to the waiting cars.

Caspar and Raina took the back seat of the Tesla, Meredith driving.

'Hold on!' said Meredith, as she floored it down the drive, laughing wildly at the acceleration.

A smile filled Caspar's face at her childishness, and the stress of the last few weeks began to peel away.

Caspar pulled a battered gold band from his pocket, and Raina went still. She kissed him, then held out her index finger so he could slide her ring into place. She rubbed the metal with her thumb, then settled against his side, finally back where she belonged.

Chapter 18

'I'm disappointed in you,' said the Grand Master, leaning back in his office chair, pinning Noah with a formidable glower.

Noah said nothing. He knew whatever he did or said, there was no way out of whatever punishment his father had planned.

'What do you have to say for yourself?'

'I'm sorry for disappointing you,' said Noah.

'Fraternizing with the enemy,' said the Grand Master. 'Forming a relationship with one of *them*.'

Noah still wasn't sure how he'd found out ... the only thing he could think was that the soldier who'd captured him had seen him and Zahora together ... that it had taken a while for the report to filter up ... 'I'm sorry.'

'No, you are not.'

Noah stared longingly through the skyscraper's wall of windows. No, he wasn't sorry. He loved Zahora. He missed her every waking second ... not to mention in his dreams.

'I'm sorry for disappointing you,' he said. That was almost true.

'I've never told you about your mother,' said the Grand Master, 'but I think now is the time.'

Noah's eyes flicked to his dad's.

'When I was your age,' he said, getting to his feet and walking to the window, 'I too went on a mission. But mine was to Africa, not Wales.'

Noah's heart stammered as he concentrated hard on every word.

'I met an exquisite, dutiful woman in the demon community I infiltrated, and we fell in love.'

Noah's blood ran cold. 'My mother ...'

'Was a demon, yes. I broke it off when I'd completed my mission and returned to New York. I gave my superiors every detail I'd learned about their settlement, their community, their beliefs, their weaknesses ...'

Noah felt sick. He knew what came next ... what always happened after a successful mission.

'But before we returned to finish what I'd started,' said the Grand Master, 'a baby appeared on our doorstep, with my name pinned to its blanket.'

'Me,' said Noah, his voice hoarse.

'Indeed.'

'What happened to my mother?' He held his breath, but he already knew.

'I killed her with my bare hands,' said the Grand Master.

Okay, he hadn't known ... A wave of nausea hit, and it was all he could do to tramp it down.

'My actions that day were the very foundation of my success,' said his dad, continuing as though he hadn't dropped a life-changing bombshell. 'My superiors saw how I handled myself, knew from my actions that I was dedicated to the Slayer cause—above all else—and those actions ultimately led me here, to this office.'

The Grand Master finally turned to look at him.

Noah didn't want this office ... never had. 'Did you love her?' he asked, the words erupting of their own accord.

The Grand Master fixed him with unforgiving eyes. 'I love our cause. Everything else is irrelevant.'

Including you, said his father's icy expression.

'The Lord works in mysterious ways, and he has provided an opportunity for you to follow in my footsteps, to prove you're a worthy successor.'

'What?' Noah choked.

'You will return to Wales and kill the girl. The Devil has infiltrated your mind ... has made you think you love her ... this demon. It's a trick ... sorcery ... evil. You will kill her, and your actions will set you free. This is the word of the Lord.'

'Thanks be to God,' said Noah, parroting the words.

'Good. You leave this evening, but first, there's someone I'd like you to meet ...'

A flutter of panic stirred in Noah's chest. *What now?*

He followed his father to the chapel. The place made him shiver every time he entered, and today was no different, especially when he saw what awaited him at the altar: A woman dressed head to toe in white, a veil covering her face.

Noah shrank back, but his father was waiting. The Grand Master threw a cloak around Noah's shoulders, then raised his hood so Noah matched the knights standing at each of the pillars around the altar. Their faces were angled down, their hands on the hilts of their longswords.

The chapel was filled with candles and roses, the romantic glow starkly juxtaposed to the knights' terrifying forms.

'You never married ...' Noah whispered to his father. He frequently visited Noah's surrogate mother—the woman who'd raised Noah—but he'd never deigned to marry her.

'Oh, but I did,' he said.

'What?'

'She lives with your half siblings in a compound on Long Island.'

'What the fuck?' said Noah.

'She's a perfect Christian wife, and I am a perfect Christian husband.'

'What about me?'

'You are my warrior son, sent to me by God to follow in my footsteps. You are divine, and you deserve a wife of the highest order.'

'I don't even know her,' said Noah. 'She can't want to marry me ...'

'Believe me, she does,' said the Grand Master. 'It's a great honor to be a part of my family. And what higher purpose can there be for a woman than to be a wife and a mother, especially to a man like you? She will live alongside my wife in a position of great honor, and you will provide for her ... visit her as you will ... get her with child.'

'Dad! I can't have sex with her,' he hissed.

'Why not?'

Because I'm in love with someone else.

'Because it's indecent.'

'It is the will of the Lord,' said his father in a low voice, as he pushed Noah down the aisle. 'And if you should refuse to complete your duty in Wales ... if you decide not to return, or set the demon girl free, your wife shall pay for your crimes ... shall be your sacrificial lamb.'

'You can't be serious,' said Noah, blackness filling his head, threatening to consume him.

But his father didn't respond, and it didn't matter, because they both knew he was.

Caspar and Raina entered their house—Maltings—and shut out the world. After hours of debriefing, the others had left them, staying elsewhere, giving them precious time alone ... to heal.

Raina led Caspar to the upstairs bathroom, the strain lightening a little as she reacquainted herself with her home. They stripped off their blood-splattered clothes and stepped into the steaming shower together, embracing as the water fell over them in torrents, hoping it would wash away the weeks of separation.

They soaped each other, exploring, looking for changes wrought by the time they'd spent apart. They were both thinner, less polished, battle hardened.

Caspar held her hand suddenly still and looked down at her with tortured eyes. 'I'll understand,' he said, his voice no more than a whisper, 'but did you ... did you and Jamie ...' He looked away.

'No,' she said, pulling his gaze back to hers, showing him it was the truth. 'We kissed, but that was all. If I'd been there much longer ...'

He wrapped his arms around her, cutting off her words, and tears ran down her cheeks. Tears of relief, and joy, and raw, unfettered emotion. He kissed her and everything else fell away. Her mind only had room for the press of his warm lips, the stroke of his tongue, the eucalyptus scent the soap had left on his skin. They lost themselves in the kiss until the water turned cold, forcing them out into the chill air.

They toweled off, then lay together naked in bed. Raina needed the press of his skin, his presence, this simple expression of love that required nothing in the world but for them to share a space together.

Caspar and Raina woke to the orange glow of sunrise through their window.

'They'll be here soon,' said Caspar, rubbing Raina's back, his fingers tingling with the need to keep her close.

Raina looked up at him, and his lips were moving to kiss her before he'd registered conscious thought. He cupped her face and tilted her head back, his movements slow, savoring every bite and suck and taste, and she purred beneath him.

Her fingers played with the hair at his nape, then her nails scraped lightly against his skin. He exhaled sharply, rolling her onto her back.

The sound of car wheels crunching across gravel floated through the ancient window, and they sprang apart, lunging for the chest of drawers, grabbing clothes.

They sprinted for the stairs, throwing open the back door just as Christa helped Callie out of a Range Rover.

'Oh my Gods,' breathed Raina, running to scoop Callie up in her arms. 'Oh my Gods.'

'Mum,' said Callie, her voice small as she clutched Raina's neck. 'I was scared.'

'I know,' said Raina, 'I know. But you're safe now.'

Caspar stroked Callie's back, feeling suddenly awkward. Callie was his daughter, but he'd only met her once, and that was before he'd known. She and Raina already had a bond ... had known each other even before Raina's demon memories had returned. He was a stranger, and he felt like one.

'Callie,' said Raina, pulling back so she could see their daughter's face, 'this is Caspar ... do you remember him?'

Callie flicked her eyes to him, then nodded, looking nervous. 'He gave me a flower.'

'He did,' said Raina, stroking Callie's hair. 'And I know this might be confusing, but ... he's your father.'

Callie furrowed her brow, then screwed up her features. 'No, he's not,' she said. 'My daddy's name is Jamie.'

The words were like a knife to Caspar's heart, but he tried to keep the devastation from his face.

'No,' said Raina, her tone kind but insistent. 'We had to pretend ... to keep us safe, but Caspar is your real father, and he loves you very much.'

'My daddy's called Jamie!' Callie pushed and squirmed, forcing Raina to put her down, and then she ran.

Raina watched Callie as she fled. Christa and Talli went after her, and she, Alerac, and Caspar followed at a distance.

'She's a feisty one,' said Alerac.

'Can't imagine where she gets that from,' said Caspar, putting on a brave face, but his shoulders were slumped, his words flat.

'She'll come around,' said Raina, taking Caspar's hand. 'Jamie bought her affection with parties and presents, but he didn't really love her ... I'm not sure he's capable of true, selfless love.'

Caspar squeezed her fingers. 'It'll take time,' he said, although Raina got the feeling he was talking mostly to himself. 'She's been through a lot ...'

'Thank you, Alerac,' said Raina, not letting go of Caspar's hand, 'for your help getting her out.'

'My nation and yours are allied now,' he said, 'at least until someone tells me otherwise. I don't know why the Aztecs tried to prevent us from leaving, but it was dishonorable, and makes me ashamed. We own our home for the first time in hundreds of years, and we owe that to this alliance. I hate to think what was required to achieve it ...'

Caspar raised an eyebrow. 'Best not to tell Raina how I decimated her hard-won reserves,' he said.

'Oh Gods,' said Raina, wincing. 'I guess it's only money ...'

'And artwork, and ancient artifacts, and IOUs ...'

'I would have happily given everything I own to be back here,' said Raina. 'Although IOUs sound ominous ...' She nudged Caspar, unable to help wondering what exactly he'd promised.

A shriek from Talli snapped their attention back to the others. 'Help!' she cried.

'No,' said Raina, taking off at a sprint, Callie's slight frame convulsing on the ground.

They reached her, and Alerac pushed the others back. 'It's magic,' he said. 'I can smell it.'

He picked Callie up and ran with her to the stone circle, placing her on the altar stone.

Raina caressed Callie's hair. 'It's going to be okay,' she said, then looked desperately at Alerac for answers.

'She's a Templar,' he said. 'They're using magic to punish her for leaving.'

'They don't have any magiks!' said Raina.

'The Registerium does,' said Alerac, 'although luckily for us, they aren't very good. But if I break their magic now, they'll just keep trying.'

'Then what do we do?' said Raina.

'Put her to sleep until we find a way to fight back … I can form a protective shield that will block their attempts to harm her.'

'Do we have any other option?' said Caspar, clutching his daughter's hand as she writhed on the stone, screaming in pain.

'None I can think of,' said Alerac.

Raina's heart hurt: They'd only just got her back … 'Do it,' she whispered.

Alerac wrapped Callie in a protective blanket of magic, then Caspar carried her back to the house. He put her in the bedroom next to his and Raina's, carefully tucking her in while Raina arranged for a nurse. Thankfully, the Pagans kept medical professionals on payroll.

He looked down at his sleeping daughter ... a perfect little form. Her lips quirked up as though smiling at something in her dream. He took her hand in his, so delicate and fragile, and emotion welled within him. It was all so much ... What if she never accepted him? What if she wanted to go back to the Templars?

The rational side of him said she would never do that ... never leave Raina. She'd get to know him ... see he loved her ... that he only wanted the best for her.

Caspar's phone rang, and he left the room, answering as he headed down the stairs.

'Cas-par!' boomed Henrik, the King of the Vikings.

'Henrik,' he said, 'I'm sorry, I've been meaning to call.'

'Pah! I hear you've been busy! Your family is reunited, you lucky son of a goat.'

'We're trying to get confirmation of what happened to Torsten, but ...'

'Torsten died an honorable death,' said Henrik. 'How many of us can boast of that in these recent times? Eh? He died in battle ...'

'And will gloat endlessly when he joins us again,' said Sofie, the Vikings' Queen.

'We'll keep looking, in case he's still alive,' said Caspar. 'I hope for his sake he's dead, and isn't being tortured ...'

'Ya,' said Henrik.

'They attacked us again ...' said Caspar.

'No!' said Sofie. 'Where?'

'We think the Templars are trying to force Callie back to them ... she's in crippling pain.'

'Poor girl,' said Henrik. 'She's been through enough.'

'We're doing everything we can ... We think the Templars are using Registerium magiks, given they don't have any of their own.'

'I wish we could help,' said Sofie. 'Our last remaining Proficient went to ground years ago. If he surfaces, we'll send him to you, but I wouldn't hold out hope ...'

'Thank you,' said Caspar.

'Come and see us when this is all over,' said Sofie. 'So we can celebrate your victory in style.'

Caspar hung up and entered the kitchen ... he couldn't think about celebrations right now. Pablo and Raina sat at the table, drinking tea.

'The nurse is on her way,' said Raina. 'Should be here within the hour.'

'Good,' said Caspar, dropping into a chair.

'I'll leave you,' said Pablo, making to get up.

'No, wait,' said Caspar. 'You're here because you want to help?'

'Of course,' said Pablo. 'I have been friends with Raina for a long time ... longer than I've worked for the Registerium. It used to be a fine organization ... neutral and fair ... but it is no longer that way.'

'Can you help us?' said Caspar. 'We've been trying to access the online archives, but with little success.'

'I can get you in, so long as they haven't changed my password already,' said Pablo, 'but I don't know what you expect to find ... it's just a list of demons and their nation affiliations.'

'Including the affiliations of all known Adepts ...' said Caspar.

'Yes,' Pablo confirmed.

'Do you have access to records from when the Registerium was formed?' said Caspar.

'No,' said Pablo. 'I'm not sure they put any of that online ... if there are any records at all ... you know what magiks are like ... always protecting their methods, lest someone come along and use their own creations against them.'

'Ira can dig around once he's in,' said Caspar. 'At least we can give him a foot in the door. Let's call him now, before the Registerium remember to change your password ... assuming they haven't already.'

Jamie paced. The edge on his anger was still sharp, even after twenty-four hours. Raina had lied to him. She didn't love him. She still loved Caspar, despite what he'd done ... and Callie wasn't Jamie's daughter ...

Even if Caspar had been lying, they'd made him look like a fool ... Raina had gone with the Pagans ... had refused to join him.

'Update,' said Jamie, as the Registrar and the Registerium's head magik entered the room. Janet trailed behind them, her movements stiff, her face a mess of black and blue.

'I attacked Callie,' said the magik. 'I felt her pain—extreme pain—but then something blocked me. I don't know who did it, or how. I've tried to find a way back, using her bond to the Templar nation as a guide, but it's like I've been locked out.'

'Then break through,' said Jamie, the magik's words like a whetstone to his anger.

'I ... can't,' said the magik. 'To do something like that ... you'd need an Adept.'

'Then find me one of those,' said Jamie. He'd been reassessing his views on magic ... maybe it wasn't without its uses after all ... maybe he should bolster his team by acquiring those with magical skills ...

The magik looked at him blankly, so Jamie turned to the Registrar. 'Well?'

'Adepts are generally well looked after by their nations,' said the Registrar. 'And those without nations fly under the radar.'

'Isn't it your job to keep track of all demons?' said Jamie.

'No, not exactly,' said the Registrar, giving a rare demonstration of his backbone.

'Janet,' said Jamie, 'I have a new assignment for you. Find me an Adept, or better yet, two. See if you can do what the Registerium cannot.'

'I'll need access to the records,' said Janet, 'and to Pablo, the record keeper.'

'Pablo's gone,' said the magik. 'He left with the Pagans.'

'What?' said the Registrar. 'Why did no one tell me?'

'I ... ah ... don't know?'

'Leave us,' said the Registrar.

The magik fled.

The Registrar fidgeted with his long black robe. 'Look,' he said eventually, visibly mustering his courage, 'I can't break the rules for you any longer ... not with the upcoming enquiry. I helped you because you said you could help me, but now ... I'll lose my job.'

'I see,' said Jamie, the urge to slit the man's throat almost overwhelming. 'That's not going to work for me ... so unless you want me to testify against you at your hearing—in which case, you can kiss goodbye to any chance of survival—you're going to help us. And you'll do it with a fucking smile.'

Chapter 19

Gemma and Elliot sat dangling their legs in their infinity pool, looking out over the ocean. They'd kept to themselves since the night of Ares' celebration, and Elliot had repeatedly suggested they leave.

'We can't leave,' said Gemma, once again. She reached for his fingers, and he reluctantly complied.

'Gem, we can't stay here forever, and we haven't found a single useful piece of information … at some stage we have to cut our losses …'

'We're inside, which is more than anyone else achieved,' said Gemma. 'We've had glimpses of their lives, their beliefs … that's useful. And they want us to stay, which means they're beginning to trust us.'

'Or having us here suits their plans.'

'You see conspiracies everywhere you go,' said Gemma, snatching back her hand.

Elliot gave her a forlorn look, and she turned her head away.

'No, I don't,' he said, 'which is why I'm so alarmed.'

'I'm going for a walk. I need … something I'm not getting here.'

Elliot's face fell and Gemma's heart gave a lurch. She hated hurting him, but they had to do this, to see their mission through, and there was something about being here, away from all the drama of their Pagan lives that called to her. She needed this peace ... and sometimes you had to take the things you needed, because no one else would give them to you ... everyone too busy looking after themselves.

Gemma's feet had barely hit the beach when she spotted Aphrodite at the water's edge. She really didn't want to see anyone, but it would be rude not to at least say hello.

'Gemma!' said Aphrodite in her usual seductive croon.

'Hi Aphrodite,' said Gemma.

'Everything okay? You look distressed ...'

Gemma held her breath, then plastered on a smile. 'I'm fine,' she said. 'How are you?'

Aphrodite fixed Gemma with a sour look—she knew Gemma was lying—and the arrangement of Aphrodite's features communicated she wouldn't let her get away with it.

Aphrodite grabbed Gemma's hand and pulled her into the water. 'Sit,' she said, plonking herself down in the surf. She tugged at Gemma's hand like a petulant child until she complied, despite the fact they were both fully clothed.

The water reached Gemma's waist, and she shivered against the bracing cold. She felt foolish, and her whole being tensed.

'Now,' said Aphrodite, still holding her hand, 'breathe.'

'I am breathing.'

Aphrodite gave her a *really?* look. 'No,' she said, 'breathe properly. You take miniscule, shallow little puffs of air, like you're scared you might use up too

258

much oxygen ... in for three and out for three. Come on, I'm not joking.'

Gemma's insides scrunched, but she closed her eyes and did as she was told. She had to admit, it did help. But Gemma didn't want help, especially not from this wild woman. She was happy by herself. Or, if not happy, then content ... or, at least, *managing*.

Tears welled in Gemma's eyes, burning as she tried to blink them away.

'Let them out,' said Aphrodite. 'Let it all out.'

A sob escaped her then, much to her horror. Gemma could deal with anything, except for this apparently ... why was Aphrodite being nice to her? Couldn't she see Gemma wanted to be alone? She didn't want her host to witness her breakdown ... didn't want the world to see her weakness.

'The ceremony the other night ...' said Aphrodite.

Gemma's body snapped to attention, then held rigid, her breathing shallow once more.

'It's okay,' said Aphrodite. 'You were uncomfortable ... I'm sorry we made you feel that way.'

'It's ...' But it wasn't fine. *Part of the job?* She couldn't say that ...

'It is what it is.' Oh Gods, that sounded passive aggressive. In for three, out for three. The water suddenly made her claustrophobic. A wave slammed into her, and she launched to her feet, pulling her hand from Aphrodite's.

'Gemma ...'

'I have to go.'

Zahora wandered the Nexus like a lost kitten, clumsily stumbling from one nation to another. It occurred to her she could probably find out all kinds of interesting things, but spying was unethical, and she had no interest anyway ... she didn't know any of these people.

It also occurred to her that what she was doing was dangerous. She'd been accessing the Nexus without using the Pagan gate. She found the gate restrictive ... didn't like it spying on her, and if the Pagans discovered she was spending so much time hunting Noah, there would be hell to pay.

She just hoped she didn't run into anyone powerful and malicious, because she still didn't really know how to defend herself.

For all her searching, she could find no sign of Noah, and the Templar headquarters had been quiet for days. She'd taken to wandering aimlessly, just in case she got lucky ... in case he'd escaped.

Now Raina and Callie were back, it was like their nation had breathed a collective sigh of relief, everyone taking a much-needed break. But Zahora didn't want a break. She wanted answers, to learn, to find Noah ... she wanted to be useful, but despite her formidable power, it seemed no one knew how to put her to work.

A guitar pierced her consciousness, and then the sound of Noah's voice singing one of the slow country songs he'd written. Was this an auditory hallucination?

Was she losing it …? Or maybe the sleep deprivation was catching up with her …

Zahora flew across the Nexus as fast as she could go, chasing the music, which was leading her … home … to her body. She slammed back into herself so hard she couldn't breathe. She sprawled on the cold floor, gasping.

Noah discarded his guitar and crashed through the water to the stone where she lay. She clutched her chest, struggling for breath, unable to get air into her lungs. She panicked, which only made things worse.

Noah took her face in his hands, looking into her terrified eyes. 'Breathe, Zaha … you're fine … it's just the shock.'

She nodded, grabbing short, staccato breaths until her body came back under her control. She wrapped her arms around him, drinking in his scent.

'Are you okay?' she said. 'I was so worried … I've been looking for you, but I …'

Noah looked confused. He didn't know about magic, or the Nexus …

'How did you get back here?'

'I came in through the passages.'

'How did you escape the Slayers? And how did you know it was them attacking us?'

'Zaha,' he said, smoothing her hair, 'please don't hate me for what I'm about to tell you.'

Zahora pulled back, knitting her brow. 'What are you talking about?'

'I'll tell you everything, but please hear me out before …'

'Just spit it out,' she snapped, trying to ignore the clawing dread.

'My dad is the Slayers' Grand Master. He sent me here on a mission to infiltrate the Pagan nation and report back.'

261

'So you could attack us?'

'Yes,' said Noah.

She recoiled. 'Is that why the Slayers attacked? Because you told them how to?'

'No,' he said, so adamantly she believed him. 'I told them nothing. They came to retrieve me because I'd stopped communicating with them.'

'But your plan was always to go back ... to tell them everything you knew.'

'To start, yes, but then I fell in love.'

She made a sound of disbelief.

'Zaha ...' He reached for her, but she batted his hand away. 'I love you. If you believe nothing else, please believe that.'

'Why are you back? To finish what you started?'

'If my father had his way ... He sent me here ...'

'To do what?'

Noah sat on the stone slab next to Zahora, facing away, not meeting her gaze. 'When my father was my age, he went on a mission to Africa, to infiltrate a nation. He fell in love with a demon woman, and they had a child.

'My father completed his mission, and like a good little Slayer, told his superiors everything. They returned and wiped out the whole settlement.'

'No,' Zahora whispered. 'They killed everyone?'

Noah nodded, still refusing to look at her. 'My father went with them ... he killed my mother in cold blood.'

Zahora watched him as he crumpled. She wanted to comfort him, but realization dawned ... 'He sent you back here to kill me ...' she said, scrambling back on the stone.

He finally looked at her, his features forlorn. 'He did, but I would never do it ... couldn't do it. I love you.' He looked as though he would reach for her again, but then stood to face her. 'I don't care what my father wants ... the Slayers cause nothing but destruction ...'

'And yet, here you are ...' said Zahora, eyeing him warily, wondering if she could make it out of the cave without him catching her ... of course she couldn't ... he was an athlete, he was blocking her way, and she'd have to wade through the water.

'You can't think I would ever ...'

She didn't know what to think.

'Well anyway,' he said bitterly, 'it gets worse.' He sat, his face turned away as he continued. 'Dad made me marry one of his most devout and dedicated followers. She is to give me perfect Slayer children and cook me meals in a compound built for flawless little wives. If I don't kill you, he'll kill her.'

Zahora felt the blood drain from her face. It made her woozy. 'You're ... married? Did you ...'

'Did I consummate my marriage?' he said, spitting the words. 'Yes.' He rubbed his face with his hands. 'In front of a fucking audience ... like a twisted throwback to the Middle Ages.'

He looked defeated, his shoulders slumped, his head down.

'And all I could think was that she was going to die, because I would lay down my life before letting anyone hurt you ... and she doesn't deserve that.'

Zahora let silence saturate the air, reeling from his words. She believed him. And if he was going to kill her, he would have done it when she was meditating, when she'd been entirely at his mercy. She crept forward, wrapping her arms around him from behind.

'I'm so sorry,' she said.

He pulled her onto his lap and clutched her to his chest. 'I was lost without you,' he said into her hair. 'I'm never leaving you again.'

'Then your wife will die ...' The words tasted like ash on her lips.

'Yes.'

'Does your dad know you're a demon?'

'I'm not ...'

'You are. Marla confirmed it, and she has no reason to lie.'

'I ...'

'Your mum was a demon ...'

Noah shook his head as he processed her words.

'You're one of us,' said Zahora, 'at least, if you want to be ... and that means the Slayers are your enemy now too.'

Caspar entered the cave to find Zahora and Noah locked in an embrace. A shot of adrenaline fired into his blood.

'Zahora?' he said.

Zahora jumped, looking around guiltily, searching for the source of the interruption.

'Could you come here for a moment please?' *And get away from that treacherous snake.*

'Um ... sure,' said Zahora, disentangling herself and wading through the water.

Caspar didn't take his eyes off Noah, who watched Zahora's every move.

'How did you get back here?' said Caspar, when Zahora was far enough away to be safe.

'My dad—the leader of the Slayers—sent me,' said Noah.

The honesty was shocking ... Caspar had been preparing for something else entirely. 'You knew?' said Caspar, rounding on Zahora.

'No. He just told me ... his dad sent him here to kill me.'

'Gods,' said Caspar.

'But he's a demon. His mum was an Animist; he's one of us.'

'Is that true?' said Caspar.

'Honestly,' said Noah, 'it's all so new ... I don't know who or what I am. But I know I'm not a Slayer. I know I could never hurt Zahora, and I guess I'm a demon ... although that still seems farfetched.'

'It won't after your first reincarnation,' said Caspar. 'You're lucky you found out before your second life ... most of us aren't so fortunate.'

Noah nodded, accepting Caspar's words.

'Zahora, we need you,' said Caspar. 'And Noah, I'm sure you understand, we'll have to keep you under close surveillance.'

Noah nodded again.

'No!' said Zahora.

'Yes,' said Caspar, giving her a *don't be an idiot* look.

Zahora balled her hands into fists, but followed Caspar out of the cave.

Zahora got as far as the standing stone, where the sight of Raina stopped her in her tracks.

'Oh my Gods,' said Zahora. 'It's really you!'

Raina's lips curved into a half-smile, and Zahora told herself to quit with the fan-girling.

'It's nice to meet you,' said Zahora. 'I've heard a lot about you.'

'Same,' said Raina.

'I'm sure it wasn't all good …'

'A lot of it came from Marla, so …'

Zahora shook her head. 'Her goal in life is to frustrate me.'

'Don't worry, the feeling seems mutual,' said Raina.

Zahora's skin prickled. 'I just want to learn,' she said defensively, 'but the old bat won't teach me.'

Raina softened. 'I know, and I've brought you someone whose methods may be a better fit.'

'Really?' said Zahora, a wave of excitement filling her belly. 'Who?'

'Alerac. But listen, if he has his way, you won't see the light of day for the next ten years … he'll work you that hard … so don't say I didn't warn you.'

'I'm ready,' said Zahora. This was what she'd been waiting for, what she'd yearned for.

'And in return, we need your help,' said Raina.

'I'm a Pagan. I'll do anything for my nation.'

'Good,' said Raina. 'Come with me.'

Raina took Zahora to one of the more spacious sleeping huts, where a little girl lay motionless on the bed, Alerac by her side.

'Oh my goodness,' said Zahora, taking in the scene, then whirling to face Raina. 'That's your daughter?'

Raina nodded. 'Alerac put her to sleep. She's magically a Templar, and they used that bond to hurt her.'

'I've cast a protection around her,' said Alerac. 'Their magic can't penetrate, but it's obviously not a permanent solution.'

'Why do you need me?' said Zahora.

'We have to find a way to release her from her bond to the Templars,' said Raina. 'But the Templars don't allow free movement of their demons, and there's no way they'll ever grant permission for her to leave.'

'So we have to break the bond using magic?' said Zahora.

'Yes,' said Raina. 'But that's not as easy as it sounds. The bonds are sealed via the Registerium, and we don't understand exactly how that works ... we're not sure anyone does any longer.'

'So we need to find out,' said Zahora. 'But we've been probing the Registerium's magic for weeks, and can't find any chink in their armor.'

'Low-level magiks tinkering at the edges,' said Alerac scornfully, 'running with their tails between their legs at the first sign of resistance.'

'I tried to attack them!' said Zahora, hotly. 'Marla stopped me.'

'And she was right to do so,' said Alerac. 'She told me of your attempt, and while I applaud your spirit, you had no plan and no training. What would you have done if you'd found a way in, and the magic had trapped you inside? No one would have ever known ...

'The Registerium was established by magiks who were crafty, old, and in possession of a dark sense of humor. You could have wasted away for all eternity.'

'Oh.'

'But we will work together, you, me, and Marla. We will be aggressive ... think like they did back then ... put ourselves in their shoes ... but we will also be safe.'

'And Rose will keep the Registerium distracted with the inquiry,' said Raina. 'And if that's successful ...'

'Which it is unlikely to be,' said Alerac.

'Which it is unlikely to be,' agreed Raina. 'But if it is successful, then the door is open for change.'

'We hope,' said Alerac, 'assuming the other nations play ball.'

'Couldn't we just put an end to the Templar nation?' said Zahora. 'Magically, I mean.'

'Oh, good,' said Alerac, 'you know how to do that?'

Zahora's cheeks heated as she shook her head.

'Me neither,' said Alerac.

'But Pablo gave us access to the Registerium's records,' said Raina. 'They might help us find someone who does.'

'Most magiks are wary of being tracked,' said Alerac. 'The old guard haven't registered for many lifetimes ... too many were targeted and killed.'

'Pablo said there were likely other records never put online,' said Raina. 'Records no one was allowed to see ... they might tell us something, assuming we can get our hands on them.'

'Boots on the ground?' said Alerac.

'We're trying,' said Raina. 'They're supposed to give members of the inquiry access to all records, but the Registerium's dragging its feet.'

'Probably destroying stuff while they have the chance,' said Zahora.

'Malcolm—our representative there—is keeping vigil outside the door to the dungeons, where they keep the records,' said Raina. 'Along with representatives from every other nation ...'

Raina exited Callie's hut, leaving Alerac and Zahora to become acquainted. Nothing made her more frustrated than feeling useless ... helpless. But magic was the one thing she'd never mastered ... it had mastered her instead.

She was so deep in thought, descending into a pit of self-chastisement, that she barely heard the call of her name. She looked up to find Leila—her human cousin—staring at her, Jon standing protectively just behind.

Leila was moving before Raina could blink, wrapping her arms around Raina's neck and laughing loudly. 'I thought I'd never see you again!'

Raina hesitated ... humans weren't supposed to know about demons ... it contravened so many rules ... but her arms wrapped around her cousin of their own accord, squeezing her tight.

'I'm sorry,' said Raina.

'Don't be!' said Leila. 'I understand.'

'But ...'

'Hey, I know everything,' she said, looking back at a sheepish Jon.

'Do you now ...' said Raina.

'Don't worry, I won't tell anyone. Who would I tell? Any anyway, no one would believe me. I'm just so glad to have you back!'

'I'm glad to be back, and I'm thrilled to see you, but ...'

'But what?' said Leila, her inquisitive eyes turning wary.

'You're in danger here, with us.'

'I'd be in more danger out in the big wide world on my own,' said Leila, hotly. 'Jon's been looking after me.'

Jon reddened. 'I've been on bodyguard duty,' he said.

'Indeed,' said Raina, raising an eyebrow.

Leila hit Raina on the arm. 'Can you stop, please? Where can we get an alcoholic drink around here? We have *so* much to catch up on.'

Raina took Leila into a side cave—one not generally used for the practice of magic. It was, however, utilized by Talli for the storage of decorations and ceremonial items, including leftover alcohol.

'It's Talli's secret stash,' said Raina, pulling a bottle of vodka out of a box of decorations. 'I think she misses her teenaged years.'

They talked and drank, the sting of vodka not exactly pleasant, but the buzz was.

'So … you and Jon?' said Raina, when the serious topics were out of the way.

Leila smiled. 'Nothing's going on.'

'But you'd like there to be?'

'No,' Leila said too quickly.

Raina laughed. 'You *like* him!'

'I do not … and anyway, he's had plenty of chances to make a move, and he hasn't.'

'You know, demon-human relationships are frowned upon.'

'What? No! Why?'

'Because you're going to die at the end of this life, and he'll live on.'

'Crickey … don't sugarcoat it.'

'It's not something to gloss over. If Jon falls in love with you, he has to deal with that loss forever. You get to slink off into oblivion and never have to think of him again.'

'Oblivion? That's where I'm going after death?'

'Who knows,' said Raina.

'You don't believe in an afterlife?'

'I don't know what to believe, but oblivion sounds blissful to me.'

'Dark,' said Leila.

Raina took a swig from the bottle, wincing as she swallowed. 'You need to leave,' she said.

'Why?'

'It's not safe.'

'I have nowhere else to go,' said Leila, her forehead furrowed as she told herself not to cry. 'And I don't want to be alone.'

'We'd send a bodyguard with you, but unless you've been hiding combat skills all these years, it's too dangerous for you to stay here.'

Leila turned away.

'I don't want you to go ...' said Raina, 'I'm just trying to keep you alive! And when this is all over— assuming that happens in this lifetime—you can come back and join us ... live out the rest of your life with us.'

'I thought that was frowned upon ...'

Raina took another swig. 'We'll pretend you're a cleaner or something.'

Leila threw a willow wreath at Raina's head. 'A cleaner? That's the best you can do?'

'Or something ... but cleaning's an honorable line of work.'

Leila shook her head. 'I'm glad you're still you ... even with ...' She waved her hand, 'hundreds of years of memories or whatever.'

Raina nodded. 'I'm still me.' She handed the bottle to Leila.

'Who would you send with me? As my bodyguard?' Leila asked, the air suddenly still.

'Do you have a specific request?' Raina asked dryly.

'It would be better if it was someone I already knew ... someone I got on with.'

'You want me to go with you?' said Raina. 'That's so sweet!'

Leila threw a dried hydrangea flower at her this time. It didn't go far.

'Oh ... silly me ... you want someone more ... male.'

'Jesus Christ, Raina,' said Leila. 'Yes, I wouldn't be unhappy if Jon was my bodyguard. But only because we've already gone through that awkward getting to know each other stage. I know I can tolerate his company, and that's no small thing.'

'Tolerate his company ... I'll tell him you said that.'

'Please do.'

'Very well. I will put your request to our leader and let you know what she says.'

'Focus, girl,' said Alerac, for the hundredth time.

Zahora was, and anyway, 'I'm not a fucking girl! I'm in my *twenties*.'

'You want me to call you woman?' said Alerac.

'I want you to call me Zahora, and not treat me like I'm twelve years old. Maybe if you refrain from calling me *girl*, it'll help you remember I'm an adult and should be treated like one.'

'You're a baby in demon terms,' said Alerac.

'A baby whose help you need.'

Alerac regarded her for a long moment. Zahora didn't care what he thought; she'd had more than enough of this bullshit ... she was done with it.

'Very well,' said Alerac. 'Now, can we concentrate, *Zahora*?'

'Yes, we can, but I already was.'

'Then why isn't it working?'

'What are you doing?' said Marla. 'I told you to wait ...'

'Getting a head start,' said Alerac.

'With what?'

'We're trying to widen the protective cocoon around Callie,' said Zahora. 'So it stretches across the whole settlement. That way, Callie can wake up, but won't be in danger, so long as she stays inside the boundary.'

'That will take a huge amount of power,' said Marla.

'We're trying to use the standing stone,' said Alerac, 'trying to draw power from it to keep the cocoon in place.'

'But *Alerac* can't make it work,' said Zahora, still smarting at being called *girl*.

'*We* can't make it work,' said Alerac. 'Maybe we need a different solution ...'

'No,' said Marla, 'I think you're onto something. How are you connecting to the stone?'

'What do you mean?' said Alerac.

'You need to establish an ongoing connection to access its power and protection,' said Marla. She turned to Zahora. 'Didn't you tell him this?'

'I thought he knew!'

'I told you, each nation has their own way of connecting with the Nexus,' said Marla. 'The Aztec way will be different to ours.'

'Which is?' said Alerac.

'We use the Pagan wheel,' said Zahora.

'Ink?' said Alerac.

Zahora nodded, showing the fresh tattoo on her arm.

'We can't do it that way,' said Alerac, 'or one of us will have to maintain the connection at all times. We'll have to do it the Aztec way.'

'Which is?' said Zahora.

'We'll draw the Pagan symbol around the area we want to protect.'

'The entire area?' said Zahora. 'It'll be huge!'

'Luckily, it's just a circle,' said Alerac.

'With an eight-pointed star inside,' said Marla, frowning.

'We'll do our best to interpret the circle, and just draw the tips of the points,' said Alerac.

Marla made a skeptical noise.

'Unless you have a better idea?'

Marla shook her head. 'We'll conduct smaller tests first.'

'Of course,' said Alerac.

Caspar carried Callie into the protective circle the magiks had drawn. He placed her gently beside the stone, then stepped back out of the way. He wrapped his arm around Raina, still not used to being able to do so, kissing her hair as she pressed close.

His heart thudded. Everything they'd ever wanted was within reach, but he knew their route was still long. And what would it be like in future lives, with Jamie always hunting them ... always trying to destroy them? He couldn't think about that now ... one problem at a time.

'The circle's in place,' said Zahora. 'We've tested it ... it should work.'

'It will work,' said Alerac, stepping into the circle. 'Zahora will create the protection, then I will remove the existing protective magic around Callie. She will wake, but will still be safe.'

'How will we know?' said Raina. 'What if no one's attacking right now?'

'We won't know for sure,' said Alerac, 'but the magic is the same type that protects her now ... there's no reason for it to be less effective.'

'Then why can't you just wake her now?' said Caspar. 'How is this new solution different?'

'Because the magic right now hugs her skin ... it's too close, too restrictive,' said Alerac. 'It would make her itch ... want to claw at herself.'

'But that won't happen inside the cocoon,' said Zahora. 'The magic's much more dispersed.'

'Okay,' said Raina, balling her fist in the fabric of Caspar's shirt. 'Go ahead.'

Zahora touched the wheel drawn in chalk on the ground, eight arrowheads pointing to the edge of the circle, equally spread all the way around. She closed her eyes.

'It's up ... I feel it,' said Marla.

Raina thought she could feel something too, but maybe that was wishful thinking ... her magical ability wasn't what it had once been ...

275

'I'm removing my magic from Callie now,' said Alerac.

Seconds later, Callie opened her eyes. 'Alerac,' Callie whispered, then cast her eyes wildly around.

Raina had to fight the urge to break the protective circle, to run through it and cradle her daughter close.

'How do you feel?' said Alerac. 'Any pain?'

Callie shook her head. 'Where am I? Where's Mummy?'

Raina's heart broke. 'I'm here,' she said. 'I'm right here.'

'Mummy!' Callie tried to get up, but Alerac held her in place.

'You can't leave this circle,' said Alerac, pointing to the chalk.

Callie stilled, and Raina pulled away from Caspar.

'It worked. Now let me in there,' said Raina. 'Now,' she snapped, when Zahora didn't immediately heed her command.

'I'm ... not sure how to,' said Zahora. 'Alerac?'

'Tell the magic to let her in,' said Alerac.

'How?'

'Think it ... will it ... make it your sole intention.'

'I ... I think I've done it?' said Zahora.

Raina didn't wait for further confirmation. She launched herself across the chalk line and ran to her daughter.

'Good,' said Alerac. 'Now, Caspar, try to cross the line.'

'I wasn't born yesterday,' said Caspar. 'Unless someone tells that thing to let me across ...'

'What's going on?' said Jon, entering from deeper in the cave system, Leila two steps behind. 'You guys having a party and forgot to invite us?'

'Jon!' said Caspar. 'You need to cross that line right now, or you're going to ruin everything!'

276

The alarm in Caspar's voice meant Jon didn't hesitate, but as his arm touched the air above the line, an invisible force threw him backwards with such ferocity it knocked him unconscious.

Leila shrieked, dropping to her knees beside him. 'What did you do?' she demanded.

After a minute or two, Jon came round, Leila fussing over him. 'You're a bastard,' he whispered.

'Thank you, Jon,' said Caspar. 'You've helped us prove a theory.'

'I hate you,' Jon croaked.

'I'll help you back to your room,' said Caspar.

'See, Mummy, he's a bad man,' said Callie's small, muffled voice, her face hidden in Raina's scarf.

Raina's eyes locked with Caspar's. She willed him not to take it personally. Callie had been brainwashed by Jamie ... didn't know Caspar yet. She hoped her eyes told him those things. Callie would come around ... she had to.

Alerac put Callie back to sleep while he, Zahora, and Marla drew a massive wheel around the compound. They checked and rechecked it, then met back at the stone to invoke the magic.

'You're the most powerful of us,' said Alerac, looking to Zahora. 'You should be the one to put the protection in place.'

'But ...' said Zahora. But the words died on her lips. Why shouldn't it be her? Hadn't she been asking for more responsibility? 'Okay.'

'I've warned everyone not to leave or enter the compound without permission,' said Marla. 'So we're ready whenever you are.'

Zahora nodded. She sat by the stone, taking comfort from its solid presence, but didn't use it to connect to the Nexus. She touched the line they'd drawn on the floor, connecting herself to the huge Pagan wheel around the compound, then threw every ounce of her intention towards it, willing the shield into being.

But nothing happened.

She went deeper into herself, feeling for her connection to the power, calling on it, but again, nothing.

She pulled herself out of the meditation and looked up at Alerac's expectant face. 'Nothing happened,' she said. 'I connected to the Nexus, and willed it like I did before, but ... nothing.'

'Magic always comes with a cost,' said Alerac, 'and we're asking a lot. Give something of yourself in return.'

'Like what?' said Zahora, alarmed.

'Vitality,' said Marla. 'Try that.'

'You want me to offer the magic my vitality?' said Zahora. 'How?'

'Just try,' said Alerac.

'Should I try using a symbol?' said Zahora. 'Maybe the Triskelion?'

'Gods, no!' said Marla. 'Never use that thing ... you'll spiral out of control. But maybe a Trinity Knot ...'

Marla wasn't wrong about the spiraling ... 'Okay,' said Zahora, drawing the three-pointed knot on the back of her hand. 'Here we go again.'

278

Zahora connected once more, then willed the magic to do her bidding. It flatly refused, with not a flutter of response. *Magic always comes at a cost.* The words echoed through her mind … *Fine.* If that's what she had to do … but how could she offer vitality?

Practically before the thought was complete, something pulled at her chest, hollowing her out. It sucked and sucked, pulling her down into the depths, dangerously close to the Sphere itself. *Stop*, she thought. *You've taken enough.* But the magic didn't stop. Not by a long shot.

Noah snuck into the caves. Zahora had smuggled him to her hut and made him promise to stay there until they could come up with a plan, but he'd grown restless. She'd been gone too long, and he worried about her.

He crept on silent feet, keeping to the shadows, pressed against the tunnel's side. He came to the cave with the standing stone and hid behind a lip in the wall, watching Alerac and Marla as they monitored Zahora. They were silent and unmoving, and the longer he observed, the greater Noah's sense of foreboding became … something didn't seem right.

'She's been in there a while,' said Marla, sounding worried.

'Give her time,' said Alerac. 'Patience …'

Zahora's body collapsed to the floor, convulsing, and Noah sprang forward without thinking.

Alerac spun at the sound of his footsteps. 'No!' said Alerac, putting himself between Noah and Zahora.

'She's in trouble,' said Noah. 'She needs me.'

'She needs time,' said Alerac. 'If you interrupt her too soon, it will all be for nothing.'

'We have to pull her out. Look at her!' said Noah, trying to push past.

Alerac held him in place, seemingly without effort. 'She's fine,' he said. 'Give her time to work.'

'The barrier's up,' said Marla. 'I can feel it.'

'I can too,' said Alerac, releasing Noah.

Noah rushed to Zahora's side as a high-pitched wailing escaped her mouth, her back arching off the floor.

'Zahora!' said Noah, taking her hand, bending to sing in her ear. He looked up—still singing—and found Marla watching. 'Start the sound bowls!' he shouted, enraged that she could stand idle when Zahora was in peril.

To his surprise, Marla did as she was told. The ringing pierced the air, and Zahora's wails ceased, Noah unsure if that was a good or bad sign.

'What's he doing?' said Meredith, rushing in from the entrance.

Noah kept singing ... that was all that mattered.

Alerac stepped into Meredith's path. 'He's helping her.'

'He's a Slayer! He's probably trying to kill her ...'

Noah's heart lurched.

'I don't think so,' said Alerac.

Meredith didn't slow her approach. As she neared Alerac, he moved his hands in a strange circular motion. Meredith didn't falter, flooring him without breaking a sweat.

'No!' shouted Alerac, grabbing Meredith's ankle, bringing her to the ground. 'He's helping her!'

Meredith kicked out, freeing herself, back on her feet in an instant. She launched herself at Noah, knocking him to the ground and pinning him in place just as Zahora opened her eyes.

Zahora took in the scene and screeched at Meredith to release him. Noah had to fight the urge to sob ... he'd thought she was lost.

Meredith backed off, and Noah went to Zahora, pulling her into his arms, holding her tight.

'Are you okay?' said Noah.

Zahora nodded. 'Tired,' she said, resting her head against his arm.

'Let go of her,' said Meredith. 'You're coming with me.'

'No,' said Zahora, holding onto Noah's t-shirt. 'He's already told me everything ...'

'What?' said Meredith, halting her approach.

'My dad is the Slayers' Grand Master,' said Noah. 'He sent me here to kill Zahora.'

'But he's a demon,' said Zahora. 'One of us.'

'I wouldn't go that far,' said Meredith, eyeing him suspiciously. 'So what's your plan? Return to your dad and pretend you killed her?'

'He'd find out,' said Noah. 'Honestly, I don't have a plan. But I love Zahora ... would never do anything to harm her.'

'Really,' said Meredith.

'I need to sleep,' said Zahora. 'The Sphere took a lot ... I had to fight ...'

Noah picked her up. 'I'm taking her back to her hut.'

Alerac took a swig of his home-brewed beer, Marla and Meredith his drinking companions as they sat by a crackling bonfire. A comfortable silence had settled over them, and they looked up at the stars, relishing the tranquility. Down time was a rare and precious thing, and Alerac felt regeneration seep into his soul.

Until the urgent sound of approaching feet interrupted ...

'Is five minutes' peace too much to ask?' said Marla, turning her eyes to the approaching footsteps.

A boy of about twelve appeared. 'We can't access the Nexus,' he said frantically. 'Or ... we can ... but ... that's all we can do.'

Marla hardly looked older than the boy herself; it was almost comical to watch their interaction.

'I guess that makes sense,' said Marla. She turned her weary face to Alerac. 'Did you know this would happen?'

'I didn't think about it,' he said, 'but as you say, it makes sense.'

'Tell the others they won't be able to use the Nexus until further notice,' said Marla. 'We know the cause of the issue, it's nothing to worry about, and we will rectify it shortly.'

'Okay,' said the boy, wheeling around and running back the way he'd come.

'We need to move Callie,' said Marla, sighing then getting to her feet. 'I'll tell Caspar and Raina.'

'I guess that explains why people don't put protective boundaries around their headquarters,' said Meredith, taking a swig of beer.

Marla left, and Alerac watched Meredith with interest. She caught him, did a double take, then turned quizzical. He leaned forward in his chair. 'How did you do it?' he said.

Meredith went still, her bottle of home-brew half-way to her lips. 'Do what?' she said, seeming to be genuinely confused. And then her features smoothed. 'Oh ... you mean in the cave?'

'Yes.'

'Just a little something I picked up in Myanmar ...' The bottle connected with her lips, and she took a long pull.

'Recently? Or when it was Burma ... or at some other time?'

Meredith smiled an infuriating smile. 'Why do you want to know?'

'Because ...' *How to phrase it ...*

'Never come across anyone who can best your magic tricks?' she said.

'Not like you.'

'I teach all the Pagans.'

'Most can't do magic as rapidly as I can,' said Alerac. 'I usually beat defenses like the one you used.'

'I'm old,' said Meredith, 'and back when I was young, all the magiks were as fast as you. Maybe your old age is taking its toll ...'

Alerac frowned. 'I doubt that.'

'Or maybe you're getting sloppy ... I doubt you get much practice these days ...'

'Are you always like this?'

'I am.'

'It's disturbing.'

'Can't deal with a bit of friendly ribbing?'

283

'Is that what you call it?'

'As opposed to?'

'Rudeness.'

'Wow.'

'Will you teach me how you do it?'

'I'm sorry ... Mr. I-don't-do-joking-around wants me to teach him?'

Alerac looked at her blankly; he didn't understand this woman. 'Yes?'

Meredith took another swig, then leaned back in her chair. 'I'll think about it.'

Chapter 20

Caspar watched Callie push roasted vegetables around her plate. She'd eaten the chicken and was stalling on the rest.

'How are you feeling?' asked Raina.

'Fine,' said Callie, dropping her fork. 'I'm full.'

'No, you're not,' said Raina, drawing out the words into a friendly warning.

Callie's face set firm. 'I am.'

Caspar was lost at sea. He had no idea how to reason with a five-year-old. Should they make her sit at the table until she'd eaten everything on her plate? Or was that considered too heavy-handed these days? Would bribery work? Or … that was probably wrong too.

'That's a shame,' he said eventually, 'because I was really looking forward to the rhubarb and apple crumble …'

Callie eyed him suspiciously. 'With ice cream?' she asked.

'I guess we'll never know,' said Caspar.

'How many bites?' she asked, pointing to her plate.

'Five,' said Caspar.

'Three,' said Callie.

'Six,' said Caspar.

Callie scowled. 'Fine ... five.'

She shoveled mouthful after unceremonious mouthful, then said, 'Done. I want ice cream *and* cream.'

'Why don't you go to the kitchen and see what they've got,' said Raina.

Callie was suddenly hesitant, her eyes darting sideways to her mother.

'It's just over there,' said Raina. 'We'll still be able to see you.'

Callie wavered, then made up her mind, looking back several times as she headed to the kitchen. Raina nodded encouragingly.

'She's so funny,' said Raina.

Caspar took Raina's hand. 'This is all so new ...'

'I know. I felt the same way to start ... I'm afraid you have little choice but to get used to it.'

'I feel ... behind.'

Raina rubbed her thumb across his skin, then moved to sit on his lap. 'You won't feel like that for long, and she's already coming round ... turns out five-year-olds are fickle creatures.'

'I'm glad to hear it,' said Caspar. 'Maybe I should bribe her with sweets ...'

'Then you'll have me to answer to,' she said, leaning down to kiss him.

Caspar got lost in the kiss, not yet used to having her near ...

'They had both!' said Callie's excited voice, breaking them apart.

Callie plonked her bowl on the table and dug in.

'Hey, where's ours'?' said Raina.

'Oh, yeah,' she said, taking another mouthful before running back to the kitchen.

Caspar kissed Raina again, only releasing her when he heard Callie's returning footsteps. He held Raina's hand as she moved back to her seat.

Callie dumped their bowls down, looking at them with suspicious fascination. She wolfed her crumble, deep in thought, and when she finished, she looked up at Raina. 'Mummy,' she said seriously.

'Yes?' said Raina, matching her tone, giving Callie her full attention.

'Why did you never do that with my other daddy …?'

Zahora woke to find Noah lying next to her, watching her sleep.

'Morning,' she said, every muscle in her body stiff as she tried to sit. She groaned.

'Are you okay?' said Noah, reaching for her arm, helping her sit, propping her against the headboard.

'No,' said Zahora, 'but I'll probably live.'

'What was that yesterday?'

'Magic,' she said.

'But …'

'I can't tell you all the details. I'm not even sure I know all the details,' she said. 'But it took a lot from me … it took vitality. Maybe that's why I feel like an ancient woman right now.'

He fussed over her, plumping her pillows. 'I missed you,' he said, bringing her hand to his lips.

'I missed you too,' she said, her eyes flicking to his naked torso, '... wait ... what are those?' He was covered in bruises, with big pink welts curling around his shoulders.

'Punishment,' said Noah.

'The Slayers?'

'My dad.'

'No ... I'm so sorry.'

'Don't be; it's hardly the first time. Punishments are a core part of Slayer training ... along with self-flagellation.'

'It's so wrong,' said Zahora, tracing the lines over his shoulders. She pushed him down onto his stomach so she could get a good look at his back.

'This is the first time Dad went so far with me though ... they reserve punishments like this for the fully initiated ... those who've proven themselves on their missions.'

'But you ...'

'Haven't proven myself yet, no. And never will. But Dad wanted to make it look like I had, so he could look strong, and so my wife wouldn't have cause to question me on my wedding night.'

Zahora wanted to be sick. 'Your dad is fucked up.'

'Mine and many others,' he said, sitting.

'I guess that's true enough.'

'You know we could just leave, right?' said Noah. 'We could hightail it out of here ... disappear ... go somewhere exotic ...'

'Noah ...'

'We could live a happy, fulfilled life. I could sing, and you could ...'

'We can't; I'm needed here. And you need to think bigger ... I know you're new to all this, but we're going to live many lives ... this is just one. If we can defeat

288

those who want to hurt us now, we can enjoy ourselves later.'

'Not if we're killed first.'

Zahora put a hand on his face and stroked his cheekbone. She pulled his lips to hers, and he came willingly, straddling her legs as he took her face in his hands.

A knock sounded from the entrance, and then the door flew open, whoever it was not waiting to be invited in.

Zahora resisted the urge to scream. It was just getting good …

'We need you,' said Marla. 'The defenses have weakened, and Callie's in pain.'

'She's exhausted,' said Noah, rolling off her. 'Can't someone else do it?'

'Doesn't look that exhausted to me …'

'I'm coming,' said Zahora. 'I'm coming.'

Gemma knocked on Aphrodite's door, and a servant let her in. She'd come to tell Aphrodite she and Elliot were leaving. After many arguments and much discussion, they'd agreed it was for the best.

Aphrodite's room was similar in layout to Gemma and Elliot's, and Aphrodite was in her infinity pool, looking out to sea. She turned when Gemma approached, her naked body distorted, but visible through the water.

Gemma turned away.

'Why does nakedness make you uncomfortable?' said Aphrodite.

The sounds of her climbing from the pool made Gemma turn back to face her. Her warrior instincts told her not to leave her back exposed to this woman. Aphrodite pulled on an almost sheer robe embroidered with flowers, then sat on a chaise.

'Please,' said Aphrodite, pointing to a second couch. 'Most demons are comfortable in their own skin, and seeing the skin of others ... we've been around too long, seen too much for such squeamishness. So there must be a reason, my Goddess of Spring.'

'I'm no goddess,' said Gemma, puzzled by the title.

'I beg to differ,' she said. 'I sensed it the moment you arrived. Why else do you think we allowed you to stay? You're special to us ...'

Gemma stayed silent. She was special to no one ... aside from maybe Elliot.

'You've suffered,' said Aphrodite. 'Your mother?'

Gemma shook her head.

'Your lover then ...'

Gemma shuddered. 'Elliot would never hurt me.'

'He hurts you even now,' said Aphrodite. 'He's holding you back from your true potential. He's suspicious of us, doesn't belong like you do, and ... he's jealous. He knows Hades is here, living with us.'

'What?' said Gemma. What the fuck was she talking about? 'Elliot's not jealous of anything. He knows I love him.'

'He's not your destiny.'

'But the God of the Underworld is?' Gemma tried to keep her tone friendly, but she couldn't hide the derision that crept in.

Aphrodite gave a non-committal shrug. 'You've suffered. Hades knows suffering ... he can help you.'

'I don't need help ... I'm...'

'Scared,' said Aphrodite. 'Terrified of finding truth, of facing your past, of naked bodies ... of everything! Let me help you ... release you from this torture. Free your true self, my goddess.'

'I am not a goddess.'

'Says who?'

Gemma faltered. *Says me.* But she couldn't say the words out loud. 'I have to go.'

We're leaving, is what she should have said, but again, she couldn't make the words come out. Because a part of her didn't want to leave ... she wanted to know more about her supposed place here, to feel valued, to be important enough that no one could touch her.

Aphrodite had hit a deep, desperate part of her soul, and it wasn't only intrigue that called her to stay, but ... hope.

'Have dinner with me,' said Aphrodite. 'Elliot has already agreed to join Ares this evening, so otherwise you'll be alone. You can't possibly have plans ... let me show you who you are.'

And even though she knew she shouldn't, knew she couldn't trust this woman, knew she should go home to the Pagans, she wanted to know who she was ... had always wanted that ... had never really known.

'Okay,' she said.

Aphrodite smiled like a cat who'd got the cream. It did nothing to settle Gemma's unease.

'Wonderful ... I'll send a dress.'

Chapter 21

As soon as the magical protection was in place at Maltings, Caspar finally felt like he could breathe. They were confined to a small area, but at least it felt like home, a place where Callie could play, where they could be a family.

Most of the leadership had come too, although Raina had relegated them to the houses in the village. She too wanted time alone, together, at last.

Meredith had stationed security around the boundary, and Zahora had to top up the magic every few hours. Those things were a small price to pay until they found a permanent solution ... which, if Caspar had his way, would be to put an end to the Templars once and for all ...

Callie had even begun to accept him, perhaps largely because of the promise of being a flower girl at a second of Raina's weddings ... a wedding Talli had insisted should take place later that day.

It had taken Talli all of about ten seconds to overcome his and Raina's half-hearted suggestions they do it at some later time, then Talli had whisked Raina away, leaving a flurry of instructions behind.

No one minded; it was good to have something positive to draw their focus.

Caspar joined Callie and the others at the barn by the stone circle, where they created winter wreaths, floral centerpieces, and laid banquet tables fit for a queen.

Zahora sat on a pile of straw in the corner of the barn and watched the wedding preparation with trepidation. This would be her first celebration with the leaders of her nation. She was elated, terrified, and downright pissed off.

The leadership hadn't allowed Noah to come to Maltings. Meredith had said it was too dangerous ... Noah was too much of an unknown ... too much of a security risk ...

He'd told them everything he knew. What more did they expect? And Noah could be useful to them ... he knew how the Slayers worked, how they trained, who their leaders were ...

Zahora had told Noah to take the time to write songs, that she would be back to hear them soon. But now she was here, she wasn't so sure that was true. The Pagans needed a powerful magik to maintain the barrier, and the only others who could do it were Marla and Alerac. Marla was still at the compound in Wales, and Alerac didn't seem inclined to take turns.

But what could she do? She'd wanted this ... to be a part of the Pagan inner circle, to help the leadership, to be important, for her skills to be recognized ...

Though not as a dog's body ...

Sleep tugged at her eyelids, and she curled up on the straw. She needed to rest before renewing the magic in a few hours, and she wanted some energy to spare for her first proper Pagan wedding.

Raina stood in front of a floor-length mirror, while Christa spritzed her with the scent of winter rose.

'Me too!' said Callie, pulling on Christa's arm.

'Okay!' said Christa, dousing Callie in the scent.

Callie twirled in her white dress, then ran to the table where two autumnal flower crowns sat waiting. 'Is this for me?' she asked gleefully, picking up the smaller crown of purple leaves, rosehips, and peach colored roses.

'It is,' said Christa, plucking it from Callie's fingers and placing it on her head. 'And one for you.' She placed Raina's crown carefully over her updo.

'Thank you,' said Raina, buoyed by Callie's exuberance. Callie's ringlets bounced as she danced in excitement, and Raina had to pinch herself, remembering the adorable little ball of energy belonged to her.

'Come on,' said Raina, doing a twirl of her own in her matching white dress, her long sleeves brushing her fingertips. 'We don't want Daddy to worry we're not coming ...'

Callie rushed for the exit. 'I'm going first,' she said, throwing open the door.

Raina laughed and shook her head.

'Wait!' said Christa, holding out a pair of Egyptian fan earrings and a gold bangle.

Raina took them and put them on, the heavy weight of the metal familiar and comforting.

Celtic folk music greeted them as Raina and Callie neared the stone circle. Callie clutched Raina's hand as they got close, suddenly shy, intimidated by the occasion. The others stood around the edge, watching their approach.

Christa took Callie's hand when they reached the circle, pulling her to the side, Raina continuing to the altar stone alone, to where Caspar and Talli waited.

The sun was setting, the sky glowing hues of orange and red, and Raina savored the moment, committing every detail to memory ... the way Caspar tracked her movements, the dying light of day, the smell of winter rose.

She reached Caspar, and he took her hand, entwining their fingers. She looked deep into his cavernous brown eyes, barely noticing when Talli started the ceremony, no idea at all what she said. Caspar stroked his thumb across her palm, and her stomach clenched, her pulse spiking. She wanted to kiss him ... couldn't wait for what would come later ... finally. They hadn't had a single private moment since Callie had arrived ... hadn't wanted to be anywhere but by her side.

Talli took their joined hands and wrapped braided cord around them, binding them together. They couldn't describe all the things they were to each other, what they promised to one another, so they simply said,

'I love you … will love you for all our lives to come.' It was all that was needed.

'Then kiss her already!' said Talli, holding her arms out, her face a picture of delight.

The band played, and Caspar leaned in, planting a chaste kiss on her lips. Raina resisted the urge to deepen it, to bite his lip, to plunge her hands into his hair.

The others clapped and cheered, and Callie ran up and hugged their legs. 'Do we get cake now?' she asked.

Raina laughed. 'Is that really all you care about?'

Callie looked thoughtful for a second, then gave a guilty smile. 'Yes.'

The banquet was torture, Caspar playing with Raina's fingers inside their binding. She ate hardly at all, thinking only of when they could slip away.

Talli had outdone herself—if that was possible— the table an autumnal display of golden leaves, rosehips, and seed heads. The candles cast a flickering light across the straw strewn around the barn, reminiscent of more ancient times.

They cut the cake, gave Callie the first enormous slice, then left. They ran for the house, terrified someone would catch them and pull them back … it was the kind of thing the others would think hilarious.

They made it, and Caspar pulled up the hem of Raina's dress, barely even taking the trouble to shut the door. 'This has to go,' he said, sliding it over her head and dropping it to the floor.

He crowded her back against the coats lining the wall and unclipped her white, lacy bra. He cast it aside, baring her peaked nipples to the chill air. His eyes turned feral as he drank her in, her breath hitching at the promise in them.

He lowered his head, invading her space ... dominating it, then kissed her eager lips. Her hands clawed at his shirt, pulling it up, sliding under, needing to feel the hard heat of his skin. He growled at the contact, pushing his hips against her, and she grabbed them, holding him to her, pressing back into his touch.

He picked her up and carried her upstairs, stumbling as she sucked at his neck. 'Raina ...' he groaned, clutching at the stair rail.

He turned them as they entered their room, pressing her against the door, her legs wrapped around his waist. His mouth nipped and licked her neck as she writhed against him, seeking friction.

She pushed him back, and dropped her feet to the floor, her hands pulling off his shirt, then making short work of the fastenings of his trousers. The fabric slid down his legs, and she discarded her underwear, then they crashed back together, fully naked.

He turned her, putting his chest to her back, pressing his arousal into the cradle of her thighs. She tipped her head back on a gasp, and his hands went to her breasts, squeezing, massaging, rolling the nipples in his fingers. She moved her hips, and he wrapped an arm around her waist, supporting her, groaning into her neck as she moved up and down.

He pressed his fingers between her legs, and she bucked, moving against his fingers and his shaft. But she wanted more. She pushed him down onto a chair and straddled him, sinking onto his length with a gasp.

She stilled, growing accustomed to the sensation before riding him with wild abandon. His hands went to her hips, and she slowed, rocking back and forth in long, sensual movements. He took her nipple in his mouth, and she fisted his hair, arching her back, offering herself up to him.

'Caspar,' she gasped, her movements becoming frantic. 'Don't stop.'

He tongued her nipple, his fingers pinching the other, and she crashed over the edge, moaning as her muscles convulsed around him. Caspar grabbed her hips, moving her once, twice, then came with a groan, pulsing his hips.

He rested his head against her chest, and she wrapped her arms around it, using him to steady herself as she caught her breath.

'I love you,' he said into her skin.

She pulled his head back and kissed him. 'I love you too.'

Raina and Caspar returned to the party—now dressed in warm coats and boots, given the Autumnal temperatures—and found Callie by a bonfire next to Talli and Christa, fast asleep and nestled under a blanket. Caspar lowered himself to the ground, leaning back against a bale of straw, and Raina sat between his legs, resting against him.

'I wondered if you two would reappear,' said Talli, wrapping the blanket she shared with Christa more tightly around her.

Raina pressed into Caspar's warmth, and he nuzzled her, enfolding her in his coat. She never wanted to leave the warm shelter of his arms.

Angry voices approached, and they all swung their heads towards the commotion.

'If you'd let me do it my way, we would have got him,' said Meredith, appearing out of the dark.

'No, you wouldn't,' said Alerac, a step behind. 'He knew we were coming ... that's why he ran.'

'How could he have known that?' said Meredith, waving an arm in frustration.

'Hi ...' said Talli. 'Want to bring the rest of us in?'

'Urgh,' said Meredith, grabbing a beer from a nearby bucket, then joining the others by the fire. 'We found a photographer with a long lens.'

'What?' said Talli. 'Who?'

'We don't know,' said Meredith, 'because Alerac can't follow orders.'

'I don't take orders from you,' said Alerac, sitting too.

'You damn well should while you're here,' said Meredith. 'We've been searching for hours, but he's gone.'

'Who would want photos of this?' said Talli.

'Maybe we'll never know now,' said Meredith, scowling at Alerac.

'Do you think it could have been Noah?' asked Leila. Raina hadn't noticed her, back in the shadows next to Jon ... although they weren't quite touching.

'No,' said Zahora hotly. She'd been slumped against a bale ... Raina had thought she was asleep. 'You wouldn't tell him our location, remember?'

'Yes, but we know he's been conspiring with our enemies,' said Meredith, who looked about ready to hit something.

'And he's missing from the settlement,' said Rose, joining them from the shadows.

'Rose!' cried Talli. 'You made it!'

'And I brought some friends,' she said. Their dogs—Charlie and Delta—ran into the circle.

The others fussed over them, and they were delighted with the attention, Charlie eventually lying next to Zahora, and Delta next to Meredith. They could obviously sense who needed comfort.

'What do you mean, he's missing?' said Zahora, in a quiet voice.

'No one has seen him in hours,' said Rose. 'They've searched the place top to bottom but can't find him. They think he must have slipped out through the tunnels shortly after we left.'

'But ...'

'Did you tell him where we were going?' said Meredith, stroking Delta's head.

'Of course not!' said Zahora. Charlie put a paw on her lap, looking up at her with sad eyes. 'What if the Slayers took him again?'

Meredith softened a bit. 'That's unlikely. They wouldn't have been able to get in ... unless they know about the tunnels too.'

'Which they don't,' said Zahora.

'Then I doubt that's what happened,' said Meredith. 'It's more likely he ran away.'

'He wouldn't ...' said Zahora, but she didn't sound sure.

'We've put Ira on the case. He'll find Noah without too much trouble,' said Rose, in a way that closed the matter.

'This is making me so excited for Yule!' said Talli, practically squealing. 'Anyone else?'

'Talli ...' Jon groaned.

'What? We missed Samhain ... and we need *something* to keep our spirits up in this Templar-caused shit storm ...'

'You need to focus on finding the magiks that set up the Registerium,' said Rose. 'That's your primary task ... not Yule.'

'The two can be achieved in tandem,' said Talli.

Leila stood and walked toward the barn. Jon watched her go, not even trying to hide it.

'I hear you're off on a romantic break,' said Talli, rounding on Jon.

'Hardly,' said Jon. 'It's a business trip, and I take my professional life seriously.'

'A business trip?' said Christa.

'Is that what Leila thinks it is?' asked Meredith.

'You'd have to ask her,' said Jon, his tone icy.

'But I thought the world would be falling apart by now,' said Talli, 'without your presence in the UK's financial district ...'

Leila rejoined, a bottle of wine and glass in hand.

'Shouldn't you be rescuing the city from certain destruction?' said Talli.

Jon scowled. 'I have other priorities,' he said. He looked down at his hands, surprising everyone with the absence of a cocky retort. 'I miss Elliot,' he said instead.

'Me too,' said Christa.

'And Gemma,' said Meredith. 'Nobody with a long lens would've got away if she'd been here, I can tell you.'

Alerac scowled and shook his head.

'I'm recalling them,' said Rose. 'We need to consolidate ... retrieving Raina and Callie was costly.'

'But worth it,' said Caspar, the deep rumble of his voice vibrating through Raina's chest. She entwined her fingers with his.

'No one's arguing it wasn't,' said Rose. 'But now we have to fight the Templars, the Slayers—who seem to be disproportionately targeting our nation—and the Registerium. A war on three fronts is quite enough to be getting on with, without involving the West Coast too.'

'And they don't seem to have hostile intentions,' said Meredith.

'Not at this moment, anyway,' said Rose. 'So I'm recalling them … it will be a weight off my shoulders when they're back—they are both assets to our nation.'

Gemma entered Aphrodite's rooms wearing the floor length plum dress Aphrodite had sent. She'd come to say she didn't want to wear it, with its sheer sections that left little to the imagination. But Aphrodite headed her off immediately, removing the replacement dress from Gemma's grasp and handing it to a servant.

Gemma would have protested, but Aphrodite drew her attention to the five others who would apparently be joining them for dinner. Gemma had assumed it would be just the two of them, and the company threw her.

'Gemma … Goddess,' said Aphrodite. 'Come … join us.'

The others—three male and two female—stood as she approached, bowing and curtsying low.

'I ... uh ...' said Gemma, not sure how to react.

'See,' said Aphrodite. 'All of us here see who you truly are. Come sit with me.'

Aphrodite reclined onto a low couch, and Gemma perched next to her, preoccupied with ensuring her dress still covered her modesty.

'Don't fret, Goddess,' said Aphrodite. 'Lie back ... relax.'

Gemma leaned against the other end of the couch, but she felt ridiculous ... awkward ... like she was failing at whatever this was.

More servants entered, carrying trays of champagne cocktails and platters of food. They served Aphrodite first, then Gemma, bowing to them both, calling them both *Goddess*.

'Drink,' said Aphrodite. 'It will help.'

Gemma did as she was told, but found herself clenching her teeth so hard she worried she would crack one.

'Thank you,' she said to the servants.

They gave her odd looks as they unloaded the food, then sat at the guests' feet.

'Darling,' Aphrodite laughed, 'they're thankful for the honor of being in your presence. You don't need to thank *them*!'

The servants nodded in agreement, and it looked genuine, like they were happy to serve.

'Grapes,' said Aphrodite, to the servant at her feet. 'Don't peel them.'

The servant did her bidding, selecting a small bunch of grapes. He offered them to her, his head down, not meeting her gaze. She took them, but didn't eat them right away. She lifted her champagne flute instead.

'To the Goddess of Spring,' she said.

The others held up their glasses and mimicked her words, all looking at Gemma expectantly.

Gemma, feeling even more awkward, lifted her champagne to her lips. It was blood red, mixed with pomegranate juice, and was sweet, and bubbly, and oddly moreish. She finished the glass in no time, hoping the alcohol would help calm her nerves.

Her servant jumped to get her another before she'd even thought to ask, carefully replacing the one in her hand. She wanted to say *thank you*, the words almost through her lips, but she tramped them back down, acutely aware of the whole room's eyes on her.

She nodded instead and took a large gulp. She could already feel the alcohol doing its work, her empty stomach speeding its progress. Her shoulders relaxed the smallest fraction.

'I didn't catch your names,' said Gemma, looking round at the other guests—all fine specimens and scantily clad.

'You need not know our names, Goddess,' said one of the women, smiling warmly. 'Call us what you will, for we are blessed to be in your presence.'

'Why do you think I'm the Goddess of Spring?' said Gemma, turning her eyes back to Aphrodite, her awkwardness morphing into frustration.

'I feel it,' said Aphrodite. 'Like calls to like after all.'

'I don't want to be rude,' said Gemma, 'but I don't feel it.' *The alcohol must really be kicking in …*

Aphrodite laughed, the sound a tinkle across the lilting background music. Had that always been playing? It was unlike Gemma not to notice …

'Darling, your senses are dull. You have suffered, and your suffering caused you to repress who you really are. I want to help you find yourself. We all do,' she

304

said, waving her arm in an arc. The others nodded and smiled. 'For your true self is remarkable indeed.'

'But ...' Well, now she thought of it, Meredith was always telling her she was great, and powerful, and in possession of fearsome inner strength. And she had suffered ... suffered badly, for many lifetimes. But that didn't mean she was a goddess ...

'*But* nothing,' said Aphrodite. 'All we ask is for you to keep an open mind. Listen, watch, *feel*, let yourself be free. Enjoy yourself for once ... for no reason other than that you can ... that it's fun!'

Why did everyone always assume she didn't know how to have fun ...?

'Another,' said Gemma, handing her empty glass to her servant. He rushed to oblige.

Aphrodite laughed again, downing her own drink. 'Tonight, we will have fun!'

The music changed and the volume increased, a pumping, thrilling cadence that enticed the others to their feet. Gemma's chest fluttered with excitement. *Yes, tonight I will have fun.*

Hours later, Gemma collapsed back onto a couch, sweaty and elated. She hadn't danced like this in too long, the music sublime. Every time one song ended, and she vowed to sit down, another would replace it that she *had* to dance to. She asked a servant for water, and they rushed to obey, returning moments later with a crystal glass.

'Tha ...' She stopped herself, raising the glass to her lips.

The encounter left a strange taste in her mouth. Even if they were happy to serve, why couldn't she thank them? She picked up more champagne and moved to the balcony, hiding in a secluded area behind a curtain of weeping branches. Everyone else was too preoccupied with dancing to notice, and Aphrodite had disappeared.

She leaned on the balcony railing, looking out into the night, the comforting sound of the sea washing over her.

'Calming, isn't it?' said a male voice from behind her.

She spun to see a man leaning casually against the wall, his hands in his suit pockets. Her pulse leapt, certainly because of the shock, but also because he was probably the most attractive man she'd ever laid eyes on. Tall, broad but not bulky, dark floppy hair, perfect cheekbones, crisp white shirt open at the collar.

She couldn't find words, so she stared.

He laughed. 'You look like a rabbit caught in headlights,' he said, his accent unplaceable. He moved to the balcony, putting his hands on the rail. Delicious hands.

'It's been a long night,' she said, turning back to face the sea.

'An entertaining night, I hope?'

'Yes,' she said, his scent washing over her.

Holy mother of ... she wanted to dive into that smell, fresh and salty and powerful. She stepped away, putting space between them.

'Wait,' he said. She stopped, and he reached up to brush her cheek. 'Eyelash.'

His hand lingered on her face, the contact electrifying. Her body swayed towards him, her lips

306

tingling, his face so close she could see specs of amber in his dark eyes.

'I ...' She pulled back, shaking her head. 'I have to go.'

She raced back through the party, Aphrodite stopping her before she could reach the exit. 'Darling, whatever's wrong?'

'Nothing,' said Gemma. 'I ... I've had too much to drink.'

'Intoxicated?' said Aphrodite, drawing the word out into a sensual caress.

'I ... yes,' said Gemma, willing her brain to forget the feel of the man's touch on her skin. 'I need to go.'

'Of course,' said Aphrodite, placing her hand on Gemma's face, exactly where the stranger had. 'Everyone! The Goddess of Spring is taking her leave.'

The dancing ceased, the others dropping into bows and curtseys, saying, 'Goddess,' in respectful tones.

Gemma flushed at the display, but something about it made her stand a little taller ... some part of her liked it.

Gemma returned to her room to find Elliot pacing. 'What is it?' she asked as she shut the door.

Elliot took in her disheveled, racily clad appearance and faltered. 'Good evening?' he asked.

'Mostly, although ... bizarre. You?'

'Ares is very serious; it makes it hard to warm to him.'

'What's wrong?' she said. 'Did something happen?'

'Ares gave me a message. We've been recalled ... Rose wants us home ASAP. They've got Raina and Callie back, and Rose wants our help for what comes next.'

'Fighting comes next,' said Gemma, sinking onto a couch. 'Endless war and bloodshed. And for what?'

Elliot's brow furrowed. 'Freedom,' he said.

'Freedom? What freedom? When have we been free to do as we please?'

'Gemma, where's this coming from?' he asked, sitting next to her, taking her hand.

She held onto him, her head foggy. 'I need to stop.'

'Stop what?'

'Being someone else's pawn.'

'We're no one's pawns ... but we are part of a nation where we have responsibilities ... where we fight for what we believe in.'

'What do we believe in?'

'Gemma! How can you ask that?'

'Winning at all costs? Revenge? Sacrificing everything to save Raina? What about the rest of us? Don't we matter?'

Elliot pulled back in shock. 'Of course we do. They would have done the same for any of us.'

'Would they?'

'Yes.'

'For any Pagan?'

'Of course.'

Gemma laughed. 'No, they wouldn't.'

'They would if they could ... and Raina helped build our nation, made it what it is today. We are weaker without her.'

'Are we weaker without me?'

Elliot looked at her in disbelief. 'Yes!'

'Do they even know who I am?'

308

'Our friends? The Pagan leaders? Of course they do ...'

'Do you?'

'Gemma ... what happened? What did Aphrodite do to you?'

Gemma stood, then paused to steady herself. 'I'm going to bed.'

Elliot stood too. 'We have to pack.'

'I'm not going.'

'You're defying orders?'

She took a breath. 'I suppose I am.'

'Why?'

'What if I am a goddess?'

Elliot placed a hand on her arm. 'My love, none of these people are what they say they are ... they're delusional.'

'How can you be sure?'

'Because it's ludicrous.'

'More ludicrous than reincarnation itself?'

'Yes; gods don't walk among us.'

She broke away from his touch. 'But what if they do? What if I am one? What if the reason I've never fitted anywhere, why I've always felt alone, like an outsider ... scared, is because I belong here?'

'Do you feel like that with me? Like we don't fit? Alone?' Elliot's face fell.

'No,' she whispered, shaking her head. 'I love you. But I need to do this ... stay here ... for myself. Or I'll always wonder ...'

'Then I'm staying too.'

Gemma's heart stopped. 'You can't ... our nation needs you.'

His features turned sad. 'You need me more.'

Chapter 22

Jamie rampaged around his loft, his entire staff avoiding him.

'Tamsin!' he screamed, as he made for her room.

'Yes?' she said, opening her door, her features wary.

He barged past her into the dingy bedroom she'd been assigned. God, it was terrible ...

'We're going on the offensive. Ramp up attacks. We will take out our enemies by any means necessary. The Slayers,' he said, chopping the side of one hand down on the palm of the other. 'The Aztecs.' Chop. 'The fucking Pagans.' Chop.

He roamed the room like a wild animal. 'What are these?' He picked up a stack of photographs from a side table.

Tamsin ran a hand through her hair, avoiding his gaze. 'They're pictures of Caspar and Raina's marriage ... from yesterday.'

He stared at the pictures, taking in every minute detail. Their entwined fingers, the look on her face, the moment they kissed. Fucking bitch had been lying to him all along ...

And there was his daughter. Callie was supposed to be writhing in pain, desperately clawing her way back to her home nation … but she looked fine. Happy. Exuberant. Were the Registerium magiks lying to him? Was the Registrar playing him too? Even now?

Callie looked gleeful, a flower crown on her head. They would poison her against him … but maybe she wasn't even his … maybe he should kill her too.

'The Registerium has some explaining to do,' said Jamie, casting the pictures aside. 'Send a team to get Callie back. Kill as many of the others as we can.'

'The whole area's protected by magic,' said Tamsin, sitting heavily on a stool. 'Even the photographer couldn't get any closer, and you know what they're like …'

'Then get me a magik who can break their little spell.'

'We're trying …' said Tamsin, her tone short.

Jamie prowled towards her and put a hand on her throat. 'What was that?'

'We're trying,' said Tamsin, her eyes pleading as he squeezed, her hands on his wrist.

'Then try harder,' said Jamie, clamping his hand tighter.

Euphoria filled him. This was what he needed. Someone at his mercy, someone to punish, someone begging … some fucking respect.

Tears welled in Tamsin's eyes. 'Jamie, please, I'll do anything,' she whispered, trying to pry his fingers away. She gave up on his fingers, her hands going to his pants.

He released her and stepped away. He wouldn't give her the satisfaction.

'We'll start with the Slayers then. They think they can dominate me … run missions behind my back … No one makes a fool of me and gets away with it.'

'I'll brief a team,' Tamsin choked, still fighting tears.

Weak creature.

'No,' he said. 'I'll do it. You find me a god-damned magik who can break that spell.'

'Is it done?' asked the Grand Master, finally looking up at his son. Noah couldn't meet his gaze. He turned his eyes through the glass. They could see water on two sides—views people would literally kill for in Manhattan—but he wasn't here to look at the view.

'I've come to tell you I'm leaving,' said Noah. 'I want no part of this organization. I will not kill the woman I love. I won't spend my life lying and cheating … I want nothing to do with this place.'

His father sat back in his chair and steepled his fingers, a smirk on his face. A prickle of uncertainty tingled against Noah's neck, but he continued.

'I came to tell you in person, out of respect for you, and also to ask that you spare the woman you made me marry. But my mind is made up, so whatever happens to her now is on you, not me. If you wish to kill her, there's nothing I can do about it.'

'Is that so …' said the Grand Master.

Noah shifted slightly on his feet, his father's expression setting him on edge.

'What if she's with child?'

'She isn't.'

'She could be. We selected her both for her brilliance and dedication, but also because she was fertile on the day of your wedding.'

'Fertile?' said Noah, not believing his ears. 'What the fuck?'

'You didn't think I would leave something as important as succession to chance, did you?' he said. 'You may have as many mistresses as you wish, but you will only ever have one legitimate wife, and she must produce heirs to continue our dynasty.'

'What dynasty?'

'The one I am creating.'

'I told you, I want no part in your plan. I'm leaving.'

'What of your child?'

'I don't have a child,' Noah ground out, 'and it's way too early to tell. We only ... a few days ago.'

'Consummated your marriage, you mean?' said his father.

'And even if she is pregnant, why should I believe it's mine? She was no virgin.'

His father nodded. 'She had been trained, it is true.'

Noah stopped dead ... went still ... he couldn't mean ...

The Grand Master laughed. 'We wouldn't saddle you with a wife without training her first ... such a thing would be barbaric! Candidates are taught to please their husbands in every possible way, both inside and outside the marital bed. It's more conducive to a happy marriage and the production of children than leaving these things to chance.'

'Jesus Christ ...'

'Do not take the Lord's name in vain.'

'You're sick,' said Noah. 'I always thought you at least had our best interests at heart. But this ... this is ...'

'Optimal,' said his father, with a smug smile. 'Don't you see? It is the natural way of things for men to lead and women to serve. It's built into our natures ... has been for all time. We have merely optimized it ... taken chance from the equation ... put ourselves in the best position to breed Slayers who will kill our enemies before they kill us.'

None of this even made sense ... he sounded like a raving lunatic.

'And if you think I'm going to let you go, you are sorely mistaken,' said the Grand Master.

Noah whirled towards the door ... something in his father's tone told him he had to get out. Now. He expected his father to say something, to tell him to stop, but the only sound was a dull thump.

Noah hit the floor, the result of years of training, worried that his father was throwing knives ... was trying to kill him.

But when he looked up, it was his father who'd been attacked, blood seeping out across his shirt. Blood everywhere.

'Help!' screamed Noah, crawling across the floor towards the desk. The side window had a round bullet hole in it. No ... this couldn't be happening ... Noah kept crawling, taking care to remain behind cover.

He reached the foot of the desk just as his father's deputy entered, taking in the scene but missing the hole in the window, immediately jumping to the wrong conclusion.

'What have you done?' he demanded.

But before Noah could reply, a hole appeared in the man's head, accompanied by a sickening crack. He went down like a lead balloon.

'Fuck,' breathed Noah. He had to get out ... to tell everyone they were under attack.

He crawled back towards the entrance, his father's secretary rushing towards him.

'Stay back!' said Noah, but she didn't listen, surging forward to see what had happened.

She crossed herself just before the bullet found her head.

'Fuck!' shouted Noah. He had to get out. He had to get back to Zahora. Why had he come? The Grand Master had never deserved his respect …

A mechanical whirring filled the air, and metal shutters fell from the ceiling, covering the windows. Thank God … he stood and ran for the stairs.

By the time Noah made it to the lobby, a crowd of senior Slayers had gathered.

'Thank God the Grand Master called for a lockdown,' said one of them.

'I hate to think what would have happened if that door had been open,' said another.

'How did he know?' said a third.

'He's dead,' said Noah. He bent over to catch his breath, to process what he'd witnessed. 'So is his deputy and his secretary. They've been shot.'

'Shot?'

'Snipper, through the window,' said Noah, trying to force air into his lungs. 'I crawled out.'

The first man looked at him suspiciously. 'Then how did he know to lock us down?'

'I don't know,' said Noah. 'But you know what my father was like … his instincts were …'

'They used a gun,' said a fourth man. 'Demons don't use guns …'

'Then who did it?' said the second man.

'Just because they haven't used them in the past, doesn't mean they can't change tactics …' said the first.

'What should we do?' asked the third, looking directly at Noah.

Noah stared back blankly.

'He's right ... you're the successor,' said the fourth. 'After your final mission ...'

His final mission? The one to kill Zahora?

'Secure the perimeter,' said Noah, falling back on his training, 'and work out who's attacking us. Go floor by floor and come back with a status report. We need to take stock, then make a plan.'

The men dispersed, and suddenly Noah was alone. He was in charge ... could take over the entire operation ... dismantle it from the inside out. But his dad ... his dad was dead.

Images swamped him ... his father's slumped form, the blood, the look on his face as Noah had rejected everything he stood for. His father had tried to hold him hostage ... the real reason for locking down the building. He'd need to search the office for surveillance devices ... if the truth got out, he was finished. And he had to get a message to Zahora.

The wedding already felt like a distant dream, although it had only been two days before ... but the outside world crashed against their bubble, forcing its way in.

Leila and Jon prepared to leave, heading to a destination unknown, for Leila's protection. The others waved them off, Raina melancholy as she said goodbye to her human cousin.

'I hope she's okay,' said Raina, as Caspar ran a hand across her back.

'They'll be fine. So long as they keep their heads down, the Templars have bigger fish to fry.'

'Fish shaped like us,' said Raina, wishing it would all end … but wishing would do nothing at all … there was one way to survive, and that was going forward into the fray.

Callie ran inside and the others followed, Alerac loudly asking an exhausted Zahora what was wrong.

'It's nothing,' she said in hushed tones, casting her eyes around at the others. 'Just a bad dream.'

'Of?' said Alerac, insistently.

'Noah, back in America, and his dad being shot.'

Alerac laughed. 'Sounds wonderful to me!'

Zahora scowled. 'Some of us aren't dark like you … I've never celebrated anyone's death.'

'You're young,' said Alerac. 'You have time.'

Caspar's phone rang. 'Ira,' he said, answering the call on speaker as they all piled into the sitting room, glad of the heat from the fire. Callie put the TV on, and Christa snatched up the controller, turning the volume down so low, Callie practically had to sit on the TV to hear it.

'News from New York,' said Ira. 'The Slayers' Grand Master has been shot, as has his deputy. They've locked down their building, and CCTV footage shows a large concentration of Templar demons in the area around the building at the time of the attack. We don't have conclusive proof, but the most likely explanation is that the Templars were behind it. The humans have sent police to the scene.'

All eyes had swung to Zahora, who was curled up on a sofa, hugging her legs.

'Thank you, Ira,' said Caspar. 'Let us know when you find out more. There's a chance the Grand Master's son was there too. We might be able to use him.'

'I'm already looking for him,' said Ira. 'Speak later.'

Ira hung up, and Zahora tried to disappear into the cushions. 'I didn't know,' she said.

'You accessed the Nexus in your sleep,' said Alerac.

'I don't think so,' said Zahora. 'It didn't feel like that ... it felt ... I don't know ... like a dream.'

'Well, whatever happened,' said Alerac, 'it was magic of some sort.'

'We have to find out if Noah's okay,' said Zahora, although she seemed tired ... like it was a great effort to get the words out. 'In my dream, he told his dad he wanted nothing to do with the Slayers, that he was leaving.'

'He went all the way back to New York just to tell him that?' said Alerac, skeptically.

A look of fury crossed Zahora's face. 'People do stupid things all the time, thinking they're acting honorably ... he wanted to make sure they didn't kill his wife ...'

'His wife?' said Caspar.

Zahora inhaled deeply. 'Noah's dad forced him into a marriage with a woman he didn't know, then sent him to kill me. The Grand Master said he would kill Noah's wife if he failed.'

'Nice,' said Meredith. 'Very fifteenth century ...'

'Sixteenth,' said Raina.

'Twelfth' said Rose.

'Guys ...' said Caspar.

'In the dream, he was trying to leave, but his dad wouldn't let him. And then his dad was shot. That's all I saw,' said Zahora.

'If it is the Templars,' said Rose, 'it's yet another example of them flouting the rules.'

'I mean, there are only three to remember,' said Christa. 'How do they find it so hard?'

'If the shooting was the Templars, they're in violation of at least two,' said Rose. 'Using guns, and risking our exposure to humans. But the inquiry into the Registerium starts next week ... I doubt they'll strike off the Templars while that's going on.'

'They probably won't even look into it,' said Christa.

'Not judging by how they've been favoring the Templars up until now,' said Talli.

'But we can't take the law into our own hands either,' said Rose, 'and we don't have proof the Templars were behind the shooting.'

'Who else would want to kill the Slayers aside from demons?' said Meredith.

'Maybe the Grand Master pissed off the wrong people,' said Talli.

'Maybe it was other Slayers,' said Raina, 'staging a coup.'

'Hopefully Ira can tell us more,' said Rose with a sigh.

Christa shifted in her seat, accidentally sitting on the TV controller, and Callie spun around in outrage.

'Sorry!' said Christa, fumbling to change it back.

'Turn it off,' said Raina. 'Callie, that stuff will rot your brain.'

'Wait,' said Talli, her eyes fixed on the screen. It was news footage from Greenland, discussing the melting ice caps.

'Gods,' said Alerac, following Talli's gaze. 'She's ...'

Raina leaned forward in her seat. 'Wow ... that's ... quite something.'

'Go,' said Rose, looking at Talli, then Christa. 'Go now. We'll find out as much as we can while you're on your way.'

'I have something to show you,' said Tamsin, bursting into Jamie's room, flipping on the light switch.

'Tamsin, it's the middle of the night,' he said, rolling over, 'but I could be persuaded ...'

'It's five in the morning,' she said, holding her phone in front of Jamie's face.

'Okay, okay,' he said, blinking against the assault of the overhead light. 'Give me a second.'

His eyes adjusted, and he looked at the video on Tamsin's phone. 'You woke me up to talk about climate change?' he asked, giving her an incredulous look.

Tamsin scowled. 'No. I woke you to tell you I've found our magik. Look at her eyes.'

'Oh ... now you mention it ... they practically glow! How can the humans ignore something like that?'

'I don't know, but this was on the BBC earlier. She's a scientist and campaigner ... has dedicated her life to saving the planet.'

Jamie rolled his eyes. 'Sounds like a Pagan to me.'

'We'd better hope they don't get there first then ...'

'Shit ... when did this air?'

'It's been looping all morning on their breakfast television.'

'Then they're bound to have seen it,' said Jamie, throwing back the covers. 'Let's go.'

I hope you enjoyed *Nation of the Sword* and, if you did, I would really appreciate a rating or review on Amazon (especially there!), Goodreads, Instagram, or any other place you can think of … authors aren't fussy! Just a rating, a few words, or a line or two would be absolute perfection, and will help others find my books. Thank you for your support.

To be the first to hear all my latest news, get book recommendations, and find out about giveaways, sign up to my newsletter here: https://www.subscribepage.com/r2a0n6_copy2

CONNECT WITH HR MOORE

Check out HR Moore's website, where you can also sign up to her newsletter:
http://www.hrmoore.com/

Find HR Moore on Instagram and Twitter: @HR_Moore

Follow HR Moore on BookBub:
https://www.bookbub.com/authors/hr-moore

Follow @authorhrmoore on TikTok

See what the world of *The Ancient Souls Series* looks like on Pinterest:
https://www.pinterest.com/authorhrmoore/nation-of-the-sun/

Like the HR Moore page on Facebook:
https://www.facebook.com/authorhrmoore

Follow HR Moore on Goodreads:
https://www.goodreads.com/author/show/7228761.H_R_Moore

TITLES BY HR MOORE

The Relic Trilogy:
Queen of Empire
Temple of Sand
Court of Crystal

In the Gleaming Light

The Ancient Souls Series:
Nation of the Sun
Nation of the Sword
Nation of the Stars (coming March 2022)

http://www.hrmoore.com

Made in the USA
Columbia, SC
29 January 2022

54997558R00193